# The Way You Say Good Morning

## Morning

**Meghan French**

MEGHAN FRENCH PUBLISHING

*To all the girls who are tired of hearing the phrase "good girl."*

*It's high time we started throwing around "good boy."*

*Disclaimer: Please don't try to drink each cocktail with each chapter. My chapters run short and the cocktails run heavy on booze. I am not responsible for your recklessness, you heathens.*

# Contents

# CHAPTER ONE

# *Delaney*

Sour Hazy: Half Sour Beer, Half Hazy IPA

I slide the heavy crate of beer bottles onto the counter, letting out a huff as I do so. Pushing the box toward the middle of the bar top, I turn and stomp back down the staircase in the corner of the room. It leads to a dimly lit storage room where Sloane and Tilly, Sip's owners, keep excess stock. Tonight, the upstairs bar is hosting a private party, and Tilly asked me to work it last week, so I need to stock the bar accordingly.

Private parties are easy to work and make me good money. You generally don't have to deal with customers in the same way, but private customers are a different brand of annoying. Instead of running the risk of dealing with a potentially overserved patron like I might if I were working the main bar downstairs, I get to deal with entitled assholes instead. Most of the guests are fine, nice even, but occasionally, an obnoxious partygoer makes up for the easier, relaxed pace of private events. Whether they get pushy about not getting their drinks fast enough or feel entitled to feel up "the help," there's usually one at every event. I send a silent plea to the universe to have tonight be an impatient guest, rather than a creep.

I really like my job. I've been bartending for years, ever since I dropped out of college. It's decent money, but the on-the-job annoyances are fewer at Sip, my current employer, than at any other bar I've worked at. I love interacting with my regular customers. The Chicago bar scene, especially on the north side of Chicago, where Sip is sandwiched between local restaurants in the middle of a busy neighborhood, is a unique community.

The back patio still attracts a fair number of guests, even in this chilly, late-October weather. Inside, patrons can lounge in booths, on high stools at the bar, or in some of the cushy, overstuffed furniture scattered around the room. Sloane and Tilly, a married couple who bought the bar together more than ten years ago, have done a great job of adding feminine touches to the typical bar atmosphere. In addition to plush seating and exposed brickwork, alternative and indie music typically pump through the speakers. The bar is an eclectic mix between grungy dive bar and artistic coffee shop, but somehow, it works.

Sloane and Tilly are amazing bosses. Sloane tends to stick to the back of the house, keeping the books and maintaining the day-to-day functioning of the place. Tilly, Sloane's wife, likes to take up residence at the front of the house, her bubbly personality bouncing around the room, reflecting off every shiny surface. They both take care of their staff. They keep us safe, even from the occasional entitled creeps, which is more than I can say for many of my previous bosses. Both women ensure no one closes up the bar alone and that we always feel supported.

One of the main reasons I love working at Sip, though, is the creative license Tilly allows me behind the bar. When it's slow, she allows me to play around with developing new concoctions using her liquor. When I make one I really like, I usually end up bringing it to Sloane in the back. Sloane's palate is far more refined than Tilly's. Tilly will tell me she loves everything I bring her, and I still haven't worked out if it's because she wants to be encouraging or if she genuinely enjoys everything I make. Sloane will at least give me a little bit more of an honest and balanced review.

Admittedly, a lot of the drinks I make don't necessarily fit the vibe of Sip, which tends to cater heavily to a beer-drinking crowd. I tend to gravitate toward upscale cocktails when I play mixologist. Half of the crowd at Sip would balk if I suggested mixing half a pint of a hazy IPA with an equal amount of a fruity sour, even if I know the flavors balance each other out and end up making a more delicious beverage. Every once in a while, though, we get a customer at Sip who indulges my cocktail creativity, but unfortunately, it never tends to be a regular, neighborhood customer, so I don't get to flex my imaginative muscles as often as I'd like.

I grunt as I lift another case of beer in my arms.

"Lift with your back, not your legs," Jeff, my barback, jokes. I scowl. He's half an hour late, which means I'm half an hour behind schedule. If Jeff had shown up on time, the beers would have already been brought to the second-floor bar. Dividing the task between the two of us would have made quick work; instead, I got to do the literal heavy lifting myself.

"Turn that frown upside down, sunshine," Jeff needles as I scoot past him. He pokes me in the side, and I glare at him. Finally taking the hint, he pulls the case out of my arms and follows me up the stairs. Jeff, much like Tilly, is an eternal optimist, but his over-the-top enthusiasm grates on my nerves in a way that Tilly's positivity doesn't. Jeff isn't a bad guy; he's just one of those *small doses* kinds of people. Still, I prefer him barbacking for me over Cassandra, who is shallow and lazy.

"I'm sorry I'm late, Delaney. I swear I'll do all the closing work for you tonight," he promises me. I grumble but accept his apology. I don't mind closing, but it takes longer after a private party because there tends to be more glassware and it's harder to clean as you go.

"You gonna share why you were late anyway?"

"D, you shouldn't ask questions you already know the answer to," he teases back. His answer tells me everything I need to know. He took some chick home last night, from who knows where, spent all night balls deep inside her, then kicked her out, never to call her again. And because he spent the night knee-deep in vagina, he slept in and likely missed his first two alarms to wake him for tonight's shift. It's almost as if I hear this story at least once a month.

"You're lucky you're the boss's nephew, or you'd be out on your ass without a job," I tell him, but my words are laced with amusement. Jeff hums his agreement; at least he's aware of his shortcomings.

"One of these days, you could take me for a spin, you know. See what all the hype is about." Jeff wiggles his eyebrows at me as I shove his chest. He fakes a stumble and a wounded expression.

"Gross," I tell him. It's a running joke between us: Jeff suggesting I go home with him, me telling him I'd rather eat glass. He's not a bad-looking guy, but I can't imagine sleeping with him. For one thing, he's too young for me, barely twenty-one compared to my twenty-eight. I don't date coworkers either, a lesson I learned the hard way involving a disastrous relationship with a high school boyfriend, a bagel shop, and far too many tears spilled in the walk-in cooler. Most importantly, though, I wouldn't be able to handle Jeff's overly smiley face above or below me during sex. I shudder. I'm not a pessimist; I'm a realist. If I wanted toxic positivity, I'd call my Aunt Karen. No thanks.

"So, who's this party for, anyway?" he asks me.

I shrug. "Apparently some hotshot. The girlfriend planned it and asked that Jamie post up by the stairs to ensure only invited guests get in." Jamie is Sip's bouncer-slash-security-slash-handyman. He's a jack of all trades, but his large bulk works well for him in a security capacity, even if Jeff and I know he's secretly a gooey teddy bear under his hard exterior.

"Probably some finance bro," Jeff suggests, and he's probably right. They tend to book plenty of events with us, and their overinflated sense of self-worth would support their misguided idea that they need "security" surrounding their party.

We continue setting up for the party in relative silence. Say what you want about Jeff's fuckboy attitude, he at least knows that I prefer to keep to myself and doesn't pester me with inane conversation.

I'm ready to get the party started so I can do my job, earn some tips, and go home alone to my cat. Who needs a fuckboy when you've got murder shows and silicone appendages (consecutively, not together) waiting at home?

# CHAPTER TWO

# *Benny*

Hemingway Daiquiri: White Rum, Maraschino Liqueur, Lime Juice, Grapefruit Juice

The first time I lay eyes on the woman behind the bar, I know she is different. Sure, she doesn't look like your average knockout bartender, although she is. A knockout, that is. Her dark hair cascades over her shoulders as they shake with laughter at whatever her coworker says to her. Her piercing green eyes crinkle at the corners, and her laugh tinkles pleasantly in my ears, like little silver bells. I could make an ASMR soundtrack from her laugh alone. The tasteful gold septum piercing glints in the overhead light, beckoning me like a siren.

It is in this moment, the first time laying eyes on her, that I know I want her. I'm not a man easily deterred from going after what he wants. I'm known for my determination, my drive, my motivation, and she is exactly my type. This woman is all the motivation I need.

I find who I'm looking for and say hello to the guest of honor. Luckily, Warner James, my right fielder, is quickly pulled into one conversation after another, making it easy for me to slip away and saunter up to the bar. I lean casually against it, waiting for the tattooed bartender to notice me. It's a private party, so it doesn't take her long to finish pouring two beers for Tyler Edwards, who tips his chin at me in greeting before walking away, presumably to find his girlfriend.

My guys are all gathered here to celebrate Warner James's audiobook release. His girlfriend, Alicia, threw together this party, which happens to coincide with the end of a hot postseason run that fizzled out entirely too soon. Initially, she planned the party to happen between rounds of the postseason because she, like the rest of us, had hoped the timing would allow us to get together before advancing to the World Series. Unfortunately, our lack of offensive prowess in the last two games of the league championship series dictated otherwise. The party has a celebratory air, but the current of disappointment still churns beneath the surface. I think we're all happy to get together and focus on something other than the crushing feeling of loss.

The last two seasons, the Chicago Foxes have made it to the postseason only to peter out before making it to the final stage. As their faithful leader, I can't help but feel the responsibility rests solely on my shoulders. After last week's loss, I holed myself up in my townhouse as much as I could, wanting to ruminate on my mistakes and figure out what I could have done differently, not only this year, but last year, too. Unfortunately, my pity party was frequently interrupted by mandatory end-of-season meetings with the owners and other higher-ups within the Foxes organization.

It's like that every season, but this year's meetings felt especially gloomy. By all accounts, we should have still been playing. Instead, San Diego advanced to the World Series and the Foxes went home.

I roll my shoulders back, attempting to shake off the loss. I plaster a smile on my face, despite feeling like scowling. I'm generally a confident, pleasant person, but these last two postseasons have rocked me. I know my players love me; they insist on taking responsibility for the losses, too. I know Chicago fans still love me. And I know the Chicago media, a notoriously fickle beast, still love me, too. I can't help but feel, however, the loyalty afforded me by most of Chicago does not extend to Foxes' ownership; at the very least, that loyalty is wearing thin. They've publicly promised the fans I will be back next season, but I wonder if I don't deliver on a World Series appearance, my time in Chicago might be done.

The beautiful bartender leans against the counter in front of me. I feel my smile morph from phony to genuine.

"Hi," I greet her.

"Hi," she returns. She quirks an eyebrow when I don't immediately place an order. "What can I get you?" She pulls a rag from the back pocket of her jeans and wipes the counter, even though it doesn't look like it needs to be cleaned. She doesn't have a ring on her left ring finger, which makes my smile spread further.

"You can start with your name," I say smoothly. She apparently does not find me as smooth as I sound in my head. She rolls her eyes but still offers her name.

"Delaney." She shakes my extended hand.

"Sam. Most people call me Benny, though."

She snorts. "How do you get Benny from Sam?"

"You don't. My last name is Benjamin." When she doesn't do anything more than nod and wait expectantly for my drink order, I ask her for her favorite drink. Again, she rolls her eyes at my shameless attempt at flirting.

"Most people are ordering beer. We have a local IPA and a lager on tap but we have bottles and cans of almost everything." She gestures behind her to a glass-fronted refrigerator which holds a wide assortment of beer. "Full bar, too, if you want liquor."

I pin her with a teasing smile, making sure it reaches my eyes so she knows I'm not being a dick when I tell her, "I didn't ask what most people are ordering. I want to know your favorite."

She returns my smile with a polite one of her own. I can't tell if she's interested, or if she's just giving me a customer service response. Her black chipped fingernails tap lightly on the counter in front of her.

"If I want to get drunk fast, I go for a dirty vodka martini with blue cheese olives. If I'm feeling adventurous or in need of an arm workout, I'll make a pisco sour. When I'm feeling moody and contemplative, I stick with a Manhattan. And if I'm feeling frisky, I go for a Hemingway daiquiri." Her lips quirk up at her last sentence, daring me.

This girl has a wide variety of alcohol at her literal fingertips, and I'm pleased to hear she takes advantage of it. Normally, I stick to beer and whiskey, but tonight, the allure of a Hemingway daiquiri calls to me. I don't know what it is, but it sounds delicious.

"Hemingway daiquiri it is," I tell her with a wink.

Delaney turns and begins mixing ingredients. I catch the flash of white rum going into the cocktail shaker and sigh in relief. I'm not a tequila man, and I couldn't tell you what's in a blended daiquiri, much less Hemingway, but I would have drank it down no matter what the ingredients. She caps the shaker and pulls it over her shoulder, shaking vigorously. I'm mesmerized by the movements and have to check myself to ensure my mouth isn't hanging open. She is wearing simple jeans and a black fitted T-shirt, but the way both pieces of clothing are painted on to her body, I'm at risk of panting as I stare at her, the shaking reverberating lightly across her arms and chest.

"What are you getting?" Mac Lawson, my bench coach, slings his arm over my shoulders, breaking my focus on the woman in front of me.

"Hemingway daiquiri. I'm told it's all the rage." Delaney snorts softly before pulling the daintiest glass from underneath the bar. I internally groan at the tiny cup as she strains my drink. The look she gives me tells me she knows exactly what she's doing, as if she's daring me to complain or somehow backtrack on my order. Little does she realize, I'm not intimidated by her challenge.

She slides the glass over to me, but not before popping a small, black cocktail straw in it, drawing a little of the liquid into it, and pulling it to her mouth for a taste. I've seen bartenders do it a million times, but somehow, when she wraps her plump lips around the straw, I've never seen anything more erotic. Maybe it's the look in her eyes when she does it, or the fact that she doesn't break eye contact the whole time, or maybe it's all in my head, but I've never wanted to be a cocktail straw more.

"Thanks, Delaney," I tell her softly. She turns, making me believe I'm the only one impacted by our interaction, and swiftly takes Mac's order. But the smile she gives him is polite and doesn't reach her eyes, not like the genuine one she gave me only moments ago. A sense of male satisfaction courses through my veins at that. She reserved her real smile for me.

I take my drink and return to the party, mingling with my players and staff, happy to share in our pride for Warner's work. The man has the deepest voice I've heard, and apparently that makes him an ideal candidate for audiobook narration, particularly in the romance genre. When he initially told us this was what he was doing in his spare time, some of the guys laughed. But it always made sense to me. I've seen the TikToks fans have made obsessing over his voice in postgame interviews. Good for him, finding a way to monetize that.

I watch him pull his girlfriend, Alicia, into his side. She leans into him, resting her head on his shoulder. I'm happy for Warner, and for Alicia, too, but a part of me is a little lonely watching my guys settle down with the women they love. When Keeley and I were married, we had that, too, before things fell apart. I've had relationships since my ex and I divorced three years ago, but most were short-lived and unfulfilling. I've stopped seeking out relationships as a result. It's exhausting to sift through dating profiles, even the ones for B-list celebrities like me. It should be comforting, using a more exclusive dating site, but so many of the women on there are looking for a relationship only to elevate their own social status, rather than looking for a true connection. After my last two relationships failed before they even got off the ground, I grew weary of online dating and dating in general. I'm not opposed to the idea, if something falls in my lap, but I've lost a lot of motivation to put myself out there for someone who is just going to go through the motions.

Mid-conversation with Hailey McClintock, I catch Delaney watching me out of the corner of my eye. My eyes flick to hers briefly, before returning to Hailey's conversation, but I can suddenly no longer remember what we were talking about. Something about zucchini squash? Fuck, I don't know. I've been in professional sports long enough, first as a player and most recently as a manager, that I have honed my active listening skills. But once I caught Delaney's small smirk from across the room, all auditory comprehension went out the window.

I finished my drink a while ago and have been spinning the stem of this ridiculous glass between my fingers for the better part of the last half hour. Sure, I could put it down on one of the many tables around here, but it gives me something to do with my hands. It's not necessarily nervous energy, but something frenetic nonetheless.

I wait for a break in the conversation with Hailey before excusing myself for another drink.

"Can you grab me a pear cider, Benny?" she asks as I stride away. I nod, letting her know I heard her, but keep my eyes on the prize standing behind the bar.

"Back again, sailor?" She doesn't smile, but her green eyes twinkle at me. The delicate glass clinks as I set it on the bar top. "What'll it be next? Frozen margarita? Strawberry cosmo? Champagne coupe?" She's teasing me, naming the girliest drinks, or at least the most traditionally feminine glassware, but it doesn't bother me.

"You got anything in those hourglass-shaped glasses?" I use two hands to mime an hourglass, which, coincidentally, mirrors Delaney's curves.

"A hurricane glass?" she asks incredulously. I shrug.

"It's that or a beer," I chuckle. Her eyes spark with mischief as she procures the requested drinkware from under a shelf on the other side of the register. Before I can process what she's doing, she fills it to the brim with a frothy lager. It's a perfect pour, with just the right amount of foamy head. The descriptor fills my brain with lusty ideas inappropriate for a private party for one of my players.

Delaney smirks as she slides the beer over to me, and again, I swear her eyes are daring me to refuse the drink, or make a comment, so I keep my mouth shut. I bring the beer to my lips and pull deeply. It's a standard, shitty beer, but it's cold and bubbly. The glass is ridiculous and impractical for the drink, although not as bad as the tiny one from my first cocktail, but in this moment, I decide I should always drink out of glassware befitting beautiful women.

I lick the foam from my lips and my blood heats as I watch Delaney's eyes track the movement.

"What time do you get off tonight?" I ask boldly. I chose my words carefully, fully aware of the double meaning behind them.

"Whenever your fancy party ends," she tosses back. If she catches my double entendre, she doesn't react.

"It's not my party."

"Guess that means you can leave anytime," she tells me, but there's no bite to her words.

"Guess so," I tell her with a shrug. I turn, but right before I walk away, I toss over my shoulder, "See you then." She laughs, and I want to commit the sound to memory.

# CHAPTER THREE
# *Delaney*

Adult Milkshake: Greasy Spoon Diner Peanut
Butter Milkshake, Peanut Butter Whiskey

One of the annoying things about working a private party is that the last-call rules don't apply as strictly, at least not at Sip. Private parties tend to wind down before the bar itself closes, but because there's not a hard stopping time, people tend to trickle out slowly, dragging the night on longer and longer. At this point, I want to go home to my cat, shower off the night, and fall asleep to the dulcet sounds of a true crime documentary. Instead, I'm stuck leaning behind the bar, watching a handful of partygoers attempt to prolong the night by sipping their drinks slowly. They might as well order another round; at least then it will give me something to do.

The toe of my shiny black combat boot taps impatiently as I watch a particularly attractive man, all cut jawline and broad shoulders, shrug into a vintage varsity jacket and help his girlfriend into her peacoat. He's apparently the guest of honor and recently recorded an audiobook. Jeff told me he recognized most of the people here as Foxes players. When I gave him a blank look, he gave me an indulgent smile, like I was a slow-witted younger sister. He explained they were all professional baseball players.

Big deal.

I've dealt with my fair share of self-important individuals, although I must admit, most of the time they aren't local celebrities. Still, I am less than impressed. So they have a cool job? Don't care. I couldn't tell you the first thing about baseball, which is probably evident since I didn't even recognize the team's name when Jeff told me. The good news is that they all seemed nice enough when they ordered, and they didn't treat me, or Jeff for that matter, as *less than* simply because we sling drinks for a living. Besides, at least one man, Benny, was pretty hot and charming himself.

I'm not opposed to the occasional hookup. In my experience, however, going home with a bar patron usually ends in disappointment. Men like to talk a good game and to some of them, bagging the bartender is like some sort of conquest, a point of pride. By the time the lights in the dimly lit bar raise, signaling the end of the night, the men rarely live up to the game they try to spit when the lights are low. But, because I'm a glutton for punishment, every once in a while I go home with a customer, determined to give it one more shot in the hopes that this time, it will be a little less disappointing than the last. I'm rarely proven wrong.

Tonight, however, seems promising, especially because Jeff promised to take care of the end-of-shift closing duties. When we work a private party, Tilly and Sloane allow us to leave once our duties are done, rather than having to wait until Sip closes. This bodes well for me and this Benny guy, who, I notice, is lingering with the rest of the stragglers.

The woman in the peacoat approaches me to pay the bill. She's been friendly and seems like a good person, chatting and checking in with me throughout the night. She offered some of the catered food to me and Jeff, which was kind but unnecessary. When she adds a couple extra zeros on the check, I pat myself on the back for reading her character correctly. The extra cash will go far in my travel fund, which right now, consists of a Costco-sized peanut butter jar under my kitchen sink, stuffed with tip money. I have no travel plans yet, but once I develop them, I'll be ready to go.

"If you ever want to go to a baseball game next season," the woman tells me with a smile, "here's my name and number. Warner would be happy to hook you up with tickets. You've done an amazing job. We really appreciate all the work you did making the room look great."

I thank her because I put in a little more effort for this party than I normally would. Granted, most people decorate their own parties instead of dropping off a box of decor the morning of the event, but given the tip she gave me, I'd happily decorate again. It only consisted of scattering book covers and what looks to be promotional materials across the room. The most difficult thing I did was hang little streamers made of circles of book pages across the doorframe, creating a makeshift curtain for guests to pass through to enter the room. It was cute and whimsical and fit the vibe of Sip.

I gather the receipt and pen, placing them in the bottom drawer of the electronic register at the back of the bar.

"Yo, Benny, you coming?" the deep voice of the audiobook narrator booms.

"Nah, I'm gonna hang back. I'll catch you guys later." I look up to see Benny waving off his friends, his blue eyes sparkling when he catches my eye.

Benny—or should I call him Sam?--is incredibly attractive. A little older-looking than me, his day-old stubble seems to have more salt than pepper, although his thick head of hair is a uniform, dark brown. The sleeves of his light blue henley are pushed up, and holy forearm porn, Batman. Thick muscles and protruding veins are covered by a smattering of black tattoos. The rose on the back of his right hand makes my mouth go dry, imagining what it would feel like wrapped around my throat.

*Down, girl.*

He smirks when he catches me blatantly checking him out. I shrug, and the smirk turns into a full-blown smile. For anyone else, that smile would be lethal, but I know a fuckboy when I see one. Still, my panties might have incinerated. Only a little bit.

"You done?" I can't tell if he is asking if I'm done with work or done checking him out, which are two very different answers.

I notice he doesn't ask if he can take me home, or if I'm even interested. The confidence on this one reigns supreme.

Instead of answering his question, I say, "Let me grab my coat. Meet you downstairs?" He nods. I hustle down the stairs and into the back room. Sloane's office door is half-cracked, and I can hear a podcast coming from her laptop. She rarely works in silence. I poke my head through the door to say goodnight before pulling on my bomber jacket and slinging my fringed purse over my shoulder. As expected, Benny is waiting for me at the front of the bar, leaning against a high-top table looking like a whole-ass snack.

I approach him and from the corner of my eye, I can see Tilly watching our entire interaction. I turn to wave goodbye to her and the look of unbridled excitement on her face makes me cringe. She's always telling me to put myself out there, to date more, and the smile she's wearing is threatening to swallow her entire face. I roll my eyes. She should know this is a hookup and nothing more.

Benny–Sam?--holds the door open for me, and we step into the chilly fall air. It's nearing midnight and the darkness envelops us like a secret.

"So, what am I supposed to call you? Sam? Benny?" I ask, breaking the silence.

"You can call me Daddy if you want." The toe of my boot catches on the pavement, causing me to stumble a bit, but I remain upright. The glow of a nearby streetlight illuminates the amusement on his face, and I scoff.

"Benny is fine," he assures me, the hint of a laugh lacing his voice. "Are you hungry?" I glance at him sideways, trying to figure out if he's making another joke or some sort of snide remark about my body.

Look, I love my body–it does amazing things for me–but I know what it looks like. I'm curvy, and for the most part, I'm not bothered by that, despite my doctor regularly informing me I need to lose weight. I work out semi-regularly, thanks to the rampant heart disease sinking its teeth into both sides of my gene pool, but I also look like I won't turn down a cookie. Because I won't. Cookies make the world go 'round.

Still, especially when meeting a new person, it's hard for my brain not to immediately go to self-destructive thoughts about my weight. Chalk it up to years of being a woman in America, paired with dear old Dad's regular comments on my appearance during my formative years. So, when Benny asks if I want to eat, I'm trying to figure out if he's assuming I'm hungry because I'm what the fashion TikTokkers call "mid-sized," and what my father would call "chunky."

Whether he senses my apprehension or not, he keeps talking. "You were on your feet all night, and the finger foods Alicia ordered were good, but nothing like the burgers at Moon Shadow. Ever been there?"

"Yeah, I've been there," I tell him with a grin. If I'm particularly exhausted or hungry after a shift, I order breakfast to go from the greasy spoon diner down the street from Sip. I'm obsessed with their Cabo skillet, but, in my opinion, you can't go wrong with any form of breakfast potatoes.

"Great; I'm starving." He grabs my hand and tugs me along the sidewalk, moving at an easy pace but with clear purpose.

When we're seated at the diner, Benny eyes me carefully when I order my skillet, sour cream on the side. He doesn't hold back in ordering half the menu for himself. I blow out a small sigh of relief. I am hungry, and I hate that I'm self-conscious about potentially eating more than my date. Not that this is a date, but some pressure is still there.

Benny keeps up a steady stream of chatter while we wait for our food, asking me questions about myself. I tell him about growing up in Michigan, where my mom was a college professor for a hot minute before my parents divorced. He tells me about his job as head coach of the Chicago Foxes. He overdramatically winces when I call him a head coach, insisting the title is "manager" in baseball, which is stupid.

"Are the other coaches called managers too? Who is your assistant manager?"

"No, I'm the only manager. Next in line is the bench coach. Now that you mention it, I'm the only coach not called coach, even though the guys will sometimes address me as such. I don't know why that is." He takes a long drag of his peanut butter milkshake, looking contemplative. "I've never thought about it, and I've been in baseball in some capacity for more than twenty years."

I whistle. "Wow, you're old."

Benny's eyes flash but he laughs loudly. "Watch it, gorgeous. I'm not that old."

"How old are you, exactly?" I ask. Age really doesn't matter to me, as long as two people are at the same life stage–and as long as their frontal lobes are fully developed.

"How old do you think I am?" Benny asks, a teasing spark in his eye.

"I dunno, like sixty?" He chokes on his milkshake and pounds his chest with a fist to clear his airway.

"Sixty! Careful there, girl." He points at me from across the table, but his eyes hold a twinkle of mischief. The dark tone of promise in his voice causes me to squeeze my thighs together.

I shrug, despite the additional moisture coating my panties. "So, if you're not sixty, how old are you? Seventy?"

"For your information, I'm forty-two, which is old enough to know what to do with that smart mouth of yours," he says darkly.

Yep, panties obliterated.

The lusty tension at the table is broken by the arrival of our food. By the time our server puts the last of Benny's dishes down, the table is covered in baskets of mostly fried goodness.

"Do you like onion rings?" he asks conversationally, as if he didn't just threaten to put me in my place moments ago.

"Yeah, they're good," I answer. He tips the basket of fried rings onto the plate holding my skillet. Three quarters of them tumble out onto my plate, and he pulls the basket away before I can scoop up a bunch and return them.

"Nope, those are yours. Fries?" he asks. When I shake my head, knowing between the spicy, cheesy skillet and the whole onion's worth of rings, it will be more than enough food, he shakes his own head at me. "Just try one. The curly fries are better than their sweet potato fries, but they're both so good they let me order half and half."

Never one to turn down a potato (see cheesy potato skillet for reference), I acquiesce, taking the loopy fry from his fingers. He watches me with a sense of pride as I take a bite. I have to agree, it's a fucking good french fry.

"If you could only watch one movie the rest of your life, what would it be?" He watches me as I chew thoughtfully, thinking through all the possibilities.

"It's hard to say. Maybe *Magnolia*?"

"What's that? The Julia Roberts movie?"

"No, that's *Steel Magnolias. Magnolia* is a movie from the nineties. It's long, but really good. All the characters' storylines are connected, like the way they are in *Pulp Fiction*, you know?"

"What do you know about *Pulp Fiction*? How old are you?" Benny's eyes are skeptical.

"I'm twenty-eight, old man," I tease. He narrows his eyes at me. I shrug. "My dad was really into movies. Back when I had more of a relationship with him, he introduced me to all kinds of films."

Benny doesn't say anything in response to my comment about not having a relationship with my dad. That's fine with me; it's not a secret, but I also don't need to be having a deep conversation with a man I'm going to sleep with once and never see again.

"Okay, so what movie would you watch?"

"That's easy. *The Little Mermaid*." He says the answer so matter of factly that I almost feel bad for the laugh that escapes me.

"Wait, you're serious? The Disney movie?" Benny smiles, a far-off, nostalgic look in his eyes.

"Yeah. It came out when I was a kid and I didn't care about it then. My sister loved it, but I didn't. But when my oldest daughter was born, she was such a girly girl. All she wanted to do every day was snuggle with me and watch *The Little Mermaid*. After every game, I'd come home, and she'd waddle over to me, holding the DVD case. It was easy. No matter how I played, no matter whether I won or lost that day, all that mattered in Genesis's eyes was whether I could watch the movie with her."

I smile. It's a nice memory. I have similar ones from when I was young, watching movies with my parents, an oversized bowl of popcorn on my lap.

"How old is your daughter?"

He tells me about his three children, Genesis, Kai, and Scarlett. Benny explains that Genesis is a senior in high school, getting ready to apply to colleges, while Kai is fifteen and Scarlett is five.

"Wow, that's an age difference with the little one," I blurt out, before realizing how rude that could be. Benny chuckles.

"Yeah. My ex and I had the crazy idea that having a third child would somehow save the marriage. It didn't." He smiles fondly, despite the somewhat sad tone the conversation takes.

"Oh." That's all I can think to say. I'm relieved to hear him say "ex," though. When he initially mentioned his daughter, I had a heartbeat of panic that Benny was married. I was getting ready to perform a series of mental gymnastics to extricate myself from the situation before hearing he was single.

"Keeley, my ex, and I have a good relationship though. She lives in Nashville with the kids. It's where I'm heading the day after tomorrow. It's where I live in the offseason, too." I can't help the small pang of jealousy in my chest at Benny's excitement. I believe he's genuinely thrilled to see his kids, and I can't help but wonder what that's like for his children, to know they have a father who not only wants to see them, but is excited about the prospect.

The meal winds down, Benny making a substantial dent in his food. When I request a box to take the rest of my skillet home, he insists on putting his extra fries, onion rings, mozzarella sticks, and chicken fingers in the box for me as well. It's enough to count as more than two meals. I'm not exactly poor, but I won't say no to free food, especially when it's from Moon Shadow.

"Where to now?" Benny asks as we slide out of the booth. I arch an eyebrow, surprised. I guess I assumed the night was going to end in sex, but maybe I misread the situation? "I meant, your place or mine," he clarifies, pulling me close and kissing my temple. It's the first real physical contact we've had tonight, besides the occasional brush of our fingers when I slid his drinks to him across the bar earlier.

"Yours," I say definitively. Benny might be hot and seem like a decent guy so far, but as a single woman living in the city, I'm not going to be inviting men I barely know into my apartment. He nods, throwing his hand into the air to hail a nearby cab.

# CHAPTER FOUR

## *Benny*

Fuck Me Hard cocktail: Triple Sec, Amaretto,
Vodka, Raspberry Liqueur, Peach Liqueur,
Cranberry Juice, Orange Juice

The cab ride back to my townhouse is quick, which isn't a surprise. Moon Shadow and Sip aren't too far from where I live, but I don't love the idea of Delaney walking in the cold night air after having been on her feet all night.

When we get inside, I offer to put her doggie bag from the diner in the refrigerator. When I turn, closing the fridge, Delaney presses herself against me and pulls my face down for an enthusiastic kiss. I can't help but groan into her mouth. The most awkward part of a hookup is when you get to your destination, whether it's your place, hers, or a hotel, and you stand there awkwardly not knowing if you should talk first, go straight for the kill, or do something else entirely. Delaney, god love her, went straight for the kill and I fucking love it.

I kiss her back with equal fervor, licking the seam of her lips and demanding entrance. She opens to me immediately, and I reward her with a press of my hips against hers. She's a little shorter than me; I know she can feel the evidence of my erection against her belly. Bending down, I scoop her into my arms, and her legs instantly wrap around my waist. Gripping her lush ass, I walk us back into my bedroom. I internally thank my past self for having the foresight to remove my half-packed suitcase from the bed. In reality, I was anticipating coming home mostly drunk and falling into bed, but sober and falling into bed with Delaney is a much better alternative.

I place her gently onto the bed and crawl my body over hers, settling between her thick thighs, knowing there's nowhere else I'd rather be. My hands explore her beautiful body while my tongue explores every millimeter of her mouth. I get to know her curves and valleys, soft peaks and gentle dips. She rocks her hips against mine, hooking her legs once again behind my back, silently begging me to pull her under the waves of pleasure I know are building.

My palm comes to her breast, and I can feel the tightening bud of her nipple through layers of fabric. She's obviously turned on—we wouldn't be here otherwise—but proof of it adds another layer of lust to my already scrambled brain. I run my thumb over the stiff peak and she whimpers.

"Benny." My name is a sigh. I bring my free hand to her hair, tugging her head back to allow me more access to her neck. When my teeth graze against the column of her graceful throat, she leans into me, seeking out more pressure. I provide it in the form of an additional tug on her hair and a rough squeeze of her breast. She moans into my mouth and rocks her hips again.

"Enough of this," I say, breaking the kiss and coming to kneel in front of her. "I'm going to strip you down and shove my tongue in your pretty cunt. If you don't want that, now's the time to say so." She narrows her eyes at me and presses her lips together. I know from the way I worded it, she's doing what I asked, but it's not enough. I need enthusiastic, explicit consent. "Tell me what you want, Delaney."

"I want that." When I give her a hard stare, she rolls her eyes at me. I want to laugh; she's trying so hard to get under my skin. "I want your tongue in my pretty cunt, Benny," she taunts.

That's more than enough consent for me, even if she is being a brat about it. I flick the button of her jeans. I unzip and slide them off her with practiced efficiency. I'm left staring down at a lacy, neon pink thong. I'm a little surprised, which must show on my face. Delaney, all tough on the exterior with her black tattoos, black hair, septum piercing, and combat boots, still has a little bit of girly girl in her.

She huffs a sigh, as if to say, *get on with it then*, and this time I can't hold back my laugh. Delaney may try to mask her lustful longing with impatience, but I know what she needs. And I'm about to give it to her.

Without waiting to remove her panties, I dive in with my tongue, tracing her seam through the lacey fabric and eliciting a throaty moan from her. Her arousal has soaked through the thong, the moisture coating the insides of her upper thighs. I can smell her sweet, musky aroma and can't wait until I can spear my tongue inside her. Taking off the thong will take too long. I need to be inside Delaney in any way I can. Immediately.

I fist the front of her panties, holding it tight between us. The rough fabric stretches across her clit, giving her the friction she's looking for. I know it's not enough, and her frustrated groan after a second of rutting her hips to no avail tells me she comes to the same conclusion. I release my grip. Hooking the soaking gusset of her panties with my thumb, I roughly pull the fabric away from her center while I bend low and shove my tongue inside. It's hard and fast, with little to no buildup, but I don't hear any complaints from her. I move my mouth upwards, sealing my lips around her clit and suck hard. There's nothing gentle about my movements and given the way she's pushing my face further into her as if she can't get enough, Delaney likes it this way.

Over and over again, I flick at her swollen clit with my tongue, pressing first one finger, then two, inside of her. She's not quiet about it, and her garbled moans and whimpers encourage me further. Crooking my fingers inside her, I stroke along her inner wall. Her legs, bent at the knee, start to tense. I coax gentle shakes from her thighs, knowing she's teetering on the edge. Her fingers grapple in my hair, tugging hard enough that it's bordering on painful, tears pricking the back of my eyelids. I'll never stop. Not when she's this close. A few more well-timed flicks of her clit have her shattering around me. Her legs slam shut around my head on instinct. The sensation is jarring and sexy at the same time, sending another bolt of heat down my spine and straight into my already rock-hard cock.

Delaney's tremors start to subside and I continue licking her through wave after wave of seemingly unending pleasure. Her thighs' grip around my face loosens and I am temporarily disappointed at the loss of pressure and heat. She sighs dreamily as I come up for air, grinning down at her.

"How are you doing, sweetheart?" I ask her with a smirk, already knowing the answer. She cracks an eyelid to glare at my open display of self-satisfaction.

"I'm okay," she says with an exaggerated shrug. It would almost be believable if she didn't have that dreamy look on her face.

"Only okay, huh? Guess I didn't fuck the brat out of you yet." Delaney's sharp intake of breath and wicked grin tells me she knows exactly what she's doing. I'm here for it. I'll play her games all night long.

In one quick movement, I grab her hips and flip her onto her knees in front of me. I smack her ass, watching it jiggle under my palm. She moans and presses her hips back into me.

"I know, beautiful. You're so ready for me." Unzipping my pants, I pull out my cock with one hand and lean forward to rummage in my nightstand for a condom with the other. I rip it open with my teeth and sheath myself quickly.

Delaney pushes back against me. She's such an eager, greedy girl. I already know I'll be thinking of this for weeks once I'm back in Nashville.

"Come on, Benny. Fuck me hard like I know you want to," she goads.

*You don't have to tell me twice.*

Fisting her thong once again, I grip it hard and give it a sharp tug. It snaps away at her hips and she gasps loudly.

"Did you just rip my underwear?" Her voice is indignant. I don't say anything in response. I thrust my hips forward, stuffing her tight pussy full of my cock in one movement. Her resulting scream is a mix of pleasure and something I really hope isn't pain. I lean forward, dragging a palm up her spine.

"I'm so sorry, Delaney. Are you okay?" Again, her hips thrust back at me.

"Don't you dare apologize. Keep going. Please."

There are times for slow, passionate lovemaking, but this is not one of them. I'm happy with any kind of sex. To me, sex is like pizza. Just as it's not possible to have bad pizza (because even bad pizza is still pizza), it's not possible to have bad sex, if everyone is getting off and getting what they need. And I'm going to make sure Delaney not only gets off multiple times, but gets exactly what she needs.

I love that she wants it hard and on the rougher side. I love that she's not a frail, wispy little thing like some of my previous girlfriends; I know she can take what I have to give her. Fuck, I'm taking everything she has to give me.

I bring my hand to the front of her chest, pushing back so she is upright on her knees. With one hand on her ample breast, the other on the cleft of her soft hips, I pound into her from behind. And like the champ she is, she meets me at every thrust, taking what she needs.

*If I'm not careful, I could get addicted,* I think, while I find myself wishing I didn't leave for Tennessee so soon. My thoughts are interrupted by Delaney's hand pressing against mine, urging it upward to her neck. I abandon the pinching and tugging of her nipple and splay my fingers across the pale expanse of her throat, holding her steady as I continue thrusting. Delaney moans, thrusting her hands into my hair with one hand and taking over for me at her breasts with the other.

I wish I installed a mirror for a headboard.

The parts of Delaney I can see are incredible, but from this position, I can't see the shake of her tits as they absorb the movements of each of my thrusts. I can't see the flush I know is spreading across Delaney's cheeks. What I can feel, however, is the slow tightening of her pussy against my cock as I slide in and out, in and out, of her warm, wet channel.

I grit my teeth, trying to hold off a little longer in order to ensure her pleasure. She's getting close. I know it, and judging by the uptick in her incoherent babbling, she knows it, too. I move my hand from her hip to play with her clit.

"Benny, please," Delaney whimpers. "Choke me, please."

*Fuck.*

How am I supposed to stave off my orgasm when she says things like that? Because I am a gentleman, I do what she asks. I apply pressure to both sides of her neck, careful to avoid her windpipe while I restrict her blood flow. Delaney explodes around me, coming with a keening wail. At the flutters rippling around my cock, I explode too, spilling into the condom and bellowing my own release.

Delaney and I both tip forward. She catches herself on her hands. I throw one arm out to the side to hold me up, so I don't completely collapse on top of her.

Holy fuck.

I might have to retract my earlier comparison of pizza to sex, because no sex after that will ever compare. I slowly slide out of her, pressing a kiss to her sweaty back. I dispose of the condom in my bathroom, bringing a warm washcloth back to the bed. She flinches when I press it against her sensitive skin.

"Oh, you don't have to do that," she protests, closing her legs.

"Delaney," I tell her sternly. "You let me fuck the hell out of your perfect body. This is literally the least of what I 'have to do.'" She closes her mouth but allows her legs to fall back open. After gently cleaning her, I toss the washcloth into the laundry basket I keep in my closet and return to the bed, settling in beside her.

"Give me a couple minutes to get my legs underneath me," she says. I give her a quizzical look. "I'll be out of your hair in a minute."

"Nope," I say simply, pulling her back to my chest and holding her tightly to me. She could push against me, and I'd let go immediately, but I don't need Delaney acting like her presence after some of the best sex of my life is an inconvenience. I'm not having it. She stiffens initially against me, but after a few seconds, she relaxes into me. I smile into her unruly mass of hair.

# CHAPTER FIVE

## *Delaney*

The Steamroller (A Delaney Kristoff Original):
Tequila, Serrano Pepper, Elderflower Liqueur, Egg
White

I wake a few hours later, annoyed at myself for having fallen asleep.

*Way to go, Kristoff. Falling asleep in your hookup's bed.* I've become a cliche.

I lift my head slightly. I'm still pressed against Benny, his soft snores filling the room. At least he's still asleep, and we don't have to deal with that awkward, morning-after dance. Do we hug? Do we kiss goodbye? No thanks. I'm happy with the old Irish exit.

A glance at the digital clock on the nightstand tells me it's three in the morning. Who even has a clock anymore? Don't normal people use their phones these days? That's what happens when you hook up with someone from a different generation, I guess. I suppress a chuckle when I think about what Benny might have to say about that last thought, then clench my thighs together all over again.

Benny might have joked about me calling him daddy, but he definitely gives off daddy vibes. The "warnings" he gave me in the diner earlier tonight left me certain about the kinds of "punishments" he might dole out when pushed. I'm equally certain I would enjoy them. Huffing a laugh, I can't help the small roll my hips complete as I think about it.

*Stop it, Delaney. You can fantasize later in the privacy of your own apartment.*

I roll toward my stomach and away from Benny, attempting to extricate myself from the bear hug he currently has me trapped in. He shifts slightly as I pull the sheet off me carefully. I look down at my half-naked body, feeling like Winne-the-fucking-Pooh. I'm in my black T-shirt and nothing else. In the throes of passion last night, we didn't even remove my top. What the hell?

Oh well. It will make getting dressed again that much faster. I try to scoot myself toward the opposite end of the bed from Benny, but the movement ends up tugging the blankets away from him, so I change tactics. I opt for a steamroller maneuver, tucking my arms into my chest and rolling myself over twice until I reach the edge of the mattress.

Success! Climbing out of bed to my feet, I turn around to see him awake and watching me, an amused smile stretching across his lips. *Dammit.*

"Whatcha doin' there?" he asks, failing to suppress the laughter in his voice.

"Uh, I'm just gonna head out," I say awkwardly, hiking my thumb over my shoulder, even though I end up pointing toward the window instead of the exit. Hell, at this point, I'd be fine jumping out the window to get out of here after that embarrassing steamroll move.

"Delaney, come here," Benny says softly, pushing himself up to a seated position against the headboard.

And wouldn't you know it? My traitorous feet listen to him. I blame it on those "daddy" thoughts from earlier. Benny's tone wasn't particularly demanding or stern, but my body was already primed to follow his instructions.

Coming to stand in front of him, he drags a hand down his face, his stubble making a scratching sound against his calloused palm. Why is that *sound* so sexy? I'm convinced at this point, Benny fucked me so hard that his penis must have rearranged my brain cells, because my mind is frazzled. I've never been one to linger after a hookup. I pride myself on being a hit-it-and-quit-it kind of girl. No muss, no fuss.

So when Benny reaches for my hand and tugs me down to sit next to him on the edge of the bed, and when my traitorous body *again* does what he wants, I sigh and give up the fight. Apparently, I'm a hit-it-and-quit-it kind of girl in every instance except where Sam Benjamin is concerned.

"You can go if you want, but at least let me give you a goodnight kiss."

"It's not nighttime. It's the morning," I stupidly point out. Yep, his dick definitely rearranged some gray matter.

"Then good morning, Delaney," he tells me softly, cupping my cheeks and pulling me gently toward his stupidly handsome face. My stupid face kisses him right back, too.

My lagging, reshuffled brain takes a moment to catch up to the fact that I'm somehow now straddling Benny. How did I get here? Did he pull me over here, or did I climb up here on my own, like a sex-deprived embarrassment?

Benny grasps the bottom of my shirt and pulls it over my head, groaning when my tits make an appearance. I'm not in my sexiest bra; it's plain black. It doesn't even match my underwear. I'm suddenly reminded of Benny *literally ripping my underwear off of me* last night. Who does that? I'm not complaining; I actually need to know. Because apparently, I've been missing out on feral, panty-ripping men my whole life.

Benny buries his face in my chest, his tongue licking a path around the perimeter of my bra. His fingers deftly unhook it at my back, and he slides the straps down my arms. The way he gazes upon my chest is reverent. My boobs are big (thanks, Mom), and I've never been a huge fan. The looks men started giving me at an early age, paired with ill-fitting tops and upper back pain have led me to believe, at least up until this point, that my giant boobs were more trouble than they were worth. But the way Benny is staring at them now? Yeah, it could change a girl's mind.

Both of his hands come to my breasts, palming them, cupping them in a way that is almost worshipful. He draws one breast, then the other, in turn into his mouth, sucking hard, and I'm instantly, automatically, wet again. Seeing as how I'm full-on straddling him (again, see torn-off panties for reference), there's no way Benny doesn't know how turned on he's making me.

Fuck it. In for a penny, in for a pound, as my grandmother would say.

I cant my hips again and Benny groans. It's his fault, really. I wouldn't be doing this if he didn't so masterfully suck my tits. And rearrange my insides earlier, so I'm left with thoughts of round two taunting me.

Keeping one hand on my breast, pressing open-mouthed kisses against my neck and chest, he gropes blindly in his nightstand drawer for another condom. He pulls one out triumphantly and rips it open with his teeth. What is with this guy and his animalistic ripping of things in bed? *Again, not complaining.*

I pull my hips back to watch him roll the condom down his shaft. When he's fully sheathed, he doesn't pull back his hands. Instead, he swipes two fingers through my wetness, groaning as he pulls them away, glistening. I watch, mesmerized, as he presses those two fingers into his mouth, groaning at the taste of me.

"So delicious. I needed another taste." Returning his hand to his cock, he slides himself through my folds, coating himself in my arousal. It's raw, it's dirty, and it's so fucking hot.

"Benny, please," I whine. I, Delaney Evangaline Kristoff, have never once begged a man for anything in my life before tonight. Men are takers. If you want anything from them, you have to take it yourself. Begging will get you nowhere. And yet, here I am, a writhing, horny mess on Benny's lap, begging for him to fuck me.

But Benny delivers.

Grasping my hip, he positions himself at my entrance and pulls me down. It's rough and hard and exactly the way I like it. The way I need it. I swivel my hips and watch in satisfaction as his eyes roll back in his head.

"That's my good girl, Delaney." His voice is raspy with sleep and lust. But fuck this guy. I'm not some bimbo so desperate for praise that I'm turned on by him addressing me the way he would a dog. *Right?* I hate myself a little bit as goosebumps erupt across my skin at the praise. Dammit, again.

I shove the thoughts out of my brain. I'll leave as soon as Benny gets me off. Then I can go home and never have to think about why I liked Benny's praise or any of the other million things he's said and done to me tonight.

He reaches down, bringing a finger on either side of my clit as he rubs up and down in time with my erratic movements on top of him. His teeth scrape against my neck, and I whimper pathetically.

"Come for me, Delaney. Milk my cock." Gross. *Milk.* One more thing that I shouldn't like, and yet, inexplicably, I do.

Tonight wouldn't be the first time I've come more than once in a night. It doesn't happen often, but it's not unheard of for me. However, after each instance, it takes more stimulation to get me there again. I don't have the time or patience to explain that to Benny and am contemplating the merits of faking a final orgasm when he slides a hand around me, gripping my ass tightly.

"You're going to come for me, one more time. No matter what it takes," he says roughly, picking up the speed in which his fingers rub my clit. Holy shit, did I voice my thoughts aloud?

Benny shoves his face into my chest, sucking hard against each nipple and, at the same time, his thumb presses against my back entrance. Fuuuuuck. He circles it lightly before pressing firmly against the puckered hole, and I detonate like an atomic bomb. I feel my orgasm *everywhere*. It's at the tips of my curled toes. It's in the tightness in my lungs, preventing me from sucking in a deep enough breath. I feel my orgasm release the tension in my *knees*, of all places. Samuel Benjamin is a talented, talented man.

"You're goddamn right I'm talented," he chuckles against my chest. Fuck. I guess I said that out loud. Sweaty and sated, I let Benny take over the movements of my hips, allowing him to drag himself in and out of my spent pussy until he's coming himself, spilling into the condom.

Tilting myself sideways, I allow myself to fall over onto the bed and off Benny's lap. I'm vaguely aware of him cleaning me up yet again, before he tosses me a clean black tee shirt from the top of his mostly packed suitcase.

"Put that on, sweetheart. You've got goosebumps." I do as he says, only because I don't have the energy to fight him. As soon as he falls asleep, I'm leaving anyway. I'll rest my eyes until I hear him drift off. I pull the pillow under my head, laying on my stomach and allowing Benny to trace soft patterns on my back through the fabric of the world's softest T-shirt.

I wake with a start. Peeking at Benny's old-man alarm clock, I see it's a little after five in the morning. Rubbing sleep from my eyes, I creep out of bed, cursing myself for falling asleep *again*. Benny is back asleep, *again*. This time, I'm extra careful in leaving his room. I swipe up my clothes from various spots in the room, not bothering with my ruined panties. It's not like they can be salvaged anyway.

I tiptoe out of the bedroom and get dressed in the living room, wincing at the idea of putting my jeans on commando. Benny's soft snores pause momentarily before resuming. I psych myself out, thinking about how embarrassing it would be if he caught me trying to sneak out twice in the same night. Morning. Whatever. I don't bother changing the rest of the way, holding my bra and shirt in hand, scooping up my jacket and purse, and ninja sprinting out of Benny's townhouse.

Admittedly, walking out of a stranger's house, black bra in hand, boots untied, and hair likely looking like a family of birds moved in, is not my finest moment. But I'll never have to see Benny again, and I can keep the memories of mind-blowing sex locked up tight.

45

# CHAPTER SIX

# *Benny*

Young Love (A Delaney Kristoff Original):
Raspberry Vodka, Tangerine Vodka, Pineapple
Vodka, Pomegranate Juice, Rosemary Sprig

I wake to the incessant sound of my phone's vibrations against the hardwood floor. Blinking away sleep, I frantically search for my phone near the side of my bed, thinking it slid off the nightstand overnight. Instead, I find it all the way across the room, half inside of my pants pocket from last night.

I barely have enough time to remember my night of heaven spent between Delaney's thighs before sliding my thumb across the phone screen to answer it.

"Dad, jeez, I've been calling you forever! I thought you said your meetings were done?" Genesis's clear voice sounds on the other side of my phone. Before responding, I glance over my shoulder, mindful to keep my voice down so as not to wake Delaney, but when I see my bed, I'm disappointed to find it's empty. I shouldn't be surprised; I literally woke up to her attempting to sneak out before I fucked her back to sleep. Still, I can't help but feel a stab of longing once I register her absence.

"Sorry, G. I overslept." I look at the clock, realizing it's after ten in the morning. I'm not surprised, seeing as Delaney and I were otherwise occupied for most of the early hours of the morning. Still, it's rare that I'm able to sleep late in the morning. I guess after the heartbreak of the season, I needed more rest than usual. "What's up?" I ask my oldest daughter.

"Well, I thought since I was going to pick you up from the airport, I would ask if you minded if I brought Garrett with me?"

I grimace, grateful this isn't a video call, and I don't have to school my expressions into neutrality so soon after waking up. There's not a good answer here. I don't like my daughter's boyfriend. He's a selfish punk and she deserves better—and I'm not saying that because I'm her father. Garrett tends to break up with Genesis if something better comes along, whether that's another girl or a more enticing social outing. He eventually comes crawling back to her when he's bored or tired of whatever shiny thing he chased after in the first place. However, I'm smart enough to know that I can't say that to Genesis. She's at an age where the slightest provocation can push her to rebel against her parents. If I tell her how much her mother and I despise her boyfriend, it will only drive her further and faster into his arms. Make no mistake, I'm not alone in my disdain for Garrett either; it's been a frequent topic of conversation between Keeley and me lately.

I love to fix problems for others. It's what Keeley always told me made her fall in love with me at first. I'm the one my kids come to with problems they don't know how to solve. And I'm the go-to guy to fix things on the Foxes. Don't get me wrong, I'm not a control freak who needs to fix everything. I know how to delegate and when to turn it over to someone who can fix it better than me. But I *like* being the one people rely on to fix things. I like feeling needed, and helpful, and responsible. It's killing me a little bit not to be able to fix this Garrett situation.

"Sure, you can bring Garrett," I say, infusing what I hope is passable cheeriness into my voice. The last thing I want is Garrett in the car when I see my firstborn for the first time in weeks. "Are Kai and Scarlett coming, too?" I ask, crossing my fingers. I'm not above using my other children as a buffer between me and the snot-nosed punk Genesis is dating.

"Scar has a birthday party, but I'll ask Kai," Genesis promises. "Three thirty tomorrow, right?"

"You got it. Thanks, G."

"You're welcome, Dad. I'm glad you'll finally be home." Those last six words melt me. Genesis and I have always been close, but she's seventeen now, and it's hard to see your child grow up and grow apart from you. I know it's natural and normal, but I don't have to like it.

After hanging up with Genesis, I text Keeley.

Keeley

Sorry. I told her she had to ask you first, hoping that might give her time to change her mind. Guess not.

Guess not.

See you tomorrow, Keels.

See you tomorrow, Sam.

I'm grateful Keeley and I can have as normal a relationship as possible after the divorce. I guess it helped that nothing catastrophic brought down our marriage, just a slow erosion of common interests. We wanted to stay together; we both were killing ourselves to make it work until one day, Keeley came to me with tears in her eyes, begging me to let her go. The worst part of it all was that it was easy to let her go. Of course, there was pain and grief and loss that came with the dissolution of our marriage. We had almost eighteen years together at the time we finally ended everything. But the last few years were filled with both of us forcing it and faking it, to the detriment of both of us and our relationships among our little family. By the time we officially called the marriage off, we were both relieved to let it go. Now, Keeley is engaged to Ricardo, with plans to marry him next fall.

I don't mind Ricardo; he's a bit nerdy, but I've come to hold an affectionate spot for him in my heart. He treats Keeley well, and most importantly, he treats my kids well. We have a decent relationship, and I'm truly happy for my ex. Some people find it weird that Keeley and I remain close and on good terms, but while we made a great couple for the first ten years of our marriage, the truth is, we're better off friends than husband and wife. I wanted to tell all of that to Delaney last night, but that's not exactly first date conversation. Not that what we did last night could be construed as a date.

Walking into the living room, I'm disappointed to see Delaney left without a trace. Not that I really expected evidence of her in the living room, or anywhere else in my townhouse, but I can admit a small part of me wished she had at least left a note or her phone number or something to remember her by.

I open the fridge to pull out an energy drink and spy Delaney's takeout bag from last night. Not exactly the evidence of her presence I was hoping for, but I guess it's better than nothing. I pull out the overflowing Styrofoam box and pop it into the microwave. If nothing else, at least I have breakfast before I head home for the next few months.

# CHAPTER SEVEN

## *Delaney*

Classic Margarita: Tequila, Triple Sec, Lime Juice, Salted Rim

"**M**om, I doubt I'm ever going to settle down anyway," I tell her, sipping my margarita at the beachfront cantina. Smoke from my mother's cigarette winds its way artfully up and into the night around us. The air smells like sea salt tinged with cigarettes. The waves lap lazily against the shore as the sun slowly sets in the distance.

I finally dipped into my travel fund, deciding on Cabo San Lucas as a destination, which had absolutely nothing to do with my favorite diner meal shared with an incredibly sexy man before a night of passionate, perfect sex. Nope, it's pure coincidence.

When I originally told my mom last week I was thinking of finally taking the trip, once the generous tip from that baseball player's girlfriend tipped the scales in my favor, she insisted we make a girls' weekend out of it. Which was fine with me. I don't have a lot of girlfriends, and the ones that I do have are not in a financial position to up and fly to another country on short notice.

I could have planned this trip further in advance, but by the time I made it through the dreary Chicago winter months, I was itching to get away. I needed a break from the gloom. I figured a change of locale might also get my brain to release its stranglehold grip on memories of my night with Benny. I am not-so-secretly hoping a vacation hookup will replace the near-nightly visions I have of Benny touching me, praising me, pounding into me…it's a problem.

After one particularly sleepless week, I said fuck it, called my mom, and asked her to meet me in Mexico. My mother needs very little motivation to spend money or take a vacation.

"Delaney," she says in her thick French accent. "I would encourage you to never settle down. Do you know, the first word in 'settle down' is not an accident. It requires you to settle. You, *mon petit chou*, settle for no man. Or woman," she adds thoughtfully.

I make the mistake of telling my mother about my encounter with Benny. There's very little I can say to shock my mother; she is French, after all. She has extremely liberal views regarding sex. Her takeaway from our tryst, though, is less than helpful.

"Move on to the next man, darling. That man surely has." I hope she's right. I want Benny to have moved on. It would make getting over our hookup easier. I hope he very publicly dates someone and shoves it in all our faces. Then I can be sad for a day or two before finally moving on with my life. I haven't pined over a man in a long time, and I vowed a long time ago to never do it again. If

Benny moves on (which *hello*, why wouldn't he? It's not like he's still thinking about our hookup all these months later.), then I can move on. Easy peasy.

"C'est fini. Il faut tourner la page, Delaney."

*It's over. Time to move on.*

She's right, but for the first time in a long time, I don't know how to do that. I guess I can fall back on the old saying my mother reminds me of next. Her voice, tinged with her accent, rings in my ears: "The only way to get over someone, Delaney, is to get under someone else."

Whoever said French is the language of love has clearly never met my mother.

# CHAPTER EIGHT

# *Benny*

The Benny (A Delaney Kristoff Original): Shitty
Lager Beer, Served in a Hurricane Glass

I've been stopping at Sip every few nights for the last week, ever since our home games started back up this season. We started the season on the road, which meant by the time we made it back to Chicago, we were in a time crunch. Everyone needed to get unpacked at their houses in addition to getting unpacked at the ballpark, all while somehow finding time to play several hours' worth of baseball each day.

Coming off spring training this year was brutal, too. The players all love spring training; the days are shorter than in-season baseball, and the weather is usually great. Springtime in Arizona is hard to beat. But for staff members, spring training typically means grueling hours. I usually made it into the complex by five each morning, and that's if I didn't want to get a workout in before the day started. Between planning for games, coordinating with my staff, and traveling to the various ballparks scattered throughout the Valley of the Sun, the days were long. With the way the last two seasons ended and the undeniable pressure to keep my job, working hard throughout spring training was a priority. Spending six weeks away from my family, knowing it will be even longer before I'm home for the offseason, is never easy either.

Needless to say, I could use a drink.

I try not to think about how Sip, my recent bar of choice, is in the opposite direction of my townhouse from the ballpark. I also try not to think about what I'll say to the gorgeous, tattooed bartender with a laugh like tinkling bells when I see her. I try not to think about how she might react to seeing me again, seeing as she made a point to sneak out the morning after, without so much as leaving her last name.

Last night, after a week of coming in to Sip and not seeing Delaney, I finally decided to ask the woman behind the bar if Delaney even worked there anymore. She gave me a sweet smile, which was almost pitying. She confirmed Delaney still worked at Sip, but she had been on vacation and should be back at work soon. I noticed she didn't tell me when her next shift was, which was slightly annoying, but a greater part of me recognized that she didn't give out that information to protect Delaney's privacy, which I appreciated. Still, that means I'm not sure she will be here tonight. But a man can hope.

I've never had a problem distancing myself after a one night stand, but there's something about my last one that has me coming back, craving just one more hit.

I pull open the door to the bar, eager to get out of the cold. The forecast called for snow flurries tonight; I'm not looking forward to tomorrow night's game. As soon as I cross the threshold of Sip, the air around me changes. It's not simply because I came in from the cold; there's something different about the atmosphere here today. There's an electric charge to the air. Instinctively, I know she is back at work, but a quick scan of the bar shows her nowhere in sight.

I walk toward one of the few empty seats at the bar when I hear her voice.

"Till, the Sunburst keg was all out, so I just changed–" she stops suddenly, catching sight of me. Her mouth hangs open slightly in a strangely adorable way. I'm hoping that bodes well for reconnecting with Delaney.

*My Delaney.*

Seeing her makes excitement spark in my blood. All I want to do is touch her. Feel the brush of her skin under mine, even if it's only to hand me another drink in a ridiculously dysfunctional cocktail glass.

"Hello? Delaney?" The man working behind the bar, who I recognize from Warner's party, is carrying a plastic crate of pint glasses. It looks like he's trying to carry them to the back, where I assume there is a dishwasher. Instead, Delaney is frozen, rooted where she stands, staring at me.

"Delaney Kristoff? Earth to Delaney?" The man tentatively nudges her with the crate, which seems to snap her back to life.

*Delaney Kristoff.*

I have a last name. Finally. Even if she refuses to give me her phone number, at least I might have better luck tracking her down through social media now that I know her last name. How many Delaney Kristoffs can there possibly be? None that could hope to hold a candle to her. *My* Delaney. Again, I pointedly ignore the small voice in my head telling me that I'm coming on strong—and possibly a bit stalkery.

She comes to stand in front of me, but she's still too far away for my liking, the two-and-a-half feet of bar top between us too much distance after all these months.

"W-what are you doing here?" she whispers. Her voice is soft, unsure.

"I heard this place makes an incredible Hemingway daiquiri," I tell her equally as softly, well aware that her coworkers are looking on, which sparks the curiosity of the handful of other patrons seated at the bar.

"We're all out," she tells me, but I don't miss the sparkle in her eye. "I can give you our special. I call it The Benny."

"Oh really?" I flirt back. "Is The Benny tall, strong and delicious?"

"Nope. It's shitty lager beer. Served in a hurricane glass," she says dryly, pantomiming the outline of an hourglass shape as she says it.

I can't help it. I tip my head back and laugh, the sound filling my chest with a lightness I didn't know I needed.

"That sounds like a solid choice," I tell her with a wink. She rolls her eyes playfully at me but reaches back to grab the requisite glassware.

As she pours my custom drink, the woman from last night bustles over, a wide smile on her face. She thrusts her hand out to me, introducing herself.

"I'm Tilly. My wife and I are the proud owners of this place. Thanks for stopping by so regularly," she says with a wink. I like her instantly. Her light brown hair is thrown up into an artful bun. She's wearing a retro style dress with thick pleats at the skirt, covered in tiny cherries. I have no doubt she's the creative stylist behind the eclectic collection of overstuffed, colorful chairs. I can't help but mirror her growing smile.

"Hi Tilly. I'm Benny. But I also respond to Sam." Tilly raises her eyebrows at the odd assortment of names but doesn't comment.

"Hey, Delaney." A man ambles over to the corner of the bar where Delaney is finishing pouring my drink. "Julian challenged me to darts. Whoever loses each turn has to do a shot."

Delaney is already shaking her head. Tilly, standing closer to me, also shakes her head. It does sound like a terrible, reckless idea. A recipe for a hangover at best. Wordlessly, Delaney fills two empty pint glasses with the same shitty lager as The Benny, only in a more appropriate vessel.

"Do you want to play with us? We can change the rules to take a drink of beer if you lose the round instead?" The guy's eyes are hopeful, and I watch as Delaney effortlessly shuts him down.

"Carl, in the words of my girl, Sabrina Carpenter, if you wanna go and be stupid, don't do it in front of me." She walks away, bringing the ridiculous hurricane glass to me and setting it on a flimsy cardboard coaster. Carl walks backwards toward the dartboards nestled in the corner of the bar, clutching his chest theatrically at the rejection. Tilly looks on quietly, pride evident in her features.

I can't help but let another laugh escape. There's something about Delaney Kristoff. She might not be my Delaney quite yet, but if I have anything to say about it, it's only a matter of time.

# CHAPTER NINE

# *Delaney*

The Hallucination (A Delaney Kristoff Original):
Absinthe, Homemade Sour Mix, Lemonade, Soda
water

He's here. In my bar. I surreptitiously pinch my arm for the third time. The results are the same as the first two times: I'm not dreaming. Maybe I slipped on something on my way to change out the keg and I'm really in a coma. Can you feel pinches in comas? I bet you can. Or maybe when I slipped, I knocked a piece of my brain offline and I'm hallucinating. There's no other explanation for Benny sitting here during my shift on a random Wednesday night.

He looks even better than the picture my memory painted for me. His stubble, his straight nose, that thick head of hair...those *tattoos*. If he's not some sort of hallucination or mirage, how am I even supposed to get work done? Admittedly, my job is not that hard, especially not on Wednesday nights. We're usually pretty dead mid-week, except for Julian and Carl's standing darts appointment.

I eye the drinks on the bar. Everyone is topped off, so I step in the back. As I'm contemplating heading into the walk-in chiller to cool my warm cheeks, Tilly pokes her head back. Her eyes are wide, but her smile is wider.

"That's the guy, right? The one you hooked up with last fall?"

I shush her immediately, worried that her voice will carry. Well, I guess that's confirmation enough that he's not a hallucination. Jury is still out on the coma thing, though.

"Yes, that's the guy," I sigh. The cat is out of the bag already. I peek out behind her. Benny sits at the bar, his beer in that laughable hurricane glass in front of him, watching the television screen mounted above the bar in front of him. He absentmindedly reaches for his drink, taking a sip like it's the most natural thing in the world, completely unbothered by his ridiculous glassware.

"I thought he was the guy. He's the one I told you was asking about you yesterday," Tilly tells me, wiggling her eyebrows. I scowl, mostly because that's my face's factory default setting. I had hoped, when Tilly told me someone came in asking about me, that it was Benny, then immediately talked myself out of the possibility.

Remember that whole "get over someone by getting under someone else plan?" Yeah, that didn't work. Not that my mother's advice is usually helpful, and not that I really got under anyone else in Mexico. I did, however, get a drink with a fellow American tourist, whose over-the-top pomposity and, quite frankly, boring personality promptly reminded me why I don't date. I got half a drink in before I was ready to call it quits, but I forced myself to stay for the whole round. Leaving a perfectly good cocktail unfinished is alcohol abuse.

Anyway, completely convinced that Benny had pushed me out of his mind as fervently as I tried pushing him out of mine, I assumed that whoever was asking about me was someone looking for something bar-related. My small social circle knows my work schedule, and they have my phone number to call me if they need me, so I knew it wasn't anyone from my personal life.

"So, your one night stand is back looking for more," Tilly's voice interrupts my thoughts. Tilly is a hopeless romantic. Sloane is, too, but at least she's a little more practical when she lives vicariously through her employees' love lives. Case in point: she doesn't even bother asking about mine because there's never anything to report. Tilly, on the other hand, is like a dog with a bone. The woman loves love. Honestly, good for her. I get why she does; she found her perfect match in Sloane. They complement each other perfectly. I, however, will not fall in love anytime soon. Or ever.

"Yeah, looking for another hookup, I'm sure. Guess I really am that good in bed." I say with a wink, deflecting.

"I'm sure you are, honey." Tilly's smile is knowing and I hate that she thinks this will go anywhere beyond–*maybe*–one more hookup. I'd hate to disappoint her. She knows I've mastered the art of the nail and bail. The old smash and dash. Hump then dump. I've done them all. Hell, I've probably invented entirely new ways to get off and get out. I'm probably nominated for an award somewhere for my services to hookup culture.

"So, tell me, why are you back here?" Sloane is leaning against the doorframe of her office, clearly having eavesdropped on this conversation. I give her a look as if to say, *you, too?* She laughs, then looks at her wife. A silent conversation passes through them.

"You know what? It's a light night. Why don't you call it a night? There's hardly anyone here, and I can't imagine more customers will be coming in." Tilly and her fucking meddling. Sloane is suddenly no better either.

"No, that's okay. I just came off a vacation. I'm sure Jeff wouldn't mind heading home early though." They think they can outmaneuver me? They should know that I invented the drip and dip. There's an award pending and everything.

"Jeff is fine where he is. That boy does not need to be let loose on the world any earlier." I shrug. "You, on the other hand, look like you have plans." I poke my head around Tilly's shoulders to look at the bar.

"I don't know. I have a feeling it's going to be a very thirsty night for some of these customers," I say, knowing full well that the handful of patrons sitting at the bar are likely to pack it up in the next hour or so.

"The only one thirsty here is you. Don't even deny it. Now if you won't leave voluntarily, Sloane here will fire you." Sloane grumbles something under her breath about always having to be the bad guy before turning back into her office.

"Fine," I huff at Tilly, knowing neither of them will make good on their threat. They love me too much. Grabbing my purse and jacket from the hook in the back, I throw them over my shoulders and stomp out to the bar. "Come on," I say to Benny, hooking my hand in his elbow and spinning him around on his stool. His eyes widen in surprise, but he doesn't fight me. He pushes back from the bar, leaving his half-finished beer. He tosses a twenty-dollar bill on the bar and doesn't wait for change. Hustling in front of me, he pushes the door open and follows me into the night.

After we walk half a block in silence, I whirl on him. "What are you doing here? What do you want?"

"Extra feisty tonight, I see," Benny says, trying and failing to hide his smile while he rubs his mouth. I track the movement, that fucking rose tattoo on the back of his hand taunting me.

"Is there a reason you're back?" I tap the toe of my boot on the sidewalk, hoping it distracts him from the flush I'm sure is on my cheeks.

"Well, firecracker, I have this thing called a job. It's a good one, so I wasn't ready to quit it just yet." He's teasing me, and while I secretly love it, I'm not going to let him know that. I can dole out a lot of shit; I'm impressed that not only can he take it, but he volleys it right back at me. Effortlessly.

"Funny. You've got jokes." Benny takes a step into my space. He's not completely crowding me, but the movement is enough to make me pay attention.

"I've got a lot more than jokes, baby." I scoff at the endearment. He steps away from me and resumes walking. "You coming or not?"

This asshole, forcing me to trot after him like some lovesick puppy. His strides are long, so I have to speed walk to catch up. Delaney Kristoff runs for no man. When I do finally reach him, he shortens his strides slightly, not enough to make me completely sure he's slowing for me or if it's all in my head. Like I said, asshole.

"Where are we going?" I try to hide my heavy breathing, our quick pace wreaking havoc on my lungs.

"Home." His response is simple, short, to the point.

"And what makes you think I want to go home with you?" I stop, crossing my arms tightly over my chest. Benny turns around and walks the two steps back to me. This time he fully crowds my space. His face is half-shadowed, partially lit by the nearby streetlamp.

"Delaney Kristoff, if you don't want me feasting on your pussy, tracing every inch of you with my tongue, wrapping you up in pleasure, and fucking you senseless for the next several hours, by all means, you don't have to follow me home. But," he gently tucks a strand of hair behind my ear. "If for some reason, you do, you stubborn, gorgeous girl, then keep up."

With that, he turns and walks away from me. Again. And, like last time, I hurry to follow him.

I decide if I am in a coma, no one better wake me up.

# CHAPTER TEN

# *Benny*



I hold the door open for Delaney, working hard to school my face into neutrality, when all I want to do is laugh and tease her and poke her a bit. She likes to act all tough, but she'd be more believable if her pupils didn't blow wide when I told her I wanted my tongue in her cunt. I didn't miss her sharp intake of breath or the way she didn't even fight me after I said my piece.

She huffs past me, still trying to convince me she doesn't want to be here. It's a valiant effort, seeing as no one has forced her across the threshold. Delaney walks through my living room without a second glance, stomping her way into my bedroom. She's adorable.

I step into the room, which, to Delaney, probably looks exactly as it did the last time she was here five months ago. This time, instead of packing up, my place is in a state of semi-unpacked. I own this townhouse, so I'm able to keep a lot of my things here year-round, but I haven't unpacked from spring training or our first road trip. The partial disarray of the room doesn't seem to bother her, or if it does, she doesn't outwardly react.

She leans against the foot of the bed, untying and loosening her shiny black combat boots. Once she tugs them off, she straightens, crossing her arms in front of her chest. I know she's trying to look like a badass here, but her crossed arms press her tits together and further upward, completely distracting me. I'd like to think I'm normally a gentleman, but I know Delaney's not exactly looking for chivalry right now.

"Alright, Benny. Here's how it's going to go. We're both going to get off, and then I'm going to leave." I chuckle. I can't help it.

"You beautiful, little liar. You're not leaving until I've coaxed at least three orgasms out of you. Then we can talk about you leaving." Her lips part in awe, pupils dilating. I wonder if she realizes she's stepped closer to me.

"I'm not sure you can last long enough for three orgasms, old man." I narrow my eyes at her. My little spitfire came to play.

Delaney turns to walk back to the bed but I catch her arm mid-turn. Before she can say anything else, my hand shoots up to her neck. I don't squeeze yet, but I use that hand and the other on her hip to push her back against the wall.

"We'll see about that. I've had five months to fantasize about your moans, your tits, your sweet, pink pussy. I know exactly what I'm doing here because I've had months to plan what I'd do to you if I ever got lucky enough to have you in my bed again." Delaney's eyes are hooded, her breathing shallow. "So, tell me, firecracker, are you going to let me eat you out? Are you going to give me that honey?"

She whimpers and a spark of triumph flares in my chest. I love her sass, her fire. I love that she gives me a hard time and makes me work for it. But more than all of that, I love it when I finally break through that tough exterior.

"I need to hear you say you want this, Delaney." I know she wants it, but with my hand around her throat, I need to hear it, too.

"Yes, Benny. Please." Her eyes widen, as if she's surprised by her own answer. I waste no time stripping her of her clothes. At the same time, her fingers fumble on my belt, her frantic movements uncoordinated by lust.

"I'm going to take care of you, baby. Give you everything you need," I promise her.

And I do.

Two orgasms later, Delaney is sprawled on my bed. We're both working to catch our breath. Satisfaction oozes out of every pore when I look at her, spent and satiated, a sheen of sweat glistening on her body. She pulls her hair off her shoulder, swiping it to the side as she fans her neck.

"I should have worn my hair up tonight," she comments between breaths.

"I can see if my daughter left a hair tie in the guest bathroom," I say, moving to get up. She throws her arm out across my chest to stop me.

"I'm not wearing your *daughter's* hair accessories after you just fucked my brains out!" Her facial expression conveys exactly how appalling that idea is.

"Delaney, it's not that big of a deal," I say, mentally patting myself on the back for glossing over her comment on adequately fucking her senseless. "I won't even make you give it back." I throw her a wink and bolt from the bed.

It only takes me about ten seconds to find what I need. Between Genesis and Scarlett, I knew I'd have something for Delaney here. Bringing the thick, black elastic to the bedroom, I detour briefly to my own bathroom to grab a wet washcloth to clean her up. Returning to bed, I already see her mentally reconstructing the walls she temporarily let down in the heat of passion. She pulls her legs together, cutting off my access to the happiest place on earth.

"Delaney, let me take care of you." My tone is stern, but her resolve is strong.

"Funny, I thought that's what you spent the last half hour doing."

"This is part of it." When she doesn't respond and doesn't open her legs further, I sigh. "Delaney, please. I need to take care of you as much as your body needs me to do this. If I'm going to fuck you this hard, then let me ensure you're okay after."

"I'm fine!" She scowls at me, but after a moment, she slowly parts her legs.

"Good girl," I praise. She scrunches her nose and pulls her whole head back.

"I'm not a fucking chihuahua." I can practically hear her eye roll.

"No, baby. You're a pit bull," I agree jovially. She doesn't seem to like that much better, but she doesn't argue and lets me finish swiping the warm cloth through her swollen folds.

The whole time, she demanded I fuck her harder, deeper, rougher. I happily obliged, but I wasn't lying when I told her I needed the aftercare as much as she did. I can only destroy her pussy so much without needing to build the rest of her back up. I suspect she doesn't hate the attention as much as she portrays. I'm guessing she's not used to it. I press a kiss to her temple and watch her eyes flutter closed at the contact.

"Stay right here. I mean it." My tone is gentler than my words. I pull on a pair of athletic shorts and walk to the kitchen. I had a little bit of food after the game this evening, but my mind was elsewhere, wanting to get out of there as soon as possible to head to Sip in the hopes that Delaney was finally back at work. Now, I'm starving. Fortunately, I arranged a grocery delivery the other day, so my fridge and pantry are stocked. Delaney doesn't strike me as a picky eater so I reach for my go-to snack.

Three minutes later, the microwave dings and the pops from inside slow. I pour the popcorn into a large bowl. I walk back to the bedroom, jostling the bowl to coat the pieces evenly in the synthetic butter. It's not remotely healthy, not the extra butter flavor I buy anyway, but it is delicious and satisfying. I prepare myself to have to stop a half-dressed Delaney from walking out my door, but I'm pleasantly surprised when I enter the bedroom and find her exactly where I left her. I beam at her.

"Come here," I coax, helping her to sit upright. I set the bowl of warm popcorn on the bed and turn Delaney slightly so I can gather her hair into a ponytail. I run my fingers through her dark tresses, noting how silky and smooth they are. I pull her hair back gently, pulling the elastic off my wrist and twisting it through her hair. She sighs contentedly and I fight the urge to spin her around and demand she make the noise again. I pull her against my chest, plopping the bowl in her lap and flipping on the television on the wall across from the bed.

I'm hyper aware that she is giving me a gift, settling in and hanging out with me. I love it. We got along well the last time we hung out—both in the bedroom and at the diner. I turn on a nature documentary, but I couldn't tell you what it was about. Something about octopi, I think. All my attention is devoted to the way her chest rises and falls under my sheets with each breath she takes, the way her eyes widen at the story unfolding on the screen, the way her pink tongue darts out to lick her lips after every few bites of popcorn. Forget the miracle of nature; Delaney herself is a phenomenon.

The supply of popped corn slowly dwindles. Delaney tries, and fails, to stifle a yawn.

"I'm only staying because you promised me three orgasms and you only delivered on two. You owe me," she says, keeping her eyes on the screen.

*Whatever you want to tell yourself, firecracker.*

"I'm a man of integrity, baby. I always deliver on my promises. I'm not quite sure you're ready for a third, sleepyhead."

"I'm not...tired," she says through another yawn.

"Okay," I tell her, my voice thick with sarcasm. I tug her closer to me until her head rests on my chest. She stiffens slightly.

"I don't cuddle." She really is a pretty liar. The entire documentary, she was snuggled up against my chest, but now that the movie is over, I guess she can't fool herself into thinking that her close proximity is due to the shared popcorn bowl. She wiggles away from me, and I let her go. I'm never going to force her, or any woman for that matter, to do anything she doesn't want to do. The rejection would sting more if I wasn't completely convinced that the only reason she's doing it is to build up her walls again.

I turn the lights off via the remote on my bedside table. Delaney's breathing evens out in no time, and I find myself drifting off shortly after.

When I wake, her head is on my chest, her dark hair spread around, most of it having escaped the confines of its ponytail and tickling my nose. I smile to myself. Not a cuddler, my ass. I send a prayer to the universe, coaxing out a few more minutes of this heaven before Delaney wakes and inevitably starts building her walls again. She's a tough nut to crack, but I've never had a problem with patience or determination.

# Chapter Eleven

## *Delaney*

The Old Smash and Dash (A Delaney Kristoff Original): Bourbon, Muddled Orange, Simple Syrup, Mint

I wake to an unfamiliar smell. Something expensive and all man. I scrunch my nose. Blinking, I try to orient myself to my surroundings and quickly realize I'm not in my own bed. *Duh, Delaney.*

The chest underneath my face rises and falls. Fuck. I should have known pillows aren't this muscular. Or hairy. I drag a hand down my face, surreptitiously checking to make sure I didn't drool on my bedmate's chest.

"Good morning, sunshine." Benny's voice is deep and sandpapery in the morning. It sends tingles to my lady parts and makes me want to throw myself out the window. I was not supposed to stay the night.

The events of last night seep back into my consciousness and I realize the only reason I stayed was because Benny tricked me into delusions of a third orgasm. This is all his fault, really. I should throw him out the window instead.

"Nope, don't you dare try to backtrack out of this," he says, tapping me lightly on the nose. Did Sam Benjamin somehow become a mind reading wizard overnight? Or have I spoken my thoughts aloud again without realizing it? I scrunch my nose in disgust.

"I was promised a third orgasm," I grumble under my breath, moving to get out of bed. I've stayed here long enough. Thick arms band around my waist before I can fully extract myself from the bedsheets. I yelp as I'm pulled back onto the bed. Benny climbs over me, triceps bulging as he holds himself above me.

He leans down and kisses me deeply. My stupid, traitorous body kisses him back with equal enthusiasm. Fine. I'll allow one more orgasm before leaving. This better be worth it.

"I promise, it's always worth it." Benny smirks at me. *God dammit, Delaney, do you have no fucking filter?* I don't even think a thought before it passes through my lips.

Benny's fingers part my folds and he thrusts them roughly inside me. I gasp at the intrusion, relishing the stretch from two of his thick fingers. He crooks them inside me at the same time his thumb comes to my clit, rubbing gentle circles before picking up speed. Garbled moans leave my mouth without my permission. Benny smiles.

"That's my girl," he praises. Not true, but it's better than talking to me like I'm a dog.

"I'm...not...your girl." My argument would be a lot more convincing if it wasn't constantly interrupted by breathy moans. In less than a minute, Benny's got me hanging on the edge of an orgasm. I have never, not ever, gotten there so quickly, not even when I'm doing it myself, and I know all the things I like.

"Keep telling yourself that, baby." I close my eyes tightly. It has nothing to do with the pleasure coursing through my veins and everything to do with not wanting to see the smug look on Benny's stupidly handsome face. Or so I tell myself.

"Not...your...baby," I grit out between gasps of pleasure. My delivery could use a little work.

"Delaney, sweetheart. Do me a favor?"

"What?"

"Shut up and come."

I really need to have a conversation with my vagina, because I come as soon as Benny demands it from me. As if the man isn't smug enough when it comes to giving my body exactly what it needs.

My legs shake as I come down from wave after wave of pleasure. With relatively little stimulation, somehow Benny has coaxed out an earth-shattering orgasm from me, right when I woke up. I open my eyes to catch him licking my arousal off both fingers and his thumb.

"Did I fuck the attitude out of you yet?" He asks me with a wink.

I'm beginning to understand why female praying mantises kill their mates after sex.

# CHAPTER TWELVE

## *Benny*

The skeet and yeet (A Delaney Kristoff Original):
Prosecco, Pineapple, Coconut Milk

If looks could kill, I'm pretty sure I'd be incinerated by now. Delaney looks ready to shoot lasers out of her eyeballs. If anyone could make that happen, I'm sure she could; she's that stubborn.

"Well, this was fun," she says dryly, attempting to sit up. I'm still kneeling between her legs, so pushing her back down onto the bed is easy.

"I'm sorry, baby. You know I was joking, right?" She glares at me. Clearly, she does not. "Delaney, any second I get to spend between these incredible thighs is a little slice of heaven for me. Let me make it up to you." I lean over her, tucking her wild hair behind her ears.

"Fine. But I better get another orgasm out of this." I grin. I'll happily give her a million orgasms before I have to leave for work; I'm still coming out on top of this deal.

"Tell me how you want it, baby." I trace a hand down her arm, relishing in the shiver it evokes. Delaney talks a good game, but I know damn well the effect I have on her.

"I...I don't care." I pause, intrigued. She was going to tell me something specific. I know it. What I don't know is why she stopped herself.

"I want to know what popped into your head when I told you to tell me how you want it. Where was the first place your mind went?"

"Uh, nowhere. Come on, let's do this." I pull back, just slightly. Delaney brings her hand to the back of my neck and attempts to tug me down further. I won't deny her a kiss, but I'm not letting her off the hook that easily. I kiss her softly, quickly, then pull back.

"I know you thought of something specific. Why won't you tell me?" She doesn't say anything, but I suddenly realize she's avoiding eye contact. "Are you okay?"

"I'm fine," she answers quickly. Too quickly. "I don't think what I want is possible." Now I'm really intrigued.

"Unless what you want involves me suddenly having a vagina instead of a dick, I think I can deliver." After a moment, I tack on, "Or if you wanted to chop off my dick. Please don't do that."

She rolls her eyes but smiles. "I promise I won't chop off your dick. It'd be a waste of a good appendage." I tip my head back on a laugh. She's not wrong. "I just...have always wanted..." She's squirming now. "...to be fucked against a wall from the front. Like, with someone fully holding me up."

That's it? I don't say that aloud but based on the way she was so hesitant to tell me what she wanted, I really thought it would be something more obscure, or at least dangerous. My cock inflates further at the idea of Delaney's fantasy, especially now that it knows it's not going to be beheaded.

Delaney must mistake my pause as hesitation. "Never mind, it's stupid. I know I'm..."

"You're what?" I growl, sure she was going to say something unflattering about herself.

"Bigger," she whispers. *Oh, my sweet Delaney.*

"Baby, look at me." She looks to the side, her green eyes suddenly overbright. Grasping her chin, I gently turn her face toward me. Her eyes immediately look down, refusing to make eye contact. "Fine, I won't force you to look at me, but you better listen, okay?" I grab her hand and press it against my erection. My dick is straining against my gym shorts; I need her to understand what she does to me. "My cock is hard as a fucking rock thinking about fucking you against that wall. Get up. We're doing this."

"I don't want to hurt you, Benny." Delaney's voice is small. Quiet. Meek. It's awful.

"Delaney Kristoff, you can either walk your sexy ass over to the wall yourself or I'm going to carry you–which, by the way, I am fully capable of doing without any risk of injury. I'm not going to drop you either." My tone is probably harsher than necessary, but I don't care. Delaney is going to figure out–sooner rather than later–that her size has never been anything more than my warmup weight in the gym.

"I can walk myself," she mumbles under her breath, but she scoots to the edge of the bed without further comment. I step down, smacking her ass along the way. She lets out a little yelp and moves faster. Discarding my shorts and rolling on a condom in record time, I prowl over to where she's standing against the wall. My cock bobs with each step; she watches the motion and licks her lips. I stifle a groan.

Bending my knees slightly, I lift her into my arms. I had no doubt lifting her would be easy enough, but it's nice to confirm I was right.

"You want me to fuck you against the wall? Or right here in the air? Because I can do either, baby."

"The wall," she pants. At least she isn't fighting me on calling her baby. "I want to be smashed up against you." Fair enough.

I hoist her up a little further, widening my stance so I can support her with one arm. I snake my other hand underneath her thigh and position my cock at her entrance. Stepping forward, I press her against the wall and thrust inside. Gravity works in my favor as I drop her slightly further onto my dick, until I'm fully seated inside her wet heat. We both groan at the sensation. I pause, letting her adjust to the fullness in this new position.

"You okay, firecracker?" She nods vigorously, eyes squeezed shut. "Can you look at me, please? I need to make sure you're okay." When she opens her eyes, my heart stutters a bit to see a watery sheen over them. "Delaney, what's wrong? Did I hurt you?"

"No, no, it's good. I promise. I just..." She sighs deeply. I'm about to panic because the tears filling her eyes are threatening to spill over. "I have always wanted to do this. And I never..." She lets out a shuddering sigh that almost breaks my heart. "I never thought I'd get to do it."

I press a kiss on her mouth, her cheek, her neck. "Delaney, I will fuck you like this every day if you want."

"Shut up. You'll hurt yourself." She pushes against my shoulder, but it has no effect; her hand slides to the side since she is wedged between my hard body and the immovable wall.

"Watch it," I tell her, tone stern. "I'm going to get insulted if you have that little faith in my strength. I can do this all day. I *will* do it all day if you want, but at some point, both of us need to go to work. But I'll fuck you like this tomorrow and the next day and the day after that." I let her see the truth in my eyes.

"Benny, just please fuck me now. Please move." I press a kiss to her lips, letting her feel my grin. I do as she asks, pulling out and slamming back in with the same amount of roughness I'm learning she loves. I wasn't kidding when I told her I'd do this again. Honestly, I'd do anything she wants if it gets me inside her again. To be frank, I'd do almost anything she wants if it gets me in her general proximity again, regardless of whether we sleep together one more time.

# CHAPTER THIRTEEN

## *Delaney*

The Hump then Dump (A Delaney Kristoff
Original): Vanilla Vodka, Root Beer, Cherry Garnish

By the time Benny and I finish our last round of sex (notice I say our last round, because your girl here lost track of how many rounds there actually were), showered together (which consisted of just a shower; I'm not sure my poor vagina could have handled much more than that), and redressed, both of our stomachs were loudly protesting the lack of sustenance from our popcorn dinner last night.

"Let me take you to lunch," Benny had said between kisses in the shower. He was so sweet with the gentle way in which he washed my hair that my brain couldn't formulate a response to turn him down. So I stupidly just nodded my head.

Now, as we walk back to Moon Shadow, where Benny and I had our first real conversation, I tell myself that I'm only going for the free food. It's not like this is a date anyway. Benny's a nice guy with a sense of obligation to feed me since he spent so long absolutely destroying my body last night. And this morning.

It's an awkward time between breakfast and lunch, and honestly, not a time that I'm used to being awake. I am used to late nights and sleeping in. My eyes are rarely open at ten fifteen on weekdays. But given the awkward time, the diner is mostly empty, so we have no trouble getting seated and placing our order.

I sip on my root beer as Benny explains that tonight is a night game, so he still has another two hours before he needs to head in to work. My knowledge of baseball (and sports in general) is limited, but he is patient in explaining the basics. He tells me about his playing days as a catcher. That explains the muscular thighs that I've been drooling over since I met him. Thinking of his thighs makes me clench my own subconsciously.

Jesus Christ. I've been with Benny on two separate occasions and all of a sudden, I'm hornier than a trumpet convention. *Get it together, girl.* For once, Benny doesn't pick up on my obvious inattention, chattering away about work.

When our food arrives, he changes the subject abruptly. The shift in conversation makes me wonder how long he had been waiting to bring it up.

"So...not into me calling you a good girl, then?" I wrinkle my nose to convey my distaste. "So what should I call you next time, then?"

The audacity of this man to assume there would be a next time. I mean, I wouldn't say no, after sufficient time to go home and ice between my legs. A girl can only take so much.

"What makes you think there will be a next time?" I eye him warily, setting down my chicken salad sandwich and wiping flakes of croissant off my hands.

"There will be a next time, firecracker." The ego on this guy. Benny swallows another bite before forging ahead again. "Tell me you don't want me between your legs again. Go ahead. Lie to me, Delaney."

I say nothing, my silence speaking volumes. Apparently, Benny can read me like a book. *Whatever*, I think, literally shaking my head to hopefully knock some of the loose brain cells rattling around in my skull back into place. Anything to put up some defenses against this man.

"I'm waiting," Benny trills. I am, once again, identifying *really* hard with a female praying mantis. Instead of literally trying to bite his head off, I glare at him. I'm all about taking the high road these days, even if channeling my inner insect might be more satisfying in the short-term. Benny laughs, then softens his approach.

"What do you want me to call you then? How would you like me to praise you?" He drops his voice, as if the elderly couple across the restaurant from us has suddenly developed extrasensory hearing and will know we're talking about sex.

"Do you need to praise me?" I arch a brow.

"Yes." Benny's response is simple and straightforward. When he doesn't elaborate, I ask why. "Why do I want to tell you how amazing you are? Because you deserve to hear it. You deserve to know that you are incredible–in and out of the bedroom." After a brief pause, he continues, as if he hasn't left my brain spiraling from the ease in which he compliments me. "If I'm going to continue to destroy your pussy, I'd like to build up your confidence along the way. And not because I don't think you're confident, but simply because I appreciate you."

I have no idea what to say to that. I'm not opposed to receiving compliments, but when your love life consists of quick, generally less-than-satisfying hookups from randos that you'll never see again, compliments and praise aren't high on my list of expectations. It strikes me that as children, we receive praise all the time, even for the most mundane of tasks. At some point, we must have stopped receiving praise regularly. Aside from the occasional "good job" I get at work, usually from Sip's management team, I can't remember the last time someone gave me real, positive reinforcement. And the way Benny is looking at me, like he truly believes everything he's saying? I'm inclined to believe him, too.

"Please give me your phone number, Delaney." He exaggerates the puppy dog eyes he's giving me, which makes me crack a smile. Just a small one, though.

"I'm not sure it's worth it to have you bothering me all the time."

"You like it when I bother you, though." His response is quick and self-assured.

"Hmmm," is all I say. Benny and I both know I'll end up giving him my number, but at least he lets me pretend I'll hold out on him. I've never played these kinds of games with an intimate partner before, but I can't deny it's a little fun.

"What are you going to do when you get home?" He jumps from topic to topic, lithely shifting with expert precision. Instead of being jarring or giving me conversational whiplash, it's nice. It makes me think he's excited to keep engaging with me. Knowing he has no obligation to keep socializing with me, it's hard not to feel like he is doing it because he genuinely wants to. It's a heady feeling and I caution myself not to get used to it.

"I'm probably going back to bed," I tell him honestly. "Seeing as you kept me up half the night."

"I'm *so* sorry," he jokes. "I can't promise it won't happen again, though." I snort, this time not with my usual derision, but with humor. Benny grins. "Are you working again tonight?"

"Yeah, my days off are Mondays and Tuesdays usually, unless we have an event. Thursdays and Fridays tend to be our busiest nights, so I don't mind working those shifts."

"What's your favorite thing to do when you're not working?" Benny asks a lot of questions, but it doesn't feel like an interrogation. He thoughtfully nods along as I speak, earning himself an A plus in active listening skills.

"It might sound lame, but I really like developing new cocktail recipes. I guess that could count as work, but I do it at home for fun. I don't really do anything with the recipes I create, but it's fun to experiment with different tastes. I like looking at a menu or sitting down to a meal and tasting something, letting it inspire me to develop a cocktail pairing."

"That's really cool. What was the last cocktail you invented?" My cheeks flush. My brain is constantly thinking of new ideas, new names, and new flavor combinations. The one I came up with as we sat down several minutes ago is not exactly appropriate for public conversations. Benny picks up on my embarrassment.

"Tell me," he encourages.

"When we got here, I had a craving for root beer. That alone is pretty sweet, but I thought a little extra sweetness could cut through the taste of liquor, making a sweet, easy drinking cocktail." Benny nods along, listening avidly. "Adding vanilla vodka and cherry to root beer is simple, but sometimes simple combinations work best. Sometimes you don't want complex, layered flavors if the situation doesn't call for it."

"It sounds good. I'd drink it. What would you call it?" I squirm a little, because as soon as I thought of the flavor profile, the name popped into my head. That's typically how it goes; I spend most of my mental energy developing the drink, naming it after whatever comes to mind first. And this morning, I've only had one thing on my mind. "The hump then dump," I tell him quietly. His eyes widen behind his coffee mug, incredulous. He coughs, inhaling the liquid into his lungs. It takes him a few more minutes of coughing and pounding his chest before returning to our conversation.

When he does finally regain his composure, his eyes twinkle with mirth.

"You're right, Delaney. You are not a good girl. You are very, very bad."

# CHAPTER FOURTEEN
# *Benny*



The crew chief for tonight's game is pissing me off. He's working home plate and squeezing the strike zone, making it nearly impossible for our starting pitcher or our middle reliever to throw more than a handful of strikes this whole game. Normally, I can put up with a narrow strike zone, knowing the opposing team is suffering the same fate, but that's not the case tonight. In professional baseball, arguing calls about balls and strikes will get you ejected from the game. It's an annoying rule, but it does help move the game along in an era where the sport is constantly trying to recruit new viewership. New fans these days want a faster pace of play, and lately, baseball has delivered.

I'm normally a laid-back manager. I have a lot of respect for the game that shaped my life and livelihood. Tonight, however, my patience is dwindling. This bullshit strike zone has put everyone in a sour mood, and we've had several calls made in the other team's favor. Sometimes that happens, and I can brush off some mistakes due to the human element of the game. Humans make errors. This error, however, will not be let go so easily.

Moments ago, Carter Perez hit a screaming double to the right field corner. It was beautifully placed; I couldn't have designed it better myself. JJ Jeffers was already on base; his lead off second allowed him to round third quickly, but the play was going to be close. The right fielder rocketed the ball into the second baseman, who pivoted gracefully and threw it to the catcher. JJ, however, is one of the fastest baserunners in baseball. He slid into home about half a second before the catcher applied the tag. He should have been safe. He *was* safe, but somehow, unbelievably, the umpire called him out.

JJ pops up, brown dirt smudged across the front of his uniform. He's already yelling at the ump. Usually, I can count on JJ to be levelheaded; he's rarely one to get upset by calls, but he and I are of the same mind with tonight's umpiring performance. I'm already launching myself out of the dugout to get between my player and tonight's officiant. I make the hand motion to request a video review of the call before ushering JJ in front of me to the back of the dugout. Carter stands on second, his baserunning never contested at the bag.

"Total bullshit, but they'll absolutely reverse the call," Mac, my right-hand man tells me. Normally, we have a staff member specifically devoted to reviewing plays and advising Mac and me whether to challenge a call on the field or not. He has to make snap decisions confidently, based on a quick review of our own video footage. Tonight, I was so confident in JJ's baserunning and my own eyes that I didn't even confer with them before requesting the replay. The umpires huddle near a small television screen, headsets over their ears, while they discuss the play with an official watching remotely from MLB's official headquarters.

Several minutes pass by. My team behind me is growing restless, as are the fans. The video replays on the scoreboard show what we all know: JJ was safe. I'm not sure how many different angles they need. Yeah, it's a close call from the angle of the cameras, but there should be enough evidence to overturn the call on the field.

Except that's not what happens.

As soon as the crew chief reconfirms the out at the plate, I'm running from the top step of the dugout to give him a piece of my mind. Look, I get it. Not every call is going to go our way, but I'm pretty sure my five-year-old daughter could be making better calls than this umpiring crew today, and all she cares about in baseball is what the mascot is doing. I've been exceedingly patient throughout this game, but I have had enough.

While I know the crowd can't hear what I'm saying over their own screams of indignation, I know the cameras are zooming in on my face. Savvy lip reading fans watching from home will be able to decipher the colorful language I'm using to describe the crew chief's performance. To his face. I don't care. Sure, I'm mad about the call, but if I get tossed from the game tonight, it will galvanize both my players and the fans and hopefully get us out of the rut we've been stuck in all game, thanks to this horrendous strike zone.

Sure enough, Barry Westerly, the recipient of my vitriol, apparently had enough of my comments when I compared his judgment to a blind squirrel looking for his own...well, you get the idea. I'm honestly surprised he let me rant for as long as he did, but it's early in the season, so maybe he thought I'd back down eventually. When he finally throws an index finger in the air, thrusting it across his body, I say a few more choice comments before stalking back to the dugout. The guys cheer me, slapping my back as I head inside.

Back in the clubhouse, I change into athletic wear, discarding my uniform in the laundry bin. I have to stay; just because I get thrown out of a game doesn't mean the workday is over. I might as well get a workout in, even though I already lifted weights after lunch with Delaney. I wasn't kidding about her being my warmup weight.

The stereo is blasting heavy metal as I finish my third mile on the treadmill. The weight room has televisions mounted from the ceiling every few feet. I've been watching the rest of the game with closed captioning on, so I haven't missed a second. Which means I didn't miss the way Warner James hit a triple immediately following my ejection, allowing Perez to score easily from second, tying the game. I also didn't miss the way, the very next inning, Hayden Oliver and Tyler Edwards both batted runs in, putting the Foxes ahead. We're still winning, heading into the eighth inning.

I foam roll and complete some cool down stretches. I'm not ready to shower yet, wanting to watch the rest of the game. We have a young guy serving as our reliever tonight, Asher Incaudo. He's not bad, but he's green. He did well during spring training, but I'm not sure he has what it takes just yet to remain on the team all season. Based on this outing, however, it looks like he'll live to see another day. He makes quick work of the inning. The Foxes will have one more chance on offense, if they can maintain the lead. I know Mac will turn it over to our closer for the final inning of play.

The end of the game goes exactly according to plan. Jameson Bates, the new closer we traded for this offseason, leaves us with no doubt why he's worth every penny of his hefty contract. Three batters up, three batters down. He makes quick work of the ninth inning, and the game ends on a high note. I can hear the roar of the crowd and the blare of this season's victory song from the weight room.

Toweling off, I grab my phone and see I have a text from Robert Davis, Los Angeles' manager, and Angel Romero, the manager for San Diego, on a group text.

Robert

Congratulations. First toss of the season honors. My money was not on you.

Angel

For sure I thought I'd get the boot first.

Angel

I agree the call was bullshit, but what's lit a fire under your ass, Benny?

Robert

He's trying not to get canned, Romy.

Romy and Davis aren't expecting a response from me; they know phones are banned for everyone except medical staff while games are still in play, thanks to a season-long cheating scam involving smart watches, secret codes, and elaborate hand gestures from another team four seasons ago. It looks like my fellow managers have continued the conversation among themselves and seeing as how Davis isn't wrong about the lingering nerves I have about keeping my job, I don't bother texting back.

Coming up through the minor leagues, I had the honor of playing with Romero almost a decade ago. We both played for Davis at various points in our careers, but that's not unique. Robert Davis is one of the longest-tenured managers in professional baseball; he's that good at his job. I'm lucky to be able to count both men as my close personal friends. Still, I'm not ready to tell them that the fire lit under my ass is due to my increased energy levels courtesy of a feisty, fiery bartender.

Players start trickling in, talking loudly and jostling each other, amped up from the win. I squeeze out of the weight room as the head strength coach walks in with JJ and Warner, ready to take them through their workouts. I slap them on their backs, congratulating them on the win.

After showering and dressing, I head to the post-game press conference where I speak in politically correct, professional terms about my disagreement with Barry Westerly. I talk about strategy for the upcoming season, answering all media questions with generalities. After decades of baseball, you learn to answer media questions without really saying anything. After the presser, I head back to strategize with my coaching staff about tomorrow afternoon's games. It's always a quick turnaround from night games into day games, so we keep it brief.

When I finally leave the ballpark, the wind has picked up and the temperature has dropped. I live close enough to the field that I make a point to walk to and from work. I live far enough away that the foot traffic from games doesn't come down my street, not that I'm home during game hours to experience it, but as I tug my beanie down low over my ears, I wonder briefly if I should have driven to work today. Then, I'm reminded if I did that, I likely would not have gone to Moon Shadow with Delaney. Despite the chill seeping into my bones, I'm pleased with my decision. While Delaney has never not been on my mind today, thinking of her now spurs me to text her. She's working, so at least I know a late-night text message won't wake her, but I am surprised when she texts me back almost immediately.

> How's work tonight?

Firecracker

> Well, I haven't gotten thrown out of the bar yet, so I'd say it's going better than yours.

I can't help my grin. Delaney watched the game tonight. Sure, it was probably on in the background of the bar, but she paid attention enough to know about my ejection.

> You watched my game.

Firecracker

> Don't let it get to your head. It was on in the bar.

> But you watched.

Delaney doesn't respond, but I can picture her adorable little scowl. I'm a block away from home when she finally texts back.

Firecracker

> Like I said, don't let it go to your head.

Grinning, I slide my phone back into my pocket. I feel like a teenager again, my crush on Delaney permeating all my thoughts. I want to be around her, hear her tinkling laugh, be the one causing it. She was originally going to be a hookup, but I can't get her out of my brain. I couldn't for the five months I was away from Chicago, and I can't now, now that I've gone more than twelve hours without her touch.

Thinking about Delaney's touch makes my mind wander to the other ways in which she touches me, and I'm suddenly hard again, with no one but myself to blame. I sigh, climbing the steps to my front door and heading to bed.

# CHAPTER FIFTEEN
## *Delaney*

Cosmopolitan: Vodka, Cointreau, Cranberry Juice, Lime Juice

I feel his gaze on me like a physical touch. I don't know how else to explain how I know Samuel Benjamin has, once again, walked into my bar. I thought maybe he'd gotten me out of his system in the last two weeks. I haven't seen him since Tilly pushed me out the door, forcing me to end my shift early and spend it between the sheets at Benny's house. We've texted in the time since, but even that has consisted of light, playful banter. He hasn't alluded to seeing me again, and I've been too much of a coward to suggest it myself.

I'm working a rare Wednesday afternoon instead of the night shift. Tilly and Sloane are hosting a queer community event at Sip tonight, so they're closing early. When Benny asked me last week about my work schedule, I had told him about the change, but when he didn't inquire further, I assumed he was being polite, rather than attempting to make plans.

I spent the first week without Benny immersing myself in audiobooks and recipe creation. I rarely let silence fill my small apartment, knowing my mind would otherwise wander back to Benny. I wasn't opposed to allowing my thoughts to flit to him late at night, while I was in bed (particularly after listening to the spicier scenes in my audiobooks), but thinking of him during the bright light of day held entirely different connotations—ones I wasn't ready to explore.

The second week sans Benny, I hit my stride. I developed a few more recipes and added them to my scrapbook, spending extra time maximizing the aesthetic effect of each page. I stopped thinking of Benny every second of every day and instead only thought of him once or twice an hour. So, things were improving, right as he has the audacity to literally walk back into my life.

Taking a seat at the bar, he orders a Hemingway daiquiri. Instead, I deposit a bright pink cosmo in front of him. He accepts it with a half-smile and an eager spark to his eyes. I suspect he loves it when I give him shit.

"What are you doing here?"

"I had the day off and wanted to see something beautiful." He winks. I don't take the bait.

"Tilly *is* looking particularly pretty today," I agree. Tilly laughs from the other end of the bar. Benny raises his martini glass to her, and she responds with a small curtsy.

"You get off in an hour, right?" I cross my arms, trying to fight the smile creeping across my lips. If Benny thinks he can come in here and throw plans at me without a head's-up, he's got another thing coming. He could have at least texted first if he wanted to hang out. He's sent me all sorts of inane texts over the last few weeks: pictures of a full popcorn bowl, his morning cup of coffee (with that sexy rose tattooed hand wrapped around it, which I absolutely ignored and definitely did not pull up and zoom in on over and over again), his solo cup of beer on a flight.

"You can't just waltz in here and expect me to drop everything to hang out with you."

"I didn't waltz in here. I walked." His eyes twinkle. I bite the inside of my cheek to keep from smiling.

"I hate you," I tell him with a glare.

"No, you don't." His confidence is bordering on cockiness, and somehow, I can't bring myself to detest it.

"You're right. But I want to."

"You can't deny that the universe keeps bringing us together," he says, taking a small sip.

"It's not the universe. It's you," I point out.

"Potato, potato." He throws me a wink, and my cheeks flush involuntarily. With that, I turn and walk away from him.

For the next hour, I try very hard not to glance at him or wonder what he is doing here and what he is planning to do when I finish my shift. Benny, on the other hand, is the picture of casual nonchalance, leaning back in his chair, watching sports highlights on the bar television.

Finally, I can't avoid him any longer. I've already cashed out my tips. Tilly and I have swept everyone else out of the bar, turned off the "open" sign, and hung the flyer announcing the queer community planning event as the reason for the early closure on the door.

"Alright, I'm done," I say, coming to stand near him, coat and purse already on.

"Great. See you later, Delaney; have a great night." My jaw drops. He must be messing with me, right? I guess he technically never invited me to do something with him. I turn to stomp off when he catches my arm and pulls me into a tight hug.

"I'm kidding! You know, I think I like pressing your buttons as much as you like pressing mine, firecracker." I roll my eyes but don't pull away from his embrace. He feels too good. He smells too good.

Allowing him to tug my hand, I follow him out of the bar and around the corner, where he unlocks and opens a car door for me. My brain hesitates for a second. I've watched plenty of murder shows; I love true crime. There's nothing more relaxing to me. But for some reason, my brain interprets getting in a car with Benny as somehow dangerous, despite readily following him to his own home on more than one occasion.

"Where are we going?" I ask warily, wondering if I should share my location with a friend.

"It's a surprise." At my incredulous look, Benny squeezes my upper arm reassuringly. "I promise you'll like it."

Still not entirely convinced Benny hasn't suddenly turned into a deranged yet charming murderer, I slowly lower into the car and buckle in. At least if we get in an accident on the way to some murder dungeon, I will be protected.

We do not, in fact, pull up to a murder dungeon. As soon as Benny parks in front of our destination, I recognize the building's facade. To anyone else, the building looks like it's undergoing renovations; the plywood over the windows is covered in colorful street art. Construction scaffolding towers over the sidewalk, creating a covered walkway. Benny leads me down an airy alleyway and comes to a stop in front of a familiar steel door. He knocks loudly, and a small window at the top of the door opens. Through the artful metal screen covering the window, I can barely make out a man's bushy eyebrows and crinkled, smiling eyes. I don't need him to open the door to know he is a jolly person; his eyes give it away.

"Benny!" he booms loudly. A metal scraping sound screeches lightly before the door is thrown open to reveal exactly what I expected: a younger, red-haired version of Santa Claus standing before us. He's large in every sense of the word: tall, rotund, and, I'm guessing, with an equally large personality.

"Hey, Ernie," Benny responds jovially. Ernie's happiness is infectious; I find myself smiling immediately in his presence.

"Come in, come in!" Ernie ushers us inside a small room roughly the size of my apartment bathroom. The walls are covered in floor to ceiling bookshelves containing a vast array of tomes. "Who is this lovely young lady?" Even Ernie's voice is large.

"Ernie, this is Delaney Kristoff. Delaney, meet Ernie Young. He's the head chef here at The Bookstore."

Suddenly self-conscious, I smooth my hair. I don't recognize Ernie or his name, but I certainly know The Bookstore, Chicago's most delicious speakeasy, and can recognize the honor of a private introduction to its head chef. I shake Ernie's hand, his palm the size of a bear paw enveloping mine entirely.

Ernie turns, no small feat for a man of his size in this tiny room, and presses three seemingly random books further into their shelves. On cue, the shelf swings back on its hidden hinges, revealing a cavernous, well-lit room. I've been to The Bookstore twice before, but never during the day. It doesn't open to the public for several more hours and seating is by reservation only, so it's almost jarring to see the normally packed, dimly lit room filled with light and nothing else.

The bar, normally backlit by moody lighting, sits empty at the front of the room. Spindly tables surrounded by luxurious high-backed armchairs sit empty as well. Still, the room is impressive in its grandeur. A few staff members mill about, rolling silverware into napkins, rearranging tables, stocking the bar. Ernie beckons us into the back, where we follow him into the kitchen.

Two prep cooks stand at a nearby stainless-steel table, chopping vegetables. Ernie turns, arms spread wide, welcoming us into his inner sanctum.

"Delaney, have you been to my speakeasy before?" he inquires. I squeak. I didn't realize he also *owned* The Bookstore. It makes his presence much more impressive.

"I have, but never during the day. Your Lime in the Coconut cocktail is one of my favorites," I tell him honestly. I've tried a hundred times to recreate it and have never been successful. There's something creamy and limey and refreshing that I can't accurately replicate. I've long since abandoned my attempts, resigning myself to return to The Bookstore the next time a craving hits.

"Ah, beautiful *and* smart!" I really like this Ernie guy; he obviously knows what he's talking about. "I don't play around with cocktails too much; I leave that to my mixology experts. But the Lime in the Coconut was invented by yours truly." He laughs at my widened eyes.

"You know what you're doing, let me tell you, Ernie. I've tried to make it myself at home and it never turns out right."

"That's right, Benny tells me you're something of a mixologist yourself." Ernie's eyes twinkle. I gape at Benny. I told him about playing around with cocktails in passing, never expecting him to remember it, much less share the information with anyone else. Especially when he hasn't even tried one of my own creations; he has no idea if I'm any good at it or not.

"Well, I only do it for fun," I say, hurrying to downplay my hobby in front of a literal legend. Ernie, however, is gracious.

"I'm sure you are incredibly talented." He claps his hands together. "Now, Benny thought we could do a bit of a cooking class together to inspire you with some flavors for the next time you feel like inventing a new drink. And if inspiration strikes while you're here, you have full access to the bar."

Now instead of gaping, my jaw fully falls open. It's not a flattering look, I'm sure, but I can't bring myself to care. I was just given carte blanche at The Bookstore's bar. Me! Behind the bar at Chicago's most exclusive, delicious, gorgeous, elegant bar. Ernie continues talking, but I'm not registering what he's saying, my too-slow brain still caught up in the dream of hearing his earlier statements.

Benny reaches across and hooks a finger under my chin, closing my still-open mouth. I can't even come up with a snarky retort or a glare for him; I'm too busy mooning over this entire experience. Ernie beckons us to a table laden with cylindrical plastic prep containers filled with herbs and various other ingredients. Chatting conversationally between steps, Ernie walks us through the creation of chicken breast stuffed with spinach and balsamic-soaked Toscano cheese, wrapped in prosciutto. By the time we taste the food, I could have eaten that alone, but Ernie serves it with the most perfectly braised broccolini with preserved lemon and I'm pretty sure I've died and gone to heaven. The flavors dance on my tongue, and, as predicted, I'm struck with inspiration. Admittedly, this meal would pair perfectly with a glass of robust red wine, but when given access to The Bookstore's bar, I'm not going to waste the opportunity by pouring a straightforward glass of wine. Instead, I'm dreaming of a bold, figgy, wine-based concoction.

Ernie must see inspiration land on my face because he shoos me toward the bar, whispering, "Have fun." Benny hangs back; I can hear their friendly chatter while I mix ingredients. I have to ask a server for fig jam, but she returns from the kitchen a moment later with my request. I take a quick taster sip via cocktail straw after stirring it thoroughly in the mixing glass. I add the tiniest pinch of rosemary salt I find in a covered container. When I taste it again, I'm pleased with the flavor profile. Straining and pouring it between three coupe glasses, I set the glassware on a tray before bringing it back into the kitchen. Benny's eyes shine with pride as I explain the tasting notes in the drinks. When they take their first sip, Ernie's eyes widen in surprise before immediately delving back in for another one. Benny's grin is wide and knowing.

"I told you," he tells Ernie. I snort.

"You didn't even know it would be good. You've never had one of my cocktails before."

"That, firecracker," Benny tells me, pulling me into his side, "is called faith." Before I can overthink what it means for him to have such blind confidence in my abilities, Ernie speaks.

"Delaney. Please let us have your recipe and put it on our menu here." My jaw drops again. At this point, I'm sure Ernie assumes I'm part goldfish. "What do you call it?" He drains his glass, licking his lips.

"The audiobook," I tell him, immediately settling on a name appropriate for the setting.

"Will you sell me the recipe?" He's not joking. I balk.

"Wha-sell? You want to buy it?" I blink rapidly, as if that will somehow make my brain process the information more efficiently. "You don't have to do that. I can just give it to you."

"Whoa, wait a minute," Benny interrupts. "You deserve to be credited for your talents."

"Benny, it took like five minutes to make." He gives me a hard look.

"Maybe, but it only took five minutes because of your years of experience. He's paying you for your years of time, not just the last five minutes." I'm suddenly embarrassed to have Benny assume Ernie will pay me. I've never thought of selling my ideas; it's always only been a fun hobby for me.

"Oh, uh, I don't know," I say, shifting my weight uneasily side to side.

"I'll tell you what," Ernie proposes. "Our standard consulting fee is one thousand dollars an hour. Let's say, for business purposes, you spent two hours behind my bar developing that cocktail. I have a feeling that putting The Audiobook on our menu will more than make up for its development fee. It's the cost of doing business. What do you say? Two thousand?"

When I don't say anything, Benny nudges me. "This is where you make a counteroffer, firecracker."

"Twenty-five hundred. And my name credited."

"Done." Ernie and I shake hands, and he gives me a business card with his email. I promise to send him the recipe tonight.

Later, when Benny and I leave The Bookstore, a line is already forming outside the entrance, the first seating crowd already arriving.

"You know, I bet you could have held out for a lot more money," Benny tells me as he pulls my hand into his.

"More? No, I'm sure Ernie only offered that much to be nice, because he's your friend." He stops, forcing me to stop with him. We're blocking the sidewalk, causing people to walk around us.

"Delaney, did I miss the part where you told me friendship involves shelling out thousands of dollars to someone you just met? I've never seen Ernie do that before, and it's not because you were there with me. It's because you earned that success."

My cheeks flame. I've never had major issues with my self-esteem, but to hear someone so blatantly and thoroughly insist I've not only earned my success, but deserve it? It's delightfully gratifying.

As we climb back in the car, I'm reminded of my momentary panic the last time I entered Benny's car. This evening's adventure was the exact opposite of a murder dungeon mishap, and I couldn't be happier.

"So, what do you want to do now?" Benny asks. I feel bold, riding the high of my cocktail accomplishment.

"Do you want to come back to my place?"

Benny's responding smile is dazzling.

# CHAPTER SIXTEEN

# *Benny*

The Audiobook (A Delaney Kristoff Original
Exclusively for The Bookstore): Merlot, Fig Jam,
Lemon Juice, Rosemary Salt, Soda Water

"**I** can't believe I finally got to have not one, but two Delaney Kristoff Originals tonight," I tell my girl as she leans against her kitchen counter. She laughs. I love her feisty spirit, but I love her laugh more than her faux-annoyed scowls and glares. We're drinking a mix of beers, but it somehow tastes good, instead of weird like I thought it might be.

"This is hardly a Delaney Kristoff Original," she says, holding up her pint glass. "It's more of an old bartender's trick than anything else."

It doesn't matter to me. I know she is brilliant, no matter how humble she may be acting right now.

"What made you want to be a bartender?" I ask her. "Did you always like playing around with recipes?"

"No, not really. I've always grown up drinking wine with dinner." Surprise must flash across my face, because she hastily adds, "Not a lot. My mom is French. It's part of her culture. It was normal growing up. I didn't get drunk until college, though. I suppose my early exposure to wines allowed me to develop my palate more than the average person. At least when it comes to French wines. Anyway, after I dropped out of college, I needed a job. Bartending was easy and I made decent money."

I nod along, cataloguing her responses. I love learning about her. I had no idea she was French, nor did I know she went to college, at least for a little bit.

"Are you going to judge me for dropping out?" She squares her shoulders, as if preparing to defend herself.

"What? No, absolutely not!" She nods, her shoulders relaxing a bit. I make note that this is a sensitive topic for her. "Are you close with your mom?"

"Yeah, we're pretty close. She lives in Maine, so I don't see her super often. She teaches French at a university up there."

"Do you speak French?" She nods. "Teach me. Say something," I demand.

"Je suis pas un singe qui danse pour toi," she fires back immediately.

"I don't know what you said, but it's sexy as fuck. Tell me something else."

"I told you I wasn't a monkey who dances for you." She smirks at my raised eyebrows but continues. "Tu veux je dise quoi?"

"What does that mean?" I whisper. I don't know why I'm whispering. I'm in awe of her.

She laughs. "I asked what you wanted me to say."

"Tell me that I'm the sexiest man you've ever seen. That you want to be with me night and day."

"Tu es l'homme le plus agaçant du monde. J'ai aucune idée de pourquoi je te veux."

"Oui," I respond dumbly. Delaney tips her head back, her tinkling laugh filling the room. Out of nowhere, a black cat nimbly leaps onto the counter by my arm. I jump. "You have a cat!" I'm really pulling out all my intelligent comments tonight.

Delaney laughs again. "Yeah, this is Kingston. He usually takes a bit to warm up to new people, but you must have passed the test." Kingston nuzzles his head against my arm. I scratch behind his ears, eliciting a motoric purring. I wonder if Delaney knows how much she has in common with her pet.

"Of course you would have a black cat," I say playfully. She doesn't respond, instead pulling Kingston into her arms, kissing his head and whispering all sorts of baby talk to him about how he's the bestest animal in the whole world. It's endearing to see her guard down. I feel privileged that she's allowing me to witness it.

We migrate to her living room, Kingston curling himself up in Delaney's lap when we sit on the couch. We talk for hours about our childhoods, our jobs, our families. I tell her about my beautiful children and their unique personalities. She bites her lip, as if she's holding herself back from asking her next question. I wait her out and she finally plunges ahead.

"Do you regret getting divorced?"

I think for several moments before answering her. A thoughtful question deserves a thoughtful answer.

"I regret my kids having to go through instability. I regret the heartache that comes with outgrowing your love. But I don't regret my split with Keeley. It allowed us both to move on to better things. She's about to get remarried, and I really like her fiancé. He treats my kids well."

"How are you able to get along with your ex-wife so well? I'm not friends with any of my exes."

"It helps we still have to maintain a relationship because of the kids. But even if we didn't have children together, I think on some level, we'd still be friendly. There wasn't any big catastrophe that led to the end of our marriage. We both grew so far apart, but with the chaos of baseball life, the long season, and frequent travel, it wasn't readily apparent at first. When I retired from playing five years ago, we finally started to see that we had evolved into such different people. Not in a bad way, but in a way that led to us no longer being compatible."

"Thanks for being so honest," she tells me quietly. I shift, putting my arm around her shoulder and pulling her into me.

"I'll always be honest with you, D." Her eyes crinkle at the corners in response to the nickname. She leans forward, pulling a scrapbook from the bottom shelf of her coffee table.

"Want to see my recipes?" I'm confused by the change in subject–and the presentation of what does not appear to be a cookbook–but I'll enthusiastically view anything she wants me to see.

Opening the cover, she situates the book between us, so the cover is resting across both of our laps. Page after page is colorfully decorated, some with three-dimensional embellishments along the edges. In the center of each page is a cocktail recipe. Each drink's name is written in a different font, always boldly pronouncing the drink's name. In addition to each recipe, Delaney has included small sketches on each page, allowing the reader to envision the glassware, garnishes, and main ingredients on a visual scale. The scrapbook is beautiful. Painstakingly detailed, it's an absolute work of art. It's visually stunning, but the amount of hours Delaney must put into each page, *after* the hours she devotes to developing the recipe, makes my head spin. Other than baseball or my children, it's hard to imagine devoting so much time to any one thing.

For a long time, neither of us speak, silently flipping through each page. I gaze in wonder at each entry, fascinated. There must be at least fifty pages, each devoted to a new, unique recipe. I smile when we reach the page containing The Hump Then Dump. Delaney sketched the drink to be served in an old-fashioned ice cream sundae dish, complete with a red and white striped straw. Sparkly red cherry appliques in the bottom corners of the page glint in the overhead lights. At an angle, behind the recipe card pasted onto the page, sits the cover of a takeout menu from Moon Shadow, where I know Delaney first received her inspiration for the drink.

"It feels so cool to be able to say I was there when you invented this drink." I trace the Moon Shadow logo with a finger.

"You can tell everyone you were the muse behind The Hump Then Dump."

"I will not be doing that," I tell her flatly.

"One day, Samuel Benjamin, you'll be able to say you knew me when. And then everyone will ask how you knew the famous Delaney Kristoff. You'll be forced to tell them the truth about The Hump Then Dump."

Closing the scrapbook, she turns on the television and finds another nature documentary. This one features desert dwellers, and we both immediately get sucked in to learning about Gila monsters and scorpions. An hour later, her head bobs with sleep, resting gently on my shoulder. I could stay here all night like this. I *want* to stay all night like this, but I know if we do, we'll both wake up stiff and sore in the morning. Still, I take a few minutes to relish the moment when Delaney finds peaceful comfort in my arms.

I nudge her gently, pulling her into my arms and walking to what I assume is her bedroom. Her apartment isn't that big, and I'm not surprised when I kick open the only inner door in the place and find her bedroom. Her room is filled with deep purples and soft lilacs. The monochromatic shades of violet blend tastefully together with black accents. I shouldn't be surprised; the talent with which Delaney assembled her scrapbook shows she has an eye for aesthetics. Somehow, though, I'm a little surprised her color of choice is purple instead of black.

Delaney murmurs against my chest as I place her gently on top of the comforter. Not wanting to disturb her any further, I pull the opposite side of the comforter over her, so she is tacoed into the bed. I'm about to step away, intending to lock up her apartment as best I can before heading home when she reaches out a hand to stop me.

"Benny, don't go." Her voice is soft and sleepy. My heart swells. I smile, knowing I can't deny her anything within my power to deliver. I pull her into my arms again, shifting her weight to one arm while flinging the covers back with the other. When I replace her back into the bed, she sighs contentedly. I'm glad she changed into sweatpants when we came back from The Bookstore; waking her up to get her changed into something more comfortable to sleep in seems like such a waste of a peaceful moment.

Circling the bed, I strip down to my underwear and climb in behind her. My arms band around her waist of their own accord, as if they know before my brain does that that's where they belong. Delaney releases another happy sigh, and I smile into her hair before falling asleep myself.

# CHAPTER SEVENTEEN

# *Delaney*

Thai Mule (A Delaney Kristoff Original): Whiskey, Lemongrass Ginger Simple Syrup, Ginger Beer, Thai Basil, Lime

I wake up, finding I've once again barnacled myself to Benny's side in the middle of the night. Unconscious Delaney is a needy bitch.

I try to ninja my way out from under his arm. Benny's arm might be casually slung around my shoulder, but my head is on his muscled chest, my top leg koalaed around his lower limbs. I'm more fused to him than he is to me, and isn't that just the perfect metaphor for our dynamic?

Benny says "jump," and I say "How high?" I can feel my mother's disappointment in me all the way from Maine for molding myself into something different from how I usually am. I would never let my guard down enough to allow a man to pick me up early from work and dictate our date. Although, that's not exactly what he did, is it? He surprised me with something he thought I would like, which I absolutely did. It's hard not to have a knee-jerk reaction to letting my defenses down, even slightly, though.

I let out a quiet, frustrated sigh. The noise, or maybe the feel of my breath against his chest hair, causes him to stir. I make it about three inches away from him before he groans. He pulls me tightly into his body.

"That's better. Back where you belong."

Luckily, I'm saved from having to fight him on this when his phone alarm goes off. I groan, the loud beeping filling my bedroom. The thick slice of morning light spilling onto my bedroom floor from the gap in the curtains tells me it's far too early to wake up, especially with my night owl tendencies.

Benny rolls over, silencing his alarm and getting out of bed right away. I should have known he was the kind of person that gets out of bed at the first alarm. No one in their right mind wakes up without hitting the snooze button at least three times. Anyone who tells you they do otherwise is a damn liar. Or a sociopath.

Benny hovers over me, standing at the edge of the bed near my head. He presses a soft kiss on my forehead.

"I've got to go to work, baby. Then I've got a team dinner after. I'll text you later."

He must let himself out of my apartment, because I wake several hours later to a text from Sloane informing me that she and Tilly are bringing in Thai food for a late lunch at the start of my shift. Tilly chimes in with a text moments later informing me that she expects all the details from my date with Benny yesterday.

I groan, pulling the covers over my head. As I do, however, I allow a smile to creep onto my face. Only a little bit.

# CHAPTER EIGHTEEN

## *Benny*

The Bob (A Delaney Kristoff Original): Pick up
The wet Barmat you've Poured Shots Over All
Night, Pour Into A Glass. Drink At your Own Risk.

The weeks pass in a blur of road games (unfortunately, with the same number of losses as wins), home games (more wins than losses), and late-night visits to Sip. Delaney has finally gotten to the point where she no longer pretends to be annoyed when I show up at her place of work after a game. Last week, she didn't even balk when I brought Mac and a few other staff members for drinks after work. We stayed out of her hair, sticking to drinking on the patio, but of course, I was the one who volunteered to grab more rounds each time. And each time, it took me a little longer to come back to the table, laden with fresh, icy pitchers.

Delaney is still resistant to the idea of coming to Foxes games. I'm not going to push her on it, despite my heavy suspicion that she'd get along great with some of the wives and girlfriends. She's similarly aged to many of my players' significant others, which simultaneously makes me feel cool and like a creep. Age is just a number, right?

What Delaney isn't resistant to, however, is the frequent video chats we engage in when I'm out of town. The look she gave me when she opened the remote vibrator I got her is still burned into my retinas. Controlled by an app on my phone, I can dole out pleasure or punishment as I see fit, from hundreds of miles away. The vibrator came with a matching cock ring, so I'm mindful to tip the scales more heavily on the pleasure side when we're wearing them. I'm no fool. Delaney gives as good as she gets, in all senses of the word.

Still, she hasn't fully embraced the idea of being my girlfriend, despite literally everything she says and does around me indicating she is. I can't tell if her resistance to the term is another way to bust my balls, or if she's still trying to guard herself, but I suspect it's a little of both. She doesn't pull away when I kiss her in public (or in private, thank god); she seems genuinely happy when I visit her at work and when I take her home with me after her shifts. I feel the need to check where she's at, so I don't get burned. I've been in enough relationships where my partner was in it for the wrong reasons. If Delaney doesn't want this, it's better for me to know now.

"Tell me something, firecracker." I jump right into it one morning when she reminds me, yet again, that she's not my girl. "Has another man been inside these thighs since I came back in town?" I run my hand lightly up the inside of her leg, stopping well short of where she wants me. I haven't slept with anyone—haven't even entertained the idea of having dinner with another woman—since meeting Delaney. If she hooked up with someone in the offseason, I can't exactly fault her for that.

"No," she tells me with a glare, offended that I'd even ask. After a brief pause, she adds, "Has anyone else ridden this dick or that tongue while we've been doing this?" She palms my junk, waking my dick from its slumber.

"Delaney. I haven't even thought about another woman since I laid eyes on you." I let her see the sincerity in my eyes.

"Good," she says simply.

It's not an agreement to be my girl, but her simple acknowledgment of her territory is all I need.

It's a rare day off for both of us. It only happened once before, when our schedules lined up perfectly, allowing both of us to sleep in and hang out. Unfortunately, it still means I have to do some work on my laptop, despite not being needed at the ballpark. Computer work has become much more pleasant when I can do it from Delaney's couch, leisurely drinking coffee with her.

"Want to put on another nature documentary? I still have about an hour or two of work." I hold my phone up to my face to unlock it, then hand it to her. She's taken a liking to nature documentaries, and my Discovery Channel app streams the best ones.

"You're handing me your phone?" I look at her, surprised. I didn't think she'd have a problem with me not queuing up a show, assuming she'd want to pick her own.

"Did you want me to pick one for you?"

"No...it's just...you don't mind me looking at your phone?" I give her a quizzical glance while my laptop powers on. "Like, you don't have a problem with me looking at it?"

"Obviously not?" She says nothing, but settles into the couch, scrolling through her options. Kingston hops up between us, nuzzling me briefly before circling back to Delaney and claiming her lap. The opening music plays, Delaney having decided on a segment about penguins. Periodically glancing up to watch penguins waddle in a line or huddle against a snowstorm, I tap away on my keyboard, responding to emails. My phone buzzes at the same time that my laptop alerts me to a new email. Delaney moves to hand me my phone back in response, but I wave her off, already opening the email on my computer. We're likely going to have some roster moves coming up, given that one of our relief pitchers is on the ten-day injured list with a forearm strain. It's more than likely a temporary move, but it requires a lot of coordination with our Triple-A team, our medical staff, and travel coordinators.

Several minutes later, my phone buzzes with rapid-fire texts. It's probably a group chat, no doubt related to work. We fly out later tonight to head to Detroit for a three-game series; the texts likely contain logistics from our traveling secretary.

"Can you tell me who it's from?" If it's logistics, I can ignore it. There's rarely information in it that I don't already know. If it's my kids on a group chat, I like to respond quickly.

"You don't care that I open your texts?" Delaney lifts an eyebrow.

"No; why would I?" When she doesn't respond, I clarify. "I'd prefer you keep whatever you see in there about the Foxes between you and me. Sometimes there's injury information or sensitive details in there that shouldn't be public knowledge."

Delaney presses her lips together, stopping herself from saying something. I've learned to give her time in these moments. She silently hands me my phone back and I confirm it is Alan, our traveling secretary, coordinating our bus and flight logistics for tonight. Most of the immediate responses are players and staff members thanking Alan for the information, leading to a near-incessant buzzing. I temporarily mute the chat, but Delaney doesn't seem bothered. In fact, she seems lost in thought, not really paying attention to the fat, fluffy baby penguins waddling around near their parents' feet on the screen.

Trusting that she will share her thoughts when she's comfortable, I return to my own screen. Mac and I have drawn up the lineup for tomorrow's game, but we're still waiting to hear back from our player development staff to know if we need to make any tweaks. Now that the season is well underway and summer is here, we tend to see more injuries spring up. It's part of baseball life, the grind of one-hundred-sixty-two games taking its toll on players' bodies. You always hope for day-to-day injuries instead of ones that land a player on the injured list, but sometimes it can't be avoided.

Sure enough, after about thirty minutes, the ending credits of the penguin documentary rolling quietly in the background, Delaney blurts out, "You don't care that I look at your phone."

I blink at her. We've established this already. I tilt my head, clarity finally dawning on me. "Do you think I have something to hide?"

"No!" she cries quickly. Very quickly. "I just...didn't expect you to trust me so easily, I guess."

I gently set my laptop on the coffee table and shift my body so I'm facing her. "I do trust you, Delaney. I hope you trust me, too. I don't have anything to hide, and it doesn't bother me if you look on my phone, as long as you're careful with the information about the team that might pop up."

"I don't care about baseball information," she says quietly, picking at her nails. I pull her hand into my lap and wait for her to continue. She gnaws at her lower lip, unsure of how to voice her thoughts.

"Other than that, there's nothing I care about you seeing on my phone. I'm not talking to other women; I'm not doing anything shady. What you see is what you get, D." She nods, appearing to debate something internally. She takes a deep breath and word vomits.

"I was dating this guy, Bob, in college. I loved him so much. I thought he loved me too." Sensing where this is going, I stroke gentle circles on the back of her hand. "I thought he was endgame, you know? He wasn't in college, he had dropped out by the time

I met him, but he was still friends with all my college friends. We had all these plans together. His dream was to open a surf and souvenir shop in Hawaii with me. It wasn't my dream, but I was along for the ride because I got to do it with him. It was so stupid, too. He had never even been to Hawaii, but he wanted to uproot everything to open a storefront there, without having done any research." Her expression darkens as if she's reliving each moment. "Before I dropped out, I took all these entrepreneur and marketing classes so we'd be ready, so we could be successful, you know?" I nod. "I dropped out. My parents weren't thrilled, but what could they do about it? I was twenty-one. I was literally about to enter my senior year of college. So fucking close to graduating." Delaney squeezes her eyes shut, as if the memory is physically painful. "Anyway, the week before we were supposed to leave, after I had bought us both plane tickets and booked a rental house for the first two weeks living on the island, I went to his house. He lived like an hour from campus, and I was still living in my apartment at school. I walked in on him fucking some girl."

I suck in a breath. I knew it was coming but still couldn't brace myself enough. I give her a sympathetic look, but she doesn't look back at me, instead staring at her lap. Worse than the words she says or the experience she's reliving, is the empty, hollow look to her as she tells it. I want to scoop her even further into my arms and hold her close, somehow willing the strength of my body to piece her back together. Instead, I cup her cheek. She doesn't move away, but she doesn't lean into me either. After a moment, I drop my hand and resume my circles on the back of her palm.

"She really was some girl. He didn't even know her name, but she wasn't the first, I later found out. Obviously, I did not go to Hawaii with him." Delaney's laugh is bitter. My own pulse pounds in my ears, though it's not loud enough to drown out Delaney's whisper. "That's the last time I'll ever allow a man to alter the course of my life."

# CHAPTER NINETEEN

## *Delaney*

The Pit Bull (A Delaney Kristoff Original):
Cachaca, Agave, Lime Juice, Ginger Beer, Ginger
Root Garnish

It's a Friday night and the regular crowd, plus some new faces, have Sip filled to the brim with bodies. The humid air blasts through the door every time a new patron steps inside. Despite the muggy atmosphere, the patio is almost as packed as the inside. Normally, I like to wear my hair down when I work behind the bar. I tend to get more tips from men and women alike, but tonight's stickiness is no match for the overworked air conditioner. It's cool enough here to keep the barflies cool, but not enough to keep the sweat from trickling down the back of my neck as I flit around behind the bar. It's a packed house, which is good. I find myself increasingly lonely when Benny is on a road trip.

*Ridiculous*, I scoff at myself. Last year at this time, I was single and mostly happy about it. Sure, I went on the odd date, but always with the goal of hooking up. A relationship was never the goal. Last night, when Benny and I were video chatting, I again scoffed when he opened the call by greeting me with his usual endearments.

"How's my girl doing tonight?" he had said with a warm smile. Benny's the kind of person who smiles with his whole body. His eyes crinkle at the corners. His plush lips stretch across his face, bunching his cheeks. His whole body relaxes and opens at the same time. You feel like the center of the universe to be on the receiving end of his smiles, and he gives them generously. It's not a surprise women are drawn to him and his players want to please him. The entire Samuel Benjamin aura is cheery happiness, the kind that makes you feel like you've done something to deserve it.

So, my scoff at his term of endearment really was more of a knee-jerk habitual reaction than a reflection of my true feelings about being his in any sense. Still–and understandably so–Benny bristled slightly at my reaction.

"I haven't taken a woman home since I met you. Not in the offseason. Not during spring training. Certainly not since being back in Chicago. None could hope to compare to what you stir within me. If you don't want me calling you my girl, then okay. But don't mistake my respect for your choice as a lack of devotion on my part."

He had said the words softly, not unkindly, but I still felt the sting of guilt for making him feel he wasn't worthy of my own devotion in return.

"I'm not resistant to a relationship with you," I had told him honestly. "But I go into everything assuming most men are untrustworthy fuckboys." I had thought he had gathered that a few weeks ago when I told him about Bob. He jerked his head back slightly, but I caught the movement on my screen.

"Why do you do that? Pull away, assume I'm only in it for sex?"

"In my experience, most guys want to hit it and quit it. It's best not to have high expectations for a fuckboy."

He pulled the phone closer to his face, letting his intense gaze travel through the screen and straight into my brainwaves. "That's because you've been fucking boys. Try fucking men and see where that gets you."

His voice was low and dangerous, turning the serious conversation into something different altogether. We had said what we needed to say anyway. Benny understands my hesitation on relationships has nothing to do with him; at the same time, he implicitly trusts that he's the only one warming my bed at night (or, more accurately, each morning). I understand Benny is utterly devoted to me, and I can't say that I hate it. It makes these road trips feel longer than they are. It hasn't even been a full twenty-four hours since I've seen him (through a screen, at least), but I miss him already. He was already working by the time I woke up; by the time his game was over, my shift at Sip had already started. He comes home in two days, and we've already got plans to check out a new French cafe that opened in Lincoln Park.

"Another vodka lemonade?" I ask one of my regulars, Michelle, as I pull my head back to the present moment.

"Please," she says, scooting her empty glass toward me. I raise my eyes in silent question to her husband, Joe, behind her and he nods, letting me know he'll take another IPA. "It's our last night of drinking!" she announces excitedly.

"Oh yeah, you going sober after this?" I ask jokingly.

"In a sense, yes. We have our first appointment with our fertility doctor tomorrow morning," Michelle tells me proudly. I stop my movements, wanting to make sure she knows I understand the gravity of what she's divulged. She and Joe have been married for five or so years, and they've been trying to get pregnant since before their wedding. Michelle's dream is to be a mother, but she and Joe have been dealt a shitty hand of cards. They told me months ago that they wanted to exhaust all their "natural" options before considering IVF. I guess that means the natural route has been exhausted. I reach across the bar top, squeezing Michelle's hand and offering her a genuine smile.

"I'm really excited for you both," I say honestly, my eyes flicking to Joe. Michelle beams at me. She's always been a ray of sunshine, but after several years of trying, I've seen the toll it took on her mental health. It's nice to see her hopeful again. "I'll miss seeing you around here, but you'll have to stop in anyway. I can turn this vodka lemonade into regular lemonade *really* easily. I won't do it for just anyone, but I've got you covered, girl." Michelle's laugh fills my heart.

The rest of my shift moves along quickly. We're busier than most Friday nights, but I'd rather have a busy night than a slow one, and not only because the tips are better. When things are slow, the shifts drag on, and I could use a distraction from how much I miss my man.

I decided last night I wasn't going to fight it. It's not like Benny is asking me to leave my job and move to Hawaii with him based on a harebrained idea to open a surf shop. I internally sneer, remembering how Bob didn't even know the first thing about surfing. Or Hawaii. Or running his own business. Not that I knew about those things, but it wasn't my dream. I wasn't surprised to learn a few years ago that Bob never even left Indiana. He apparently is living out of his parents' basement and, last I heard, not working or even looking for a job. If I didn't feel so much hatred toward Bob, I might pity him.

# CHAPTER TWENTY

# *Benny*

French 75: Gin, Lemon Juice, Simple Syrup, Champagne, Lemon Twist Garnish

I love Mondays. I might be the only person in the world who feels this way, but Mondays are Delaney's days off and when they coincide with mine, I wake up with an extra spring in my step. Delaney still needs a shot or two of espresso to feel that same spring, especially if we're getting up earlier than ten in the morning, but I don't mind. Sneaking out of bed to run to the cafe down the street from my townhouse to get her caffeinated is the only way I'll ever sneak out of bed.

"Good morning," I tell her softly as she starts to stir. I've been up for more than an hour and am wrapping up my work for the morning. She mumbles something I can't make out, rubbing her hands adorably across her face. She didn't seem to notice when I disappeared for twenty minutes earlier, but she promptly suctioned to my side as soon as I returned, all while remaining unconscious. "I put your cold brew with an extra shot of espresso in the fridge. Want me to grab it for you?"

"Yes, please." Delaney is very much like her feline companion. They both need an inordinate amount of time to wake in the morning in order to be functional. I don't mind. It gives me time to ease into the day, finishing what I need to get done to ensure limited work interruptions during Delaney Time.

We'll have to leave in about an hour to make it to our lunch reservation at Le Matin. Kyle Crawford, one of our starting pitchers, informed me of the new French restaurant after he found himself breakfasting there after one of his many hookups. I snort to myself thinking about it. If there ever was a fuckboy, it's Crawford. I make a mental note to never introduce him to Delaney. Not that I'm worried he'd steal my girl; I'm concerned for his well-being after a potential encounter with her.

Delaney hums happily as she drinks her coffee. Initially, she ordered them black and bitter as fuck. When I finally convinced her to try the half-sugar syrup the coffee shop used, she was pleasantly surprised and now orders her iced coffees like this all the time. I smile, thinking about her go-to order serving as the perfect allegory for her personality. A little hard on the exterior, maybe even a little bitter, but kind and compassionate when you get to know her. She comes across as distant, but I know it's a clever facade to avoid interactions with those she doesn't like. She's told me enough stories about her regulars at Sip for me to know her tough girl act is (mostly) all an act. She knows her regular patrons' backstories, about their families. She knows that Jim is about to propose to his boyfriend. She knows all the ins and outs of Griffin's attempts to save his marriage and win back his wife. Delaney told me about Heather, who is working toward a huge promotion at her job. And last night, I heard about Michelle and Joe. So no, Delaney might seem hard on the outside, but she's not fooling me. She's a big softy.

I turn in bed, gathering her in my arms and settling her between my open legs. She sighs contentedly as I run my fingers through her hair. This has become our morning ritual when we have time. With the news running in the background, she drinks her coffee while I play with her hair. Sometimes I braid it, Delaney serving as a far more patient and wiggle-free customer than my usual hair-braiding recipient, Scarlett. Most times I end up tossing it into a loose ponytail. And sometimes, I wrap that ponytail around my fist, and Delaney abandons her coffee for more fun pursuits. With no time for that this morning, I stick to tunneling my fingers through her thick hair, lightly massaging her scalp. She groans in pleasure, flopping loose-limbed against my chest. I press a kiss to her crown, urging her to get out of bed so we don't miss our plans. I could stay in bed for a week with Delaney and never get restless. Still, I know she'll enjoy the French cafe as much as I do.

When we walk in, my suspicions are confirmed. It seems legitimate, but never having stepped foot in France, I look to Delaney to verify its authenticity. She nods, bright eyed and excited as the hostess brings us to our table. Le Matin is decorated in French blues and bright yellows. Black and white photos of Parisian land-marks are framed on the walls. We're seated under a stunning pho-to of the Basilique du Sacré-Coeur de Montmartre. Delaney tells me about visiting France in the summers growing up, especially following her parents' divorce. She chatters away, pausing only to place an order to the French-speaking waitress who turns out to be the owner's daughter.

Delaney assures me everything is authentic here and encourages me to try reading any of the menu items aloud. She and the waitress snicker at my terrible pronunciation but gently correct me. I know a decent amount of Spanish–you pick up a lot in baseball–but since none of my players or teammates have ever fluently spoken French, I'm hopeless. Still, I want to learn, and she is patient in teaching me. We linger in the cafe, Delaney teaching me snippets of conversational French.

"Wait, but you said..." I pause, asking the waitress to repeat herself.

"Votre cafe," she supplies helpfully. "Your coffee."

"But you," I say, flicking my eyes to Delaney, "called it 'ton cafe?' Are there two words for coffee?"

The waitress smiles at me. Delaney shakes her head. "No, there's not an English equivalent, strictly speaking, but in French, it's called vouvoyer and tutoyer. It's a level of politeness you give to strangers or to people who are in a more respected station than you." When I give her a confused look, she continues. "So, you would use the verb form "tu" with me, because we're familiar."

"Fuck yeah, we are." I wink at her. In true Delaney fashion, she rolls her eyes at my juvenile sex joke.

"But you would use "vous" for strangers or people you want to address more formally, like a boss or someone."

I cock my head to the side, mulling it over. "I'd like you to teach me the 'vous' versions," I tell her.

"But 'tu' is probably more useful for you, since you're only really talking to me. You would use 'tu' to address me since we're equals."

I give her a soft smile. "But we aren't equal, baby. You shine above me in every way."

She stares at me. I expected her to fight me, to roll her eyes, to do something other than stare at me as if she can't figure me out. The waitress says something in rapid-fire French and Delaney nods silently, in a daze. I don't know what she said and I'm sure she wouldn't tell me if I asked. But D's smile is huge and genuine and her jade eyes overbright, so I'm hoping it was a good thing.

# CHAPTER TWENTY-ONE

# *Benny*



Later that week, I visit Delaney at work, as usual, after our game ends. We played terribly. It was a complete shutout by the other team, and both our offense and defense sucked. There's no other way to describe the performance. I'd like to blame it on our opponent's exceptional record, but the truth is, we've been playing down to our competition all month. The teams we should have no problem beating suddenly become formidable opponents. Luckily, we've been playing well against some of our tougher rivals, so at least we haven't been completely hopeless. Still, I can't say I'm not nervous.

After the game, Mac and I met with DeAndre, our mental skills director. He assured us it was something he was going to continue working on with the guys and this was just part of baseball. Seeing as how all three of us are former players, his last comment wasn't entirely necessary, but it still served as a good reminder not to get too caught up in the minutiae of the grind.

*Easy for him to say,* I think. His ass isn't in the hot seat this season. Foxes' ownership and front office management have generally been good to me, and I feel like I have the support of the fans and the city in general. Still, there's an unspoken pressure that I had better bring my team to the championship round this season. It's been a pressure that I've largely been able to let simmer on the back burner, but as the season moves along, the intensity has slowly increased. Eventually, it's going to hit a full, rolling boil. I can only hope we are on a winning streak when it does.

I could use some time off. The midseason break is coming up in two weeks. I usually do something with my family during it, often meeting them somewhere in the country for a few days of fun and relaxation. This year, Genesis asked me to come home to Nashville instead. She's leaving for college this fall, and she wants to maximize her time with her friends. I can't say I blame her, but I'm a little nervous that my baby's last midseason break before college will be spent with her friends instead of me. When I expressed this concern to Keeley, she reassured me that she'd talk to Genesis. I'm also crossing my fingers she'll talk to her about leaving Garrett out of our family activities, but I know she won't.

I take a seat at the only remaining barstool. For a Wednesday, Sip is relatively busy. I caught Delaney's eye right as I walked in, but it takes her a while to make her way over to me. She knows I don't mind; I'm not here for the drinks, I'm here for the bartender. After the fourth interruption, where Delaney has been tasked with refilling a drink or closing out a tab, she finally heads my way. Stopping in front of me, she pulls her hair off the back of her neck and fans her face. Wordlessly, I pull the hair tie off my wrist and hand it to her. She smirks before tossing her hair into a messy bun at the top of her head.

"Thanks," she murmurs. "Want anything to eat or drink?" I know the kitchen is closed by now, but Delaney won't hesitate to run back there and put something together for me if I ask.

"Nah, I'm good. I ate at the ballpark." I pull a water bottle from my backpack, cracking the seal. I lean toward her. "I'm here for the view."

She pushes me back playfully, rolling her eyes but laughing all the same. She's got another hour and a half left before she's done at Sip. The bar closes in an hour, but the owners always let me stay so I can leave with her. I help her by flipping the chairs upside down onto the tables so she can quickly mop as her last activity on shift. Anything to help her get out of there and home with me faster. We've been alternating whose place we head to after her shifts. I don't mind staying at Delaney's, but my place has a bit more room. Luckily, Kingston is self-sufficient and doesn't seem to notice if Delaney comes home several hours later than usual.

I alternate between watching sports highlights on the bar's televisions and watching Delaney. I love seeing her interact with her regulars. She's got a friendly camaraderie with a few in particular; others seem intimidated by her. I don't blame them. She's beautiful and feisty and doesn't take shit from anyone. As soon as I think those thoughts, I must have manifested them into reality, because Delaney's voice rings out sharply over the music.

"Justin, I said no. Don't make me kick you out." My eyes zero in on the offender. Justin is leaning over the bar at the far end, away from me, trying to grab the open bottle of beer in Delaney's hand. She holds it out of his reach before promptly dropping it in the trash can behind the bar. I settle in to watch the show, knowing she can take care of herself. This is going to be entertaining as hell.

"What the fuck, Delaney? I was going to drink that!" he howls at her, clearly intoxicated.

"And I have neither the time nor the crayons to explain to you how getting cut off at a bar works." I bark out a laugh, quickly covering my mouth. "I told you two drinks ago that you were cut off. I didn't realize these assholes were still ordering for you." Justin narrows his eyes at my girl. My muscles coil and tense as I watch their interaction. I don't move in yet, knowing she can handle herself, but I stay ready to intervene, in case this dickwad gets any ideas. Jamie, the bouncer, apparently feels the same way. He moves in closer, but doesn't say anything yet, following Delaney's lead.

"You're such a fucking bitch," Justin yells, shaking his head and attempting to laugh off his shame.

"Yeah, yeah, I'll cry about it later," Delaney says, entirely un-affected. Justin lunges toward her, but Jamie's arm is around his neck in a flash. I doubt he could have reached Delaney, given there's three feet of bar top separating them, but she instinctively stepped back anyway. Jamie drags Justin backward and out the door, promptly depositing him on the sidewalk, and blocking the doorway to thwart any attempts of reentry. Justin's asshole friends meekly ask to close out their tabs. Delaney closes them out with a heavy glare. Two signed receipts and several muttered apologies later, they join their friend on the sidewalk and usher him into a cab.

Jamie returns inside, and I make a mental note to get him tickets to Foxes games whenever he wants. He's a big guy who has never been more than a squishy teddy bear when I've seen him. His speed tonight was impressive; I've never seen him move the way he did, and I appreciate it. I also appreciated how he let Delaney handle the situation until it was absolutely necessary for him to intervene. My girl can hold her own, even if she shouldn't have to.

Delaney doesn't need a knight in shining armor. She *is* the knight in shining armor. She can save herself anytime she needs to. But she could use a supportive court, someone to help her off her steed, to tell her she's done a good job, and that she can relax.

Later, when she is relaxing in my arms, I pull the blanket against her and trace designs across her back in the way I know she loves. She repeatedly told me she was fine after the altercation at Sip, but I still feel the need to check in one last time.

"Are you sure you're okay?"

She sighs deeply against my chest. "Yes, Benny. I promise I'm fine. It's not the first time I've tossed out a drunken, disgruntled customer, and it won't be the last."

"Okay, but you'll tell me if you're not fine?" I meant it as a question, but it comes out more as a statement.

"Yes, *Dad*. I'll be fine." I palm her ass, giving her a warning squeeze although tonight we know I'm all bark and no bite.

"The midseason break is coming up. It's in two weeks." She lifts her head to peer at me. "I have a few days off and promised my kids I'd go home to Nashville to see them."

She doesn't say anything for a minute. "Okay, that should be fun for you." She gives me a smile.

"Firecracker, please don't freak out, but I'd like you to come with me. I want you to meet my family. I want to spend more time with you and have all my favorite people together in one spot."

"Oh, um, I don't know," she begins. I knew she'd freak out. She hasn't exactly been dragging her feet about the relationship, but I also don't want to spook her too much. "What are the dates?"

I push myself up to a seated position, almost dropping my phone in my haste to pull up my calendar. Delaney is hesitating due to logistical, scheduling reasons, not because she doesn't want to do it. I try to play it cool, try to make my elation not quite so obvious, but I must fail spectacularly, because she pokes my cheek and gives me a grin.

"As long as I have enough notice to get my shifts covered, I'd love to come. Thanks for inviting me, Benny. It means a lot to me." I want to pick her up and spin her around the room like they do in all the Disney movies Genesis forced me to watch with her. Instead, I settle for pushing her back and pinning her to the mattress as I kiss her intensely enough that she feels every ounce of my gratitude.

A knock sounds at my hotel room door. I assume it's the pizza I ordered and am a little surprised they brought it all the way to the room. Normally, food delivery couriers leave it at the front desk. It's the only reason why I got dressed again after my shower, anticipating having to go down and fetch it. I'm also impressed with the speed in which it was delivered. I ordered it only about fifteen minutes ago, right before I hopped in the shower.

When I open the door, I'm equally disappointed and confused. Confused because instead of pizza delivery, JJ Jeffers stands at my door. And disappointed only because he's not holding a large sausage and pepperoni pizza, not because the man himself is disappointing. As if to prove my physical state, my stomach lets out a loud rumble.

"Hey, JJ, what's up?" We're in New York, and the hotel the team stays at is a swanky high-rise in midtown Manhattan. There's no reason JJ shouldn't be out with his teammates or his brother, who lives here, enjoying the nightlife, especially considering I requested a "show and go" tomorrow morning, meaning no workouts. The players will show up as late as possible to the ballpark; we could all use a break.

"Hey, Benny. Are you going out tonight? Am I interrupting?"

I shake my head. "Nah, I ordered a pizza. I'm looking forward to throwing on a movie and staying in." It sounds like a great plan; Delaney is working late, so I won't be able to video chat with her tonight. I might as well pig out in the privacy of my own room.

"Do you mind if we chat about a couple things that I think could help boost the guys' morale?" I widen the door in invitation and gesture to the minibar. Even though JJ has the same setup in his room, he opens the fridge and peruses the selection. Finally settling on the world's most expensive bottle of shitty domestic beer, he twists off the top and hands me one before doing the same for his own. The mini bar prices are even more exorbitant at this hotel than any other we stay in all season–and we stay at some nice places–but since JJ is drinking with me, I wonder briefly if I can write it off as a business expense?

JJ takes a seat at the desk, and I notice about two seconds too late that my *craft project* from earlier is sitting on top. The label is twisted to the side, so for all JJ knows, it's a random paint can sitting on my hotel desk. That's not incredibly fucking weird, is it? Fortunately, he doesn't spare it a second glance, and I'm saved from an awkward explanation.

"What were you thinking?" I ask, directing his gaze back on me. JJ is a great teammate, player, and leader. He's the kind of guy you always want on your team as a player and, quite honestly, the kind of guy you love to coach. He's laid back enough where he's coachable and redirectable, but serious about his on-field performance. He's kind and gets along with everyone. The Foxes have put together a great group of men, but I suspect it's JJ's unofficial leadership–alongside Caleb Andrews–that has helped shape the team into the lovable people they are both on and off the field. I'd like to think I had something to do with shaping who they are as well.

"There's some rumbling that everyone is exhausted." I nod, having picked up those vibes myself. It's why I called for the show and go. JJ takes a long drink of his beer. When he pulls the bottle away from his mouth, he absentmindedly taps his wedding band against the glass.

Clink, clink, clink.

I smile. JJ is obsessed with his wife (as he should be). I'd like to think I'm equally obsessed with Delaney. I talk openly about her to the team, despite many of them only having met her in passing at Sip, if at all. Still, JJ's devotion to his bride is admirable, and I make a mental note to show Delaney more of my adoration. She's not into big, showy gifts, but I will arrange for coffee and an egg sandwich to be delivered to her tomorrow when she wakes up. I'll have to schedule it late enough in the afternoon to ensure she's awake to receive it. Come to think of it, maybe I'll order some Moon Shadow to be delivered to Sip tonight. She doesn't eat a ton on shift if she's super busy, despite getting a dinner break.

"So, what do you think?" JJ is looking at me expectantly, and I realize that I've entirely spaced out. I shake my head as if to clear the cobwebs.

"Shit, I'm so sorry. I completely spaced and missed everything you said to me." JJ laughs, setting his empty bottle on the desktop. He starts retelling his idea for a mini tournament, golfing off the upper deck of Foxes Field. He's apparently willing to bankroll the prize money. I'm sure the grounds crew will love golf balls being launched across the outfield the morning before a game day, but they'll have to deal with it. It's a fantastic idea. As JJ elaborates on logistics, he absentmindedly picks the peeling label from the paint can on the desk.

As if suddenly realizing what he's doing and recognizing that a paint can in a luxury hotel room is a little strange, he spins the can around. His eyes catch sight of the label, and I swear to god, JJ Jeffers, grown ass man and All-Star shortstop, starts giggling like a little girl. He turns the can toward me to show me the label, as if I don't already know what it is.

*Dick in a Can: Mold YOUR Dick into a One-of-a-Kind Dildo!* the label proudly announces. While I wait for JJ to get ahold of himself, I can't help the grin spreading across my face. It *is* ridiculous.

"Dude. What the fuck is this?" he exclaims between wheezes.

"I'm pretty sure the label is self-explanatory, JJ. What do you not understand about it?"

"Did you...did you make a *mold* of your dick?" His face reddens as he tries to gather some semblance of control over his laughter.

"As a matter of fact, I did." No use denying it, might as well embrace it. "What can I say? My girl likes the heat I'm packing so I thought I'd surprise her by making her something for when I'm on the road." JJ's jaw hangs open, but after a moment, he closes it and looks at the can thoughtfully.

"That's a genius move. Where did you buy this?"

"I'll send you the link." I open my emails to my order confirmation, finding the link easily and texting it to him.

"Was it...hard to make?" His eyes twinkle, and I'm one hundred percent certain he intended that pun.

"A little. Don't look in my bathroom. There's blue powder all over the place from when I opened the contents and mixed them a little too vigorously." JJ stifles a laugh with a cough. "The hardest part, pun fucking intended, was staying hard long enough for the material to set around my dick. So if you can do that, you should be good."

JJ nods, finally composing himself. "So now what? You stuck your dick in some goo, and it hardened around it to make a mold?"

"Pretty much," I shrug. "Once everything is completely dry, I'm supposed to send it back to them and a week later, they send me the completed toy. You can add all sorts of customizations. Add vibration, different colors, glitter." I wonder briefly if I should be earning some sort of commission on this product. JJ is likely not the only Fox who will want to try this once the word gets out.

"Glitter?" JJ snorts. I level him with a look.

"If you think your wife won't want a little bling to your battery-operated dick, I think you'll be surprised." JJ dissolves into another fit of giggles. Remember when I said he was serious enough and a strong leader and all that? I take it all back.

"So...what...color...will you...be going with?" He says between rounds of laughter. A tear leaks from the corner of his eye.

"Delaney's favorite color is purple, so obviously, I chose the violet offering. But that's all I'm telling you," I say as I swipe my paint can away from him, cradling it against my chest like a small, precious child. JJ holds his palms up in surrender.

"It's a great idea, man. I'm coming to you if I have any issues making it."

"Please don't," I say as he stands and makes his way to the door. When he finally leaves, I look over his shoulder to see he's already got the website open and is placing an order for himself.

# CHAPTER TWENTY-TWO

## *Delaney*

Blow Job Shot: Amaretto, Irish Cream Liqueur, whipped cream Topper. Must Take The Shot without using your Hands.

I've been running around like a chicken with its head cut off for the last hour. I'm not a planner, okay? I've known this trip was coming up for two weeks, yet I waited until almost two hours before I have to leave to start packing. If I'm truly honest, part of the delay is nerve-related (the other part? Personality and a professional degree in procrastination.).

This is probably why college–the parts I completed, any-way–was so difficult for me. Never one to crack the spines of my textbooks before ten at night, I also wasn't exactly eager to study at all. Until I realized somehow time got away from me and it was the night before finals. Sure, I wasn't a total idiot; I got through many of my classes by using common sense and having a vague memory of classroom discussions. But if I had applied myself? I'm sure I could have made the dean's list. Part of my problem, I can see in hindsight, is that I never identified a passion. For so long, I remained an undecided major. There were courses I *liked,* and

I put more effort into those classes, but none that I loved. None that I could see channeling into a career. So as much as I'd like to blame my poor study habits on something outside of my control, like ADHD, I know it's really that I wasn't cut out for college. I still haven't really channeled my passion into a career.

I like working at Sip. I love working for Tilly and Sloane. But if they decided to close the business and open, say, an art studio, I wouldn't follow them. I don't really understand art. I like crafting, but only as it pertains to my cocktail recipe scrapbook, and since when were either of those things viable careers? Bartending isn't a passion: it's a means to an end. It allows me to meet cool people, feel somewhat useful, and make decent money. Said money allows me to travel and eat at delicious restaurants whenever I want and generally not have to worry about making rent or paying my utilities. And really, isn't that what life is about? Now, if I could find a job that revolves around eating, traveling, and doing little else? Sign me up.

Benny still thinks I have a viable side gig going if I sell my cocktail recipes. I, however, am a little more based in reality. After working in various city bars for the last seven years, I know most people want something straightforward. They're not willing to shell out more than ten bucks on a risk, and my drinks are new and sometimes unusual, which makes them a risk. People come to a bar for two reasons: to socialize or to get drunk (oftentimes both). Benny insists I'm thinking about it the wrong way; that I need to consult with independent restaurants who will pay me a consulting fee. I don't think there are that many out there willing to consult with someone whose only experience is slinging shitty beer in a neighborhood bar and tinkering about with different liquors in her tiny apartment kitchen.

Still, that $2500 from Ernie was nice; it looks nice, sitting in my travel funds jar under my kitchen sink. It felt nice to be recognized for my creative efforts, even though I know he mostly did it for Benny's benefit. The look of pride Benny wore when I introduced the drink at The Bookstore flashes in my mind. He's a good guy. I momentarily consider that I shouldn't give him such a hard time, but then I remember that riling him up is one of the simplest pleasures in my life, and he not-so-secretly enjoys it, too.

I jolt myself out of my thoughts. I had absentmindedly sat on the corner of my bed, fingering the soft silk of a low-cut blouse, lost in my own memories, instead of packing. See what I mean about procrastination? My eyes flick to the television on mute in the corner of the room. Foxes players are trailing off the field, having won their game. Benny asked me to show up about an hour and a half after the game ends so we could leave for Nashville.

I've walked with Benny to the ballpark before, usually when we spend the night together and before I head back to my place and get ready for work. I've never attended a game, mostly because the timing doesn't work out with my shift schedule. I don't know the first thing about baseball and since Benny isn't playing, I don't feel too bad about not being there. He insists it doesn't bother him, as long as he gets to see me before and after games. He's introduced me to Eric, the head of Foxes security, when I've walked him to work, and a few members of his coaching staff when they've come in to Sip after a game. The last thing I need is the players' wives forcing conversation with the boss's girlfriend because they think they have to in order to help their husbands' careers. I can fake it as good as anyone else–I do it all the time on slow nights at Sip–but it's easier when I'm getting paid and there are other distractions, like drinks to pour and other customers to serve, to break up the awkwardness of forced conversation.

Stopping myself from sitting down, *yet again,* I hurry to finish my packing. Benny gave me very vague guidelines when I asked him what I should pack. *Comfortable clothes and a bathing suit.* Real helpful, Ben. I had rolled my eyes when I told him that, but before I could probe him for more details on what, exactly, I should expect to wear in front of his family, he pulled me onto his lap and dared me to roll my eyes at him again. Of course, never one to back down from a challenge, I did, and we spent the next hour tangled in the sheets together. Time well spent, except now I'm at a loss, never having revisited the conversation.

Sighing deeply, I throw one more pair of denim shorts and a band T-shirt in my bag. At the last second, I decide to throw in my favorite deep purple sundress in case we go out at night. I love a good summer sundress if it shows off my best assets (my boobs) and is forgiving everywhere else. I realize I don't have shoes that go with it, typically preferring to throw on my trusty black Converse low tops. I shrug. It'll have to do.

I'm not immune to worry about judgment from Benny's family. He repeatedly insists I have nothing to worry about, but I hope they don't take one look at me and think I'm not good enough for him. I think we're a good match, but on sight alone, our differences probably stand out more than our similarities. Benny is tall and sexy and extremely athletically built. I'm shorter and on the cookie-enjoying side of the scale. Benny is a silver fox (he'd probably have a lot to say about that label since his head is covered in thick, dark hair, but his stubble gives away his age more than anything); I look my age.

Tossing my makeup bag in my suitcase and flipping the lid closed, I lug it to the front door of my apartment. Sloane and Tilly already agreed to watch Kingston while I was away, so I had hauled his food, toys, and the cat himself to Sip before my shift yesterday. He spent the rest of the night with Sloane, behind her closed office door. He didn't even care when I came to say goodbye to him at the end of my shift; he barely lifted his sleepy head from her lap to acknowledge me. Ungrateful jerk.

Benny's text letting me know he is ready to leave whenever comes through while I'm in the rideshare on the way to the ballpark. He tells me to meet Eric in the lobby of the administrative offices, and he will bring me down to him, where he saved me some of the postgame meal.

When I get out of the car, Eric is waiting for me. I don't know how much the Foxes are paying him, but it's probably not enough. He's always around; he must work ungodly hours. He greets me warmly and insists on rolling my suitcase for me. He tells me about his wife's pregnancy and how much he's looking forward to a few days off to hang out with her. It makes me wonder what it's like for all the wives and girlfriends having to essentially raise children without their partners for most of the year. Sure, it's easy to write it off when you consider the players are making millions of dollars and can hire extra help, but what about the Erics of the baseball world? His wife sacrifices so much time away from her husband for his job. I hope they both think it's worth it.

"Benny, I've got a fan here who says she *had* to meet you, immediately," he jokes, bringing me to the door of Benny's office. I've never been here; I've never even been past the main lobby. Eric took me down one floor in the elevators and through wide, winding hallways to get to Benny's office. Housed down the hall from what I assume is the locker room, his office seems so *normal* for what I assume is the high importance of his job. Seeing as we're technically underground and on the interior of the building, the lack of windows makes sense, but it's also a little stifling. It's no wonder he is working with the door open.

"A fan, huh? I don't know if I'm up for a meet and greet," Benny jokes back, standing from a large wooden desk in the corner. An overstuffed blue couch sits opposite the desk. The office would look a little less cramped with a smaller piece of furniture, a loveseat even, but Benny told me last season, especially in the postseason, he had many long nights that necessitated sleeping here instead of at home. I shudder at the thought of having to sleep at Sip overnight. It's a decently nice bar, but not *that* nice.

"Hi, babe," Benny greets me, eyes dancing with mirth. "Thanks for grabbing her, Eric. I appreciate you staying for that; I was not anticipating an ownership phone call right when we're all trying to get out of here." He pulls me into a hug.

"No problem, I know how it is," Eric says with a shrug. "Enjoy your trip."

"Enjoy the time with your wife," I call after him as he leaves.

"I'm sorry, sweetheart. I know I told you I was ready to go, but the team owners wanted a bit more information on a couple of players before we break. The trade deadline is in a couple weeks, and I guess they didn't realize they didn't have the information until now." He rolls his eyes at me, letting me know how he feels about their poor planning.

He pushes a white, Styrofoam container toward me and gestures to the couch. "I got you a little bit of everything I thought you'd like. Take a peek and if you want anything else, tell me quickly because I'm sure they're already cleaning up the kitchen."

"This should be fine," I promise without even opening the lid. If I get hungry on the road, we can always stop quickly. Besides, I stuffed my backpack with a bunch of road trip snacks. I'm pretty sure whoever coined the term "hangry" did so after meeting me. I'm always prepared with food.

Opening the container, steam wafts out. I settle back into the couch as Benny makes his way back over to me, handing me a plastic fork and pulling off the lid to a blue electrolyte drink. I struggled to open the lid one freaking time, and now he opens the bottle every time before handing it to me. He presses a soft kiss to my forehead before rounding his desk again and tapping away at his laptop.

I'm midway through a bite of the most decadent macaroni and cheese I've ever tasted when Benny's desk phone rings. Sighing, he picks it up. He must have recognized the extension, because he greets the caller by name. The cleaning crew is already vacuuming the hallway. Loud Spanish music blares over the dull roar of the vacuum. Benny looks at me pleadingly, and I stand, swinging the door shut. I lock it after the briefest of hesitations; I have no idea if this is the kind of place where the cleaning crew goes into offices with closed doors, but the last thing Benny needs is another interruption. I know he's eager to get home to Nashville, and he's already annoyed at the delay. He mouths a quick thank you to me before focusing his attention on the call. The tiniest of furrows creases the area between his eyebrows, the only indication he is frustrated. His voice betrays nothing though, his tone professional yet friendly. I, on the other hand, want to yank the phone away and yell at the caller to respect Benny's extremely limited vacation time. Knowing that won't help him in the long run, despite how *extremely satisfying* it will feel in the moment, I focus back on my food.

In addition to creamy mac and cheese, Benny sourced me roasted garlic broccoli, some sort of sliced pork, a small pile of Greek salad, yellow rice and beans, roasted red potatoes, a few slices of strip steak drizzled with some sort of peppery sauce, and a small hunk of perfectly seasoned white fish. Sometimes I think Benny forgets that just because I enjoy food, my stomach is not nearly as big as his. Still, I appreciate the variety and make sure I sample a little of everything.

"Sounds good. Yeah, you too," Benny says before hanging up and sighing deeply. "Okay, let me finish this email really quickly and let's get out of here before they remember something else and call back."

"Do you want any of this?" I gesture to the food. Despite eating my fill, it barely looks like I made a dent (although all the macaroni and cheese has mysteriously disappeared).

"Nah, I ate during the first phone call." He pulls a trash can out from underneath his desk. I close the container and rise from the couch, dropping it in. I peer over Benny's shoulder to view the photos in the frames neatly lining his desk. Most of them are his children; he's shown me photos before, but every time I see them, my breath is taken away by how objectively beautiful they each are. The last photo makes me smile. Benny is in uniform, being carried on the shoulders of his teammates. Based on the teary-eyed expressions of the men in the photo, they must have just won an important game.

I take in the rest of the office. Compared to the photos on the desk, the rest of the office is rather nondescript. Blue and orange walls in Foxes' colors add a splash of brightness, but other than that, the walls are bare. A glass bowl of what looks to be fruity Japanese candy sits on the mostly empty hutch behind the desk. I open a piece, popping the chewy, intensely mango-flavored treat in my mouth. Spying a drawer obstructed from closing by a thick fabric cord, I go to close it properly, tucking the cord inside. However, when I see that the cord is attached to a stopwatch, I can't help but pull it out.

Twirling it around my finger, I lean over Benny's shoulder. I'm pleased to see him wrapping up his email. As soon as he hits 'send,' I move in front of him and lean against his desk. From his seated position below me, he must catch the devilish look in my eye because his responding grin is full of sin.

"Wanna see how quickly I can get you off?" I dangle the stopwatch in front of him like a hypnotist. Benny hesitates only half a second, enough time for him to flick his eyes to the door to confirm it's still locked.

"Hmm, want to make it interesting?" I knew he would play with me. I want him to go into his only break of the season relaxed, not annoyed at the many delays and interruptions. I grin. "We can see who gets off fastest. See who can hold out the longest?"

I pretend to consider it for a moment, twisting my lips to the side in mock contemplation. "Fine, but to keep it fair, no sex. Only hands and mouths. First your turn, then mine." Benny's eyes are blazing with heat, his ice blue irises quickly getting swallowed by the black of his pupils as I see them blow out in real time. He snatches the stopwatch from where it dangles, mostly forgotten, between us and shoves it firmly into my hands.

"I agree to your terms. I'll have you bent over my desk while I eat you out from behind, screaming my name in record time." I school my face into neutrality, not wanting him to see how his dirty words affect me. We're only playing for bragging rights, but my competitive streak is probably only matched by Benny's own, and I came to win.

"Get on your knees and press start," he commands. It's one of the few times I obey him unquestioningly. Even in bed, I tend to give him a little bit of sass, just to let him know I won't give up too easily. Tonight though, my unwavering obedience must surprise him, because when I do as he says, he drags a hand down his face, a long, slow "fuuuuuck" escaping his lips.

Ten minutes later, when we'd both gotten off admittedly far quicker than usual, I throw a triumphant fist into the air, having held out against Benny by a minute and thirteen seconds—and I was barely able to do that.

Benny pulls me onto his lap, rolling his desk chair back far enough for both of us to sit comfortably. I catch my breath as he presses gentle kisses to my neck, stroking my hair reverently. He murmurs soft praises and congratulations against my skin. I allow my eyes to close as I drag my own fingers through his hair, sighing contentedly.

# CHAPTER TWENTY-THREE

## *Delaney*

The Midseason Break (A Delaney Kristoff
Original): Prosecco, Peach Puree, Muddled
Raspberry, Popsicle (any fruity flavor)

Benny falls asleep before we even leave the city limits. The drive to Nashville isn't that long, especially on a weeknight, but he's exhausted. I'm used to staying up late, so driving the whole way doesn't bother me. I pop on my audiobook, keeping the volume in the car loud enough to hear, but quiet enough so as not to wake him. He snores softly, arms folded across his chest, the brim of his hat low across his face. Occasionally, I sneak glances at him in the momentary brightness of highway streetlights, his features temporarily lit to show off his straight nose, plush lips, and that stubble I love so much.

Somewhere around southern Indiana, my book gets to the good part. Every romance reader knows it's getting good when the hero talks the heroine through it; this scene is particularly intense. I'm so engrossed in the story, I barely notice Benny arch his back and stretch his arms overhead. He says nothing–thank god he doesn't interrupt and, for once, has no comments–but when the chapter

163

ends and the narrators move on to more mundane content, Benny arches a brow at me.

"Don't judge my book. Don't make fun," I say, cutting off whatever taunting comments Benny is about to make.

"Baby, judgment was not where my mind was going. I know what kind of books you read. I'm wondering how long you've been sitting here, listening to this, and if your neglected little pussy is as wet as I think it is as a result." He drags a knuckle along my slit, over my clothes, and I try and fail to repress a shiver.

"Benny, I'm driving," I whine, as if he didn't already know that. What can I say? I immediately lose brain cells when he touches me. He ignores my plea but withdraws his hand, returning it to his phone. He doesn't drop the subject though, scrolling through his phone and murmuring, his deep voice barely loud enough for me to hear over the continued narration of the story.

"I bet you're sitting there, that beautiful cunt dripping, and you can't do anything about it. Such a responsible driver, Delaney. Keeping your eyes on the road and your head in the game, when what you want to do is picture my fingers, or my tongue, or my cock, driving into you, filling you up, making your eyes roll back."

I swallow roughly, shaking my head the tiniest bit, as if I'm trying to convince myself that's not what I want at this exact moment. Benny continues scrolling but doesn't stop his dirty words.

"How long has your poor soaked pussy been sitting there, getting wetter and wetter with this book," he gestures to the center screen to indicate the audiobook, "while the person who can do something about it naps, completely unaware, two feet away?" He says the last bit without bite, but I glance his way anyway.

Is he upset that I didn't wake him? Or annoyed that I'm listening to this in the first place? This isn't news; he's known I read smut for a while now. Benny doesn't look back at me but must sense my gaze out of his periphery.

"Eyes on the road, baby." I roll my eyes at his bossy tone. "I can feel your eyes rolling. Just like I can sense your nipples hardening. Don't you think it'd be better if we make those eyes roll a different way? Maybe while you're screaming my name, hmm?"

His arrogance is simultaneously annoying and arousing. And he's right; my nipples could cut glass. I know this without having to glance down at my chest, but I do anyway, and sure as shit, they're about to cut twin holes through the front of this shirt. I squeeze my thighs together, keeping a steady foot on the gas, trying to get some sort of relief for the ache in my core. I absolutely was getting turned on from my audiobook (who wouldn't?), but Benny's somewhat bossy narration of his own thoughts is what's pushing me past the point of entertainment and hurtling straight to distraction.

"Benny..." I whine again, not sure how to even finish my sentence. He chuckles and continues staring at his phone.

Asshole.

I'm about to open my mouth again to tell him that, when he interrupts with thoughts of his own. "Baby, you are a writhing, needy mess over there. If you think for one second that I'm not going to take care of my girl when she's like this, you've got another thing coming. Here's what you're going to do." He flashes his phone screen toward me, where I can see his maps app showing a destination less than seven miles away.

"You are going to park at this rest stop in six point four miles. Then you're going to park your gorgeous, glistening pussy right over my face, and I'm not coming up for air until you've given me at least two orgasms. I want your juices running down my chin. I want you a babbling, stuttering mess while you make a mess of my face. And then I'm going to impale your swollen, needy little pussy with my cock, where you're going to ride me hard until I fuck a third orgasm out of you."

# CHAPTER TWENTY-FOUR
## *Delaney*

The Rest Stop (A Delaney Kristoff Original):
Vodka, Blueberry Energy Drink, Layered
Grenadine, Maraschino Garnish

The audiobook is still narrating, but I couldn't tell you what is happening in the story if my life depended on it. My right foot presses a little harder on the gas pedal as we speed closer to the rest stop, darkness enveloping us along the way. Benny's hand caresses my right thigh, never quite reaching high enough to be where I need it, but high enough to keep the steady beat of arousal thrumming through my veins. He laughs at my grumble of frustration when he starts another slow descent of my thigh, instead of continuing upward.

"Fuck you," I mumble under my breath. My words come out breathy and the exact opposite of threatening.

"Oh, you will soon enough, baby."

I press a little harder on the gas. There's hardly anyone on the road at this time of night, thanks to our, *ahem*, delayed start earlier today. There's only one semi-truck at the rest stop he directs me to. I park at the far end, away from the truck but still grateful for the heavy tint to Benny's windows. I may be turned on beyond all measure, but I'm still not willing to give some random trucker a free show. I throw the car in park and slam my palm a little harder than necessary against the power button to the audio. Benny smirks arrogantly, well aware of what he's doing to me. He's damn proud of himself.

"Frustrated, baby?" I growl in response, which only makes his smirk enlarge into a full-blown grin. "Someday you'll realize taking care of you is my favorite job," he tsks. "Now get those shorts off and get on my face. Now." The last word is spoken with the tiniest of threats, and I swear, I feel another gush of wetness in my panties.

My fingers fumble over the buttons of my jeans; I can't get them undone fast enough. My brain momentarily flashes back to how I used to fight his advances, push him away, resist him at every turn, and now, here I am, a soppy, whimpering mess who can't get her clothes off fast enough.

My thoughts are interrupted by Benny's press of the small button beside his seat as he reclines his chair further back.

"I cannot wait for you to sit your ass on top of me so I can tongue-fuck the life out of your gorgeous cunt."

The look he levels me freezes me on the spot. It's a mix of lust, heat, desire, and something else that I can't quite place.

"Need some help there, darling?" He gestures to my shorts, half unbuttoned. I roll my eyes at him and continue undressing. He grabs my throat in a flash and pulls my face toward him. He devours my mouth, our tongues tangling, and draws out a moan from deep inside of me. "Someday I'm going to punish you for all the times you roll your eyes at me," he promises.

"Don't threaten me with a good time," I retort, resuming my frantic undressing. He laughs.

"Noted," is all he says before hauling my naked lower half over the center console to settle on his face, as promised. Two swipes of his magical tongue have me coming already, my arousal gushing into his mouth. I knew it wasn't going to take much, given how worked up I was, but I've never come this quickly.

"There she is," he murmurs. He licks me through a powerful orgasm before slowly inserting two fingers in me and curling them. My own fingers scrabble against the ceiling, trying to find purchase against something, but I find no real handhold as my hips grind against his face.

He groans, the vibrations reverberating through my entire body, and my hips pick up the pace of their own accord. His fingers match the movements of my hips, writhing against my inner walls. I'm close again. Benny has always been incredibly talented, but this has to be a new record for quickest orgasms in succession. My new release is building, building, building, pulling me tauter and higher. When he presses his thumb against my back hole, I detonate. He changes nothing, and it's one of the things I love most about his talents–he finds a good thing and keeps at it. He devours me as I shake above him, and he only lets up once my release is well and truly over.

My voice is hoarse from screaming his name and my body–my muscles, my nerve endings, my thoughts–completely spent. I slide down Benny's body, finally giving him space to breathe, and he was right. My release covers his lips and chin–even a little on his neck.

He licks his lips and gently pulls me by the back of my neck down to his mouth. He tastes of me, and I moan breathlessly against him as I work to undo his belt buckle and fly.

"Baby, that was so perfect," I praise him, not even caring how breathless I sound. "I needed that so badly," I admit.

He smiles softly at me. "I know, Delaney. I'll always give you what you need, even when you don't know you need it," he tells me, slamming into me on a powerful thrust.

# CHAPTER TWENTY-FIVE

# *Benny*

Espresso Martini: Vodka, Coffee Liqueur, Chilled
Espresso, Simple Syrup, Espresso Bean Garnish

By the time we rolled into the driveway of my house last night, it was nearly two o'clock in the morning. Delaney fell asleep after I insisted I drive the last leg after our rest stop adventures, but she was awake for the last hour or so of the trek. My house is on the outskirts of the city, along the Cumberland River. It was hard to see much in the dark when we arrived, but I can't wait to have coffee with her when she wakes up. I know she'd love to curl up near my outdoor fireplace as we watch the morning kayakers float by from my second story balcony.

I sneak downstairs to brew some coffee, sending a text to Keeley to confirm lunch with the kids. She promises to bring them and Martin's Bar-B-Que Joint over promptly at noon. My mouth waters in anticipation, but I'm mostly excited for Delaney to meet the most important people in my life. I know she's nervous, and I'd be concerned if she wasn't at least a little anxious. More than two decades of professional sports have taught me that a little bit of stress can be a good thing. Still, I want to make sure Delaney–and my kids–are as comfortable with the whole situation as possible.

Returning to my bedroom, Delaney is still asleep, her arm flung haphazardly across her face, her hair fanning out in all directions. She requested one of my shirts to sleep in, and it looks incredible on her. I palm my cock into submission, knowing there's little time for that right now if we want to be dressed and presentable by the time Scarlett, Kai, and Genesis come over. I groan internally as I sit down on my balcony, coffee in hand. I really hope Genesis is not planning on bringing Garrett. She didn't call and ask, so I'm hoping that means she didn't think to bring him, or she did, and Keeley quashed that idea before she extended the invitation.

My coffee is mostly finished by the time I hear the slider door open, and I'm graced with Delaney's delicious presence. Pulling the pot of coffee off the stone table, I pour fresh mugs, handing one to her and kissing her cheek.

"Sleep okay?" I ask, already knowing the answer. Now that Delaney is no longer pretending to hate cuddling, she embraces her inner koala even further. Any day I wake up without a face full of her disheveled hair is a sad day for me. She's got me conditioned to crave the tickle of her dark mane against my skin.

She nods sleepily and settles in at my side. We watch the last of the morning kayakers and jet skiers bounce along the river. I can't wait for my family to get here; then, I'll have everything I need right at my fingertips.

After coffee, we shower and get ready. Delaney changes her outfit three times, so I know she's nervous, but I know everyone will love her. She's in the middle of changing her shirt for the fourth time when the doorbell rings, followed by the opening of my front door and a high-pitched yell from my youngest daughter. She's tiny, but her lungs were made for screaming.

"DADDY! Where are you?"

# CHAPTER TWENTY-SIX

## *Delaney*



I freeze. There was only so much I could do to prepare myself for meeting Benny's kids, but I'm still not ready. I'll probably never be ready. But they're here, and there's nothing else I can do but take Benny's outstretched hand and follow him down the stairs.

His youngest daughter, Scarlett, squeals and launches herself at her father, scrambling up the stairs on all fours to get to him. Dropping my hand, he lifts her into the air and pulls her into a tight squeeze. My heart suddenly is both heavy and full. Benny needed this time with his family, and I'm so happy he gets to have that. At the same time, I can't remember my own father ever squeezing me like that. Sure, he hugged me and told me he loved me, but any outsider can look at Benny and the way he looks at the five-year-old clutched in his grasp and know he'd kill for her. Maybe my own father felt that way when I was Scarlett's age, but he long ago gave up his devotion to me or my mother.

Maintaining his hold on Scarlett, Benny bounds down the open staircase and uses his free arm to pull his teenagers into a bone-crushing hug.

"My babies. I've missed you!" He plants kisses on both kids' heads, oblivious to their initial groans of embarrassment, but I see their smiles peeking out from under his shoulder. They both might act embarrassed, but I know they love their father's over-the-top displays of adoration. My breath catches in my throat to see so much love in one room.

"Hey, Sam," a voice calls. A gorgeous woman walks back into the front hallway, dusting her hands off on her fitted jeans. She must have dropped the lunch in the kitchen to give her children a moment with their father.

"Hey, Keels," Benny leans over to give her a side hug. I'm stunned—not by Benny's continued affection for his ex-wife. I expected that and know they continue to have a good relationship. My daze is due to the flawless woman standing in front of me. Her brown eyes are framed by tasteful blue frames. Her tank top and designer jeans, paired with her red hair tossed up in a loose ponytail, make her look effortlessly fabulous. I let loose a tiny sigh of relief at seeing she's as curvy as I am; my self-esteem wouldn't have survived if she was model-thin. Still, I self-consciously tug at the bottom of my jean shorts, hoping I'm not showing too much skin.

"Guys, this is Delaney," Benny announces proudly before naming off his children and former wife, each of whom greets me warmly. Their genuine, immediate affability is a tribute to Benny and makes me realize I had little to worry about. Don't get me wrong, I'm still terrified of not making a good impression on the loves of Benny's life, but I'm a little appeased so far.

"Should we eat?" Keeley suggests. "I don't want the food to get cold."

We all trail after Keeley into the kitchen. When we arrived last night, Benny had given me a brief tour of the house, which is on the larger side without being obnoxiously oversized. The open-concept kitchen is cavernous, with a long farmhouse table situated in the middle, past an oversized eat-in island. Genesis busies herself taking dishes from the cabinets, while Kai helps his mother open the various food containers. Benny is murmuring something to Scarlett, still in his arms. The kitchen is immediately filled with the smells of barbeque sauce and grilled meats. I spy a stack of napkins at the end of the table, in a little wicker basket, and make myself useful by passing them out. I'm grateful to have something to do with my hands, instead of awkwardly waiting around while everyone else, who is far more comfortable being here than I am, prepares for lunch. Benny catches my eye and gestures for me to sit. He pulls out the chair next to me and places Scarlett beside the empty chair. Everyone but Scarlett and me starts dishing out food. It's a free-for-all of Southern fare, the smokey, saucy delicacies being plopped onto each plate without regard for its recipient's preferences. I guess everyone eats a little of everything in Benny's family. I raise an eyebrow when a plate piled high with a little of everything, including a large scoop of collard greens, is set in front of little Scarlett, who doesn't bat an eye at the green vegetables. Plates full, we all settle in to eat. My mouth is watering, but my stomach is a jumble of nerves. I haven't said much beyond my initial greeting. I think Keeley can tell I'm nervous, because she offers me a gentle smile before launching into the latest updates on her children's lives.

"Genesis, did you tell your dad you received your roommate assignment?" Then, looking at me, she explains, "Genesis is attending the University of Tennessee in the fall."

"That's great! Congratulations," I tell her brightly. I really am happy for her. Benny sings her praises all the time, so I know she's smart and well-rounded. I'm not surprised that she's going to college. "Are you going to study photography?"

Genesis beams first at me, then at Benny. "You told Delaney about my photography?" Her tone is full of awe, as if she had no idea how proud of her Benny is.

"Of course he did," I tell her before Benny can answer. I'm as enthusiastic about Genesis's talents as her dad is. "He showed me your online portfolio. It's incredible."

"Oh, um, thanks," Genesis says shyly, tucking a strand of her brunette hair behind her ear. Kai pokes her in the side.

"She likes to pretend she's modest, but everyone knows she's got skills," Kai teases before shoveling a huge mouthful of macaroni and cheese into his cheek. He clearly gets his appetite from his father.

"Kai, I hear you play baseball, too," I suggest. After seeing how loving the Benjamins are, it's hard to be shy around them.

"Yeah, catcher, too," he says around another mouthful. "I was on JV this year, which is better than the freshman team, but I'm hoping to make varsity next year."

"I'm sure you will. Junior varsity as a freshman is quite an accomplishment," I tell him earnestly. Keeley shoots me a smile from across the table.

As the minutes go by and we get sucked into natural, easy conversation, my anxiety dissipates. I'm filled with relief; Benny repeatedly reassured me that his family would love me and that they are easy to get along with, but until I experienced it for myself, I didn't fully believe him. Scarlett tells us about her summer camp adventures, Genesis shares the little bit she knows about her new roommate, and Kai mentions he "might, kind of, sort of" have a new girlfriend. Keeley remains relatively quiet but laughs along with the rest of us.

When lunch ends with all of us stuffed to the gills, Keeley takes her leave, with promises of a family dinner tomorrow night in downtown Nashville.

"I'm glad you're here," she tells me genuinely with a squeeze to my arm as she turns to leave. I mumble a thanks while trying to keep the tears that have suddenly filled my vision from spilling over. My throat too choked to say anything more, I nod gratefully. Now, nerves jangle in my stomach for another reason: I want Benny's family to not only tolerate or approve of me, but to like me. I want a relationship with these people as much as I want to have a relationship with Benny. I'm startled at how quickly the desire pops into my head.

We spend the next several hours on the water. Scarlett and I dig in the little patch of sand near the shore adjacent to the dock that juts out from Benny's property. The rest of the surrounding area is filled with grass and mud; I suspect he imported several pounds worth of sand for his littlest one. She's an expert sandcastle builder, she tells me. Benny and Kai have taken out the jet skis, zipping back and forth, chasing each other across the somewhat choppy river. Genesis lounges on the dock, sunbathing and texting.

"What a dick," Genesis mutters under her breath. It's still loud enough for Scarlett and me to hear.

"Genesis said a bad word!"

I don't know how to handle this. I've never been a babysitter or been around small children in any real capacity before. I'm an only child with no close family members. I work at a bar. My interactions with small children are minimal at best. Am I supposed to agree with Scarlett? Is dick really a bad word? I guess to a five-year-old, maybe. Shit, I better watch my own language.

"Uh, is everything okay?" Genesis really isn't that much younger than me. I'm horrified to realize she and I are closer in age than Benny and I are. I wonder if people will find that awkward. Do *I* find that awkward? I guess, but not enough to do anything about it.

"Stupid Garrett," Genesis grumbles.

"Mom said we're not supposed to call people stupid!" To my utter terror, Scarlett locks eyes with me, as if she expects me to do something about Genesis's choice of adjectives. Genesis isn't watching our interaction, her eyes glued back on her phone, fingers flying across the keyboard. A deep groove settles between her eyebrows. If I wasn't studying her so intently (mostly to avoid Scarlett's waiting stare), I might have missed it, but I see the telltale tremble of Genesis's bottom lip. *Fuck.* I certainly am not equipped to redirect her questionable language; there's no way I'm equipped to play therapist. Still, I can't ignore her distress. This can't be too different from the drunk girls I play therapist to at Sip, right?

Pulling in a deep breath, I softly suggest that Scarlett build me the biggest tower and the deepest moat for our castle. She happily agrees, all thoughts of Genesis promptly forgotten. Cautiously, I walk over to where Benny's oldest daughter is lying on her stomach, propped up by her elbows, and sit down.

"Genesis, are you okay?" She glances up at me, startled that I've settled next to her without her noticing. She flips onto her back, flinging her arm across her face to block out the sun.

"It's just Garrett being...Garrett," she finishes lamely. I've heard Benny's mostly incoherent grumbles about Garrett enough to surmise he's not the Benjamins' most favorite person, but I've been spared the details.

"Do you want to talk about it?" I have no idea if what I'm asking is even appropriate–I just met her–but apparently, she doesn't find the question intrusive. Either that or she's so desperate to talk to someone about this, she'll settle for me.

"God, he's just so...infuriating! He's my boyfriend. Sort of. Or maybe not anymore." A single tear leaks out of her eye, tracking toward her temple. If I had a dollar for every time I saw a woman unnecessarily cry over a subpar man, I wouldn't need the job that allows me to encounter these women. Hell, if I had a dollar for every time *I* cried over a subpar man, I wouldn't need a job.

"How long have you guys been dating?"

"Two and a half years. But we haven't been together that whole time. I guess you could say it's more of an on again, off again thing."

"I see," I say neutrally. I've long come to realize that when people want to vent, they don't want your opinion. Because if I had a dollar for every time a woman cried over a subpar man, only to bring said subpar man back into the bar with her the following week, as if everything was magically changed, I also might not need my job.

"Garrett tends to forget about me when something better comes along," Genesis spits bitterly. *What a fuckwad.* I mentally pat myself on the back for filtering the thought before it came out of my mouth; I have no doubt Scarlett would have something to say about *that* word choice. "But then every time we get back together, things are so good that I forget about the annoying stuff. Until it happens again. But then I see him, and I want to be with him, and I can't help it."

"He sounds very wishy-washy," I say. Genesis's eyes widen and she nods vigorously, as if my words are wiser than they are.

"Yes! Exactly! And my friends keep telling me that he keeps coming back because I allow it, but I can't help it. Sometimes I wish I didn't love him." I know the feeling well, but I don't say that to her. I feel for her; it's hard to know what to do when your head is at war with your heart.

"What would make you happy?"

"What would–what?" She seems surprised I'd ask her that, which makes my heart break a little for her.

"Well, most people get into a relationship to be happy. Or at least happier than they would be being single, right? Are you happier with Garrett or without?" Genesis takes a long time to mull over my words.

"I don't know," she says softly. To me, that's enough of an answer, but I can't make up her mind for her.

"Mmm," I say neutrally. Genesis shifts, adjusting her bikini. She really is beautiful. She has her mother's coffee eyes and her father's thick brown hair. She's slender in the way only a teenage metabolism can support. Most importantly, she seems kind and caring. Benny's grumbles about Garrett make sense; that douchecanoe doesn't know what he's missing.

"I thought we'd be together forever. You know, high school sweethearts like my mom and dad. But now he's saying he doesn't really want to do a long-distance relationship in college, even though we're both staying in-state." I don't point out that despite her parents' high school sweetheart status, they are no longer together. I'm not a monster. She sighs deeply. "I guess I used to think that our conflicts were like little romantic challenges. Like, despite the odds, we made it. That if we could break up and get back together so many times, we'd eventually figure it out, and there would be nothing that life could throw at us that we wouldn't be able to handle together."

"And now?" I prompt gently.

"Now...I'm just tired of dealing with him. Now, I think he's an immature asshole." It's hard to disagree, given what I know about him. I nod. Genesis flips back over but doesn't return to her phone. Sensing the conversation has reached its close, I squeeze her forearm gently before returning to check Scarlett's progress.

A few minutes later, Benny and Kai come splashing toward the dock, careful not to create too much of a wake. Benny listens intently as Scarlett details all the features of her newest sandy creation before clapping his hands and suggesting we make dinner.

# CHAPTER TWENTY-SEVEN

# *Benny*

The Garrett (A Delaney Kristoff Original): Anise Liqueur, Green Chartreuse, Malort. If the above ingredients are unavailable, just mix together the most unappealing liquors around. Mmm, tastes like regret.

When I get out of the shower, Delaney is on the patio outside the kitchen, talking on the phone. Her voice wafts up to me through the open balcony door. Her voice has a slightly higher pitch; that, and the melodic tilt of the French language, tells me she's speaking with her mother. My ears strain to pick up any familiar words, but it's no use. Either Delaney is speaking too quickly, or she isn't using the common swears and insults I've mastered so far.

Now, Scarlett, Kai, and I are in the kitchen mixing ingredients when Delaney walks in, wrapping up her phone call and saying goodbye to her mother. Kai's eyes are wide.

"What language was that?" he asks her when she joins us at the island.

"French," she says with a grin. "What are you guys making?"

"You speak French? Can you teach me to say something?" Without waiting for a response, Kai plows ahead. "Teach me the good stuff, please, Delaney? Like, what's a really good swear?"

Delaney catches my eye and laughs out loud. I know she's thinking of all the times I asked her for the same lessons. I shrug, shooting her my own secret smile. She beckons Kai over to the table and I watch him try on various French pronunciations. Delaney is patient and kind in her teaching, and I feel a laugh bubble out of me. Kai can't quite get the hang of the "R" sound, but his enthusiasm is admirable.

Scarlett, perched on the counter near me, stirs the ground pork with a spoon as I periodically add in more chopped vegetables. When Kai and Delaney return, I explain the steps to make dumplings and ask Delaney to take over the vegetable mix while I work on pork with Scarlett and Kai tackles chicken. Between Kai's appetite and mine, we need to prepare enough to feed an army. After Delaney attempts to toss her hair behind her ear with her forearm, I wipe my hands on a nearby towel and stand behind her, gathering her thick locks and securing it with the elastic I always seem to have on my wrist.

"How'd you learn to make this? It seems like an ambitious choice."

"My mom grew up right outside of Chinatown in San Francisco. Her neighbors often babysat her and insisted she learn. It was a regular staple in my household growing up, and there's something relaxing about building a food assembly line with your family. We make it together as often as possible."

As if to prove my point, Kai pulls out the industrial sized vat of soy sauce from the fridge, splashing a bit of the dark liquid into his mix. Pride fills my chest; much like me, Kai cooks by feel, rather than by measurement.

When we all sit to eat, the kitchen table groaning under the weight of endless pan-fried and steamed dumplings, stir-fried beef and broccoli, steamed rice, and sesame snow peas, Genesis finally makes her appearance. Her eyes are red-rimmed, but she gives a forced smile, and I know now is not the time to push her. Her phone vibrates frequently throughout the meal before she finally turns it off without glancing at the screen. She smiles at me, letting me know she's okay, before tipping more dumplings onto her plate.

Happy chatter soon joins the myriad smells wafting from the table, culminating in a sensory-rich atmosphere I wouldn't trade for the world. There's something to be said about eating a big, home-cooked meal after spending the day in the sun. Since I rarely have time to cook, especially with my kids, I cherish this moment. When we finish eating and all clean up together, it doesn't feel like such a chore. In the midst of all the chaos occurring in my kitchen, people squeezing by one another to get to the sink and the dish-washer, bringing dish after dish from the table to the counter to be wrapped up and cleaned, silverware scraping against now-empty plates, I take a moment to breathe everything in. My kids, my girl, my house. I've never felt so lucky.

After dinner and roasting marshmallows in the outdoor fireplace off my bedroom, we curl up on the couches. The night sky slowly darkens, and I take Scarlett to bed, ignoring her protests as I help her wash the sticky marshmallow off her face. Delaney had made the kids mocktails for dinner, and Genesis is still sipping her second one as I refill Delaney's wine. I settle into the plush swivel chair between Genesis and Kai, across from Delaney. I have everything I need with me right here.

"So," Genesis begins, setting her copper mug on the table with a small clink. She's got her serious face on. "I want you all to know that I broke up with Garrett today. For good this time."

I immediately school my face into neutrality, worried a spark of joy may have slipped out before I could put on my mask. Kai is not so guarded.

"Thank fuck," he says loudly. I shoot him a warning glare at the curse, but we both know I have little room to talk. Delaney voices my thoughts.

"How are you feeling about it?" she asks cautiously. She, too, has a carefully placed mask of neutrality obscuring her true opinions. I haven't told her much about Garrett, but I trust she shares my feelings on the little turd.

"Good." Genesis blows out a breath. "Relieved, honestly. I feel like a weight has been lifted. I guess the more we got back together, the more worried I felt each time, like it was only a matter of time before we broke up again. I didn't even realize how bad I'd been feeling until I told him I wanted to end things, for real, and I felt...happy about it." She looks at Delaney as she says the last part, and something meaningful passes between them. No longer sporting a neutral expression, Delaney allows a small smile to creep onto her beautiful lips.

"I'm glad you're happy, Genesis," she says gently.

"I am too," I quickly agree, realizing I haven't said anything this entire conversation. "It will be good for you to go off to college with a clean slate. Nothing to hold you back." Delaney nods. It feels good to have a united front, even if what we're united against is a weasely eighteen-year-old boy.

"Thanks for helping me to sort my thoughts, Delaney." Genesis's voice is quiet but authentic. My gaze flicks to her, looking for some sort of explanation that doesn't come. "Garrett didn't take the breakup too well. He had a lot of unkind things to say about me, so it made me realize I made the right decision. Obviously, I blocked him," she adds quickly.

My eyes flash and I catch Kai grinding his teeth. I'm glad they have each other. Sure, Kai is three years younger than Genesis and hasn't fully grown into his body yet, but there's something reassuring knowing they were at school together and he could have had her back if she needed it. I guess I should have put more stock in my daughter having her own back; clearly she can handle herself.

Later, when we're crawling into bed, I ask Delaney what happened with her and Genesis earlier in the day.

"Not much," she shrugs, downplaying her contribution. I shake my head. Keeley and I have been secretly hoping Genesis would wake up and smell Garrett's bullshit, but whatever Delaney said to her must have stuck. "I only asked her if she was happy."

I gawk at her. Maybe it was the simplicity of her approach, or the fact that Delaney isn't Genesis's parent. Whatever it was, it worked. I could kiss her for supporting my children in the way they needed. Then I realize that, in fact, I *can* kiss Delaney pretty much anytime I want.

So I do.

# CHAPTER TWENTY-EIGHT

## *Delaney*

The Scarlett (A Delaney Kristoff Original Mocktail): Cranberry Juice, Pineapple Juice, Lemon Lime Soda, Orange Peel Garnish

The rest of the midseason break was fun and carefree, and I'm not ready to pack up. I may have fallen a little bit in love with Benny's kids these last four days, which more than shocks the hell out of me. I've never been around kids, although I guess Genesis and Kai aren't strictly kids in the way Scarlett is. Even Scarlett, though, was fun and funny, in a different way from her siblings. The biggest surprise of the trip, however, was how much I like Keeley. She's one of those warm, overtly friendly people that you can't help but be drawn to. Her fiancé, Ricardo, is equally nice. A little on the dorky side, but kind and thoughtful.

As Benny loads our suitcases into the car, I watch shamelessly as the muscles in his forearms ripple with the load. My luggage is significantly heavier than it was when we arrived. Benny insisted on taking me downtown to buy me my first pair of cowgirl boots. Of course, he purchased the most luxuriously buttery leather pair for me and the sparkliest pair for Genesis, who insisted they would look great at the bars she would certainly never be going to in college. Benny didn't bat an eye when Scarlett requested not one, but two pairs of boots in both blue and pink; the girl knows she's got her father wrapped around her little finger. Not to be left out, Kai and Benny picked out their own plainer and more masculine boots as well.

The kids went home with Keeley and Ricardo after dinner last night. A big part of me was sad to see them go, although I was grateful for the extra time alone with Benny. We hit up Broadway, new boots on our feet, and he surprised me with some very smooth dance moves. I'm excited to find out what other skills he's been hiding from me. So far, I've unearthed his dumpling making and two-stepping prowess in the last few days alone.

Now that it's time to go back to Chicago, I'm a little sad. Benny warned me the pressure on the Foxes would ramp up after the break. He's mentioned little things here and there about how, despite the team making the playoffs the last two years, he feels some stress about what might happen if they don't make them this year, or if they make the playoffs but don't secure a World Series win. He tries to play it off like he's unaffected, but I think he's more worried than he lets on. I can't imagine him not being successful in whatever he does. He is so naturally talented at everything.

I smile, thinking about how he takes everything in stride. Yesterday morning, Scarlett and I were snuggled on the couch, watching an episode of Bluey and coloring on clipboards perched in our laps. When Benny walked in, Scarlett scooted over for him to join us. When he sat next to her, she picked up her marker and began coloring his skin, tracing the thick black lines and filling in color between his tattoos. He just laughed and let her continue. When I sprang up and brought in my eyeshadow palette and makeup brushes, Scarlett's eyes practically bugged out of her skull. She had asked me in hushed tones if she could use the shimmery colors on her father. Without waiting for Benny's permission, I simply told her of course, and we both got to work, covering his arms in a bright amalgamation of pinks, purples, browns and greens. Admittedly, some of the coloring work looked better than others, but when Genesis walked in on our artistry, she smirked and plopped at her father's feet, filling in the ink on his leg. When Kai walked in, he documented everything, snapping photographic and video proof, for "blackmail purposes," he insisted, but I suspect he wanted it simply for the happy memories. Scarlett even started filling in the flowers on my arm, seamlessly transitioning from Benny's tattoos to my own. Benny caught my eye briefly in that moment and I had to look away, swallowing against my suddenly too-tight throat.

See? It's things like this, things I didn't even think were possibilities, that made me fall the tiniest bit in love with Benny's kids. *I'm not even in love with Benny,* I think. Maybe I'll use him to hang out with his kids.

Benny scoffs and I cover my mouth. Apparently I said that last part aloud. Again. Thank goodness my filter was firmly in place when the kids were here at least (and for the first half of that thought).

We walk back inside to grab water before finally heading out. We stretched the trip out as long as we can, leaving at the last possible minute to ensure we had the longest vacation possible, but we can't hold off anymore. Grabbing some granola bars from his pantry, Benny stops, glancing at something on the top shelf. I watch him slide out a stepstool, climb on top, and pull down a silver juicer, the electric cord wrapped around the base several times. He hands it to me before hopping off the stepladder.

"Do you want this? It might be useful for some of your concoctions, if you wanted to use fresh juice."

I beam at him. I've always wanted a juicer but refrained from getting one, telling myself space at my apartment was limited, which is still true, but likely that if I got a juicer, it would be too expensive of a purchase for my little hobby. Tucking the juicer safely behind the passenger seat, I clamber into the front seat and buckle up.

My mind repeatedly wanders to memories of the weekend, but I can't help it when some old insecurities creep in. Seeing how wonderful Benny's family was, how intensely attractive his ex-wife is, I can't help but reflect on myself and engage in the dangerous practice of comparison.

I don't light up whatever room I'm in. While that bodes well for me against getting murdered (at least according to *Dateline*), it doesn't clarify why Benny wants to be with me. And because I lack the normal filter between my brain and mouth whenever I'm around him, I blurt that statement out. No buildup, no preamble. Just "I don't light up the room."

Benny blinks, trying to decipher my meaning. "Okay...can you not...reach the light? Do you need me to change out a lightbulb for you?" My instinct is to facepalm, but not at Benny. At myself.

"On murder shows, the victim's friends always say, 'she lights up the room.'" I'm met with a perplexed glance before Benny shifts his gaze back onto the road. "I don't do that," I point out.

"Do you want to do that?"

"No! But don't you deserve that?" I cry.

"Don't I deserve a murder victim?" He's not purposely trying to be dense; I know this is because I'm doing an absolutely shit job of explaining myself. I take a deep breath, willing my thoughts to reassemble themselves into something logical before speaking again.

"Why do you even want me?"

Benny offers me an indulgent smile, finally catching on. "You mean, aside from the fact that you're an absolute smoke show? I love our dynamic, D. You're my firecracker. You give me a hard time; I work even harder. You make me laugh. You make me *happy.*" His words echo my advice to his oldest daughter. "You don't light up the room? Who cares? You light me up inside. I feel alive around you. You ignite my soul."

# CHAPTER TWENTY-NINE
## *Delaney*

The Switch (A Delaney Kristoff Original): Lemon Flavored Vodka, Hazelnut Liqueur, Lemon Juice, Sugared Rim

Ever since returning from the mid-season break, things between Benny and me have been incredible. We seem to have reached a point of ease between us, where neither of us is afraid to hide our obsession with the other. At the same time, Benny's been busier than ever at work. I know he's nervous about keeping his job beyond the end of the season. He has another year on his contract, but he insists if the Foxes don't make it further in the postseason than they did last year, he won't be retained in Chicago next year. The idea is nerve-wracking, but at the same time, I have complete faith in his leadership and coaching abilities. So yes, at the same time we are sinking into the comfort of our relationship, we also feel a simultaneous pressure, a stab of niggling anxiety about where we will be in a few months. Not only geographically, but where our relationship will be once we're no longer in the same city.

We've mentioned it; we've stated that it's a possibility that he won't be in Chicago next year, but then we've promptly abandoned all conversations around it. Benny is shoving his worries down like a champ; I'm following suit.

Each night, Benny works late, regardless of what time the game ends. He goes to work early, too. When he's not actively coaching, he's involved in meeting after meeting in preparation for the trade deadline. He tried to explain to me once all that goes into the trade deadline, the conversations, the logistics, the maneuvering and scouting reports, but my head was spinning, and I barely kept up.

He explained that as a player, when he was traded, it was logistically easy: he showed up where he was told to go, the two teams' travel secretaries coordinating with each other to arrange his flights. Usually, the new team arranged for a company to pack up Benny's things and move them to a new apartment in a new city. It sounded exhausting, and that was only the logistics. Benny was traded a few times in his long playing career. He told me the worst part was moving his family, especially if he wasn't expecting to be traded. Apparently, these things can change at the drop of a hat, and a player's potential to be traded is based on a number of factors, only one of which is on-field performance.

I can't imagine what it must have been like for Benny—or anyone—to uproot his life with next to no notice, to have to forge relationships with new teammates in the middle of high-pressure situations like a playoff run. I have no doubt he has the perfect personality to adapt to the changes, but that doesn't mean it wasn't hard. Now that he's grown used to a little more stability as a staff member, I can tell he's nervous about not knowing what's coming at the end of the season. He's gotten quieter about work, more cautious about what he says about next year.

When we are together, we're usually both so exhausted from our respective jobs that we collapse into bed together. It's not even the fun kind of collapsing into bed these days; it's the literal version of sleeping together, where we fall asleep before our heads even hit the pillows. We still wake tangled in each other, but Benny usually rushes off to work before we can do anything about it.

He's been on the road for the last week, the team playing games in Philadelphia and Washington, D.C., before finally coming back home tonight for an off-day tomorrow. Benny is planning on working, mostly from home, tomorrow. I'm picking him up from the airport in his car tonight and we're staying at his place. He gave me a key when we came back from the midseason break, insisting I use his place whenever I want, even if he's not in town. I've been tempted to take him up on his offer, especially following particularly long shifts at Sip, which is much closer to his place than my own.

He insisted I bring Kingston with me tonight, so we could all spend the day together tomorrow as much as possible between his virtual meetings and endless phone calls. Because I took an early shift today, covering the lunch and early evening crowd, I was able to bring Kingston and his things over to Benny's house earlier today. I'm hoping it gave him enough time to explore the place and get over his little kitten rage at being brought somewhere new without me. Little does he realize the alternative was to bring him in the car in his cat carrier, which is akin to waterboarding my stubborn pet.

I'm waiting impatiently in the airport parking lot for Benny's plane to touch down. The private, chartered plane terminal was a bitch to find, hidden behind the freight shipping terminals at O'Hare. The parking lot is miniscule, and I took one of the only remaining spots left. I've restlessly played sudoku, checked Tik-Tok, and scrolled through a Buzzfeed listicle. I'm anxious to see my man and spend time with him; it feels like he's been gone forever. Even before he left, he was busy, so I can't help but feel a little disconnected from him. I can't help it; I miss him when he's gone. His good-natured personality makes sure I don't take myself too seriously, and I find myself craving his presence more and more.

Finally, after waiting approximately one and a half eternities, I see Benny exit the plane. The terminal is tiny, so I can watch the deboarding process through the chain-link fence surrounding the parking lot. Benny is in the first handful of people to exit the plane and take the stairs onto the tarmac. Even several hundred yards away, I can tell he looks good. His light-wash jeans mold to his lower half in a way that is both incredibly sexy and still, somehow, professional. His lavender polo frames his burly arms in the most flattering way; I watch like a pervert as he reaches up to adjust his backpack strap, biceps bulging as he totes along a rolling carry-on suitcase. He's laughing at something someone in the small crowd around him says as they all walk toward the terminal building. I know Benny spots his car, but with the dark tint to his windows, there's no way he can see me eye-fucking him from the parking lot.

After another year or two, he finally exits the terminal building, which spits him out into the parking lot. His smile, directed more toward his car than me specifically, again thanks to that window tint, is radiant. I slide out of the front seat, happy to hand him the reins and let him drive home.

"Delaney." My name comes out half-excited, half a sigh, as if all he has been waiting to do is hold me in his arms and mold his body around mine. I sink into his embrace, filling my lungs with his scent. I close my eyes and inhale the luxury: strong arms, masculine scent, the feeling of home. For several moments, we stand there like that, his front door open, suitcase forgotten near the trunk of his car. A squeal, followed by running feet, interrupts my happiness bubble and I lift my head to see a somewhat familiar, gorgeous brunette launch herself into the arms of an equally toned Black man. He spins her around enthusiastically before pressing her against the car and capturing her mouth in a bruising kiss. I've seen a lot of drunk, horny people make out in darkened corners of the bar, but this is so intense, I feel like I have to look away, yet at the same time, I am somehow entranced by what I'm seeing.

Following my gaze, Benny chuckles. "That's Warner and Alicia. They hosted the party the night I met you. They got engaged over the midseason break." Their love charges the air around us; I can practically feel it crackle against my skin. I watch as Warner presses his forehead against his fiancée's, whispering words we can't make out. It's intoxicating, watching them.

"Come on, my little voyeur, let's get you home." Benny squeezes me one more time before releasing me to lift his bags into the car.

When we get home, he orders takeout from Moon Shadow, despite my protests of not being hungry. He knows me too well; I may not be hungry now, but he knows by the time I am, I won't have the patience to wait for delivery. Promising he'll eat with me when I do get hungry, Benny leads me to his bedroom, a different kind of hunger written on his face.

Pulling my back to his chest, he stands behind me, pressing open mouthed kisses to my neck while undressing me painfully, torturously slowly. My hands scrabble behind me, caught in indecision between running my hands over his body and blindly pulling his clothes off. When we're both undressed, we fall into bed. I'm frantic, desperate for release, but he apparently wants to torture me tonight, taking his dear, sweet time, working me up without doing anything other than kissing me, skimming his hands across my skin. Facing him, lying sideways on the bed, all I want to do is mount him and have at him, but Benny has other plans.

"Please, Benny," I groan in frustration. He tuts, but smiles.

"I love when you beg me, baby."

"I beg for no man." He grins, remembering as well as I do the number of times I've begged for him. Rather than calling me out on my hypocrisy, he hums noncommittally as his hands draw further down my body. Feeling devious, I snap my legs closed. He looks up in surprise, but before he can question me, I sit up, leaning forward to pin him back on the mattress.

"I think it's high time *you* beg *me*," I tell him. His eyes darken instantly. He doesn't fight the hold I have on him, my palm pressing into his shoulder. He could–easily–but, like always, Benny is down to play with me.

"Please, D," he starts, his voice raspy with desire. Fire courses through my veins. "I'll be a good boy for you." His hands hover over my sides as he watches me. "I'll do anything you want, please let me touch you."

I feel heady with power and sling a leg over his torso. My exposed center gushes a little more at his words. I know he can feel it, my needy cunt pressed against his disgustingly perfect abdomen, but he doesn't remark. He doesn't even smirk, which has got to be a first for him.

"Please, baby. Tell me what you want and I'll do it."

*This guy is good.* I can't tell if he knows it or not, without his characteristic smirk, but I decide to reward him either way.

Flipping over, I boldly back up, until I'm hovering right above his mouth. He groans greedily, knowing what's coming next.

Leaning forward, I brace myself with one palm on the bed next to his hips, stroking one finger of my free hand down his length. His cock bobs at the contact and I relish my newfound power.

Benny runs his hands up my thighs, attempting to pull me toward his mouth. I stiffen. "Ah, ah," I chastise. "You don't get a taste until I do."

He groans under me, but I hear his head plop back down onto the pillow. "Such a good boy," I coo.

I lick a long line up his shaft, swirling my tongue around his head once I reach the top. The moan he lets out is deep and otherworldly. His fingers flex on my hips, digging in enough to bruise. I hope it does. Benny is teetering on the edge, hanging on by a very taut thread, and I get to be the one to pluck at it, to cut it in half.

"Please, Delaney. I need a taste. I'll make it so good for you." His voice cracks. Hearing him on the knife's blade edge of control does something to me. My insides are molten. My head feels like it's floating. Is this what he feels like when he bosses me around? I love when he takes control, but this feeling right here? A girl could get used to this. "Can I please taste you?" His words reach a fevered pitch.

"You may," I tell him simply, and before the last syllable fully leaves my mouth, he is slamming my hips down onto his face and devouring me with a desperation I've never experienced. I moan loudly when his tongue finds a perfect cadence against my clit. Looking forward, his tip is leaking more precum than ever before.

There's no mistaking what's happening here: Benny is as turned on as I am. He likes to dominate and be dominated as much as I do. Unable to withstand another second without him in my mouth, I tilt my head down and devour him with as much enthusiasm as he consumes me. Wrapping my arms around his bent thighs, I fondle his balls from below. His responding groan reverberates across my sensitive flesh. I take him deep, sucking hard, before swirling my tongue across his head again. His hips buck up into my mouth, twin to the rhythm in which my own rut against his face. He flattens his tongue and lets me ride it the way I need to.

No words are spoken, our mouths otherwise occupied, but the sounds filling this room are pornographic. Squelching moisture, heavy breathing, lusty moans and high-pitched screams when he hits that spot just right.

Popping his dick out of my mouth, I warn him I'm close. He redoubles his efforts. Not to be outdone, I resume the ministrations on my end. His hips snap relentlessly upward and I know he's close, too. My muscles contract, tighter, tighter, tighter. Benny stiffens, his thrusts stilling as he empties into my mouth, groaning deeply and shaking his head frantically against me. I don't know if it's him reaching the finish line or the extra sensations of his moans and movements, but I tip over the edge right after him.

Over and over, wave after wave of pleasure and euphoria crashes over me. Benny prolongs my orgasm, maintaining pressure and speed, as the last spurts of his release coat the inside of my mouth.

When I finally roll off him, collapsing onto the bed, sated and brainless, he crawls over to me, peppering kissing along my neck and face. When we both finally catch our breath, he looks at me, eyes blazing.

"We are one hundred percent doing that again."

# CHAPTER THIRTY

## *Benny*

Tequila Sunrise: Tequila, Orange Juice, Grenadine

The food was delivered an hour ago, and aside from running to the front door to retrieve it, Delaney and I couldn't bring ourselves to clamber out of bed for hours. She finally started complaining of being hungry a few minutes ago, so I peeled myself away from her to heat up the Moon Shadow I'd put in the fridge. Now, coming back into the room with our reheated diner food, I want to stop in the doorway and admire her.

She looks freshly fucked and it might be my favorite version of her. Although, come to think of it, I love it when she's bragging and giving me a hard time, too. And when she's hard at work, testing and retesting new recipes, her tongue slightly protruding from the corner of her mouth. I also love the version of her when she's laughing and carefree, like when I twirled her around the dirty dance floor of a crowded bar on Broadway in Nashville. Hell, I love every version of Delaney. I'll take her any way I can have her, as long as I get her.

Between bites of my burger and her standard breakfast skillet, Delaney and I catch up. Our bodies already took the last few hours to reacquaint themselves, but I need to connect with her beautiful mind. I need to hear her thoughts and emotions, even if it's her reflections on the mundane aspects of everyday life. After making her promise to make me her newest cocktail invention, we somehow get on the topic of my fairly public dating life.

My divorce was public, but not in a salacious way. In the cities I've played for, and in Chicago, the only city I've coached for, there's been an interest in my love life that I can't quite understand. The fervor around it has died down, now that my bachelorhood is no longer the new shiny thing (or, now that I'm older, which I refuse to believe is the case). The media and fans tend to move on quickly, and between the excitement of my players and their personal relationships these days, the heat is off me. I'm glad about it, too. I can live my life in relative normalcy.

"Who did you date before me?"

"Her name was Justine. Still is her name, obviously. I think we lasted about a month and a half?" It's hard to remember a time when Delaney didn't consume all of my attention. Maybe Justine and I dated for a longer or shorter period than I remember. Time is relative, but I know the intensity of my feelings for Justine never reached even a fraction of what I felt for Delaney the first night I met her.

She nods, swallowing a particularly drippy piece of poached egg. Her tongue darts out to lick the excess yolk from the corner of her mouth. "What happened?"

Her question is innocent, but I can't help the flash of mild pain when I reflect on my dating life between Keeley and Delaney. It's not Justine in particular; she was just the most recent in a line of women who used me for their own upward social mobility. I shrug.

"I started to catch on that she was only using me to boost her social image. I realized she only kissed me, only touched me, in public, whenever she thought cameras would be nearby." Delaney's gaze hardens. I was worried she would pity me when I told her the truth, but apparently, she's feeling righteous anger on my behalf. It's an odd sensation, to have someone want to fight your battles for you. I'm perfectly capable of fighting them on my own, not that this is even a battle, but it's nice to know she understands where I'm coming from. "I want someone who wants me in public and private. The only thing worse than someone performing for the cameras is someone who wants me in private, but never in public."

"Is that what you think this is?" she asks softly.

"What? No! Why would you think that?" That's not where my head was. I was referencing yet another one of my dating disasters.

"Because I haven't gone to your games."

*This again?*

"Absolutely not," I tell her, letting her see the sincerity in my eyes. "I really don't have an opinion on whether you come to the games or not. I'd love to have you there if you want to be there. I'd love to have you at home if you're more comfortable with that.

Whenever you want to go to a game, you let me know and I'll reserve tickets in the family section for you. But just because you don't come to the games doesn't mean I think you're embarrassed to be with me…I more meant that because I've experienced that side of things with other women, too."

"Who?" Delaney's voice is sharp, and it makes me smile. This woman really would fight my battles for me if I asked her to. Hell, she'd probably do it even if I didn't ask.

"That would be Gabriela, the first woman I dated after my divorce was finalized. I was finally ready to put myself back out there, and I met her on a dating website. She was great, really sweet. But she hated being seen in public with me. Once, I was in line for coffee and she happened to be in the same coffee shop. She practically leapt away from me when I went to greet her with a kiss on the cheek." Delaney's brow furrows. "When I saw her later that night, she acted like nothing had happened. I don't know if she was cheating; I never found out. But it sucked nonetheless."

Delaney sets her food aside and curls into my torso. I gently place my empty container on the nightstand and use my free arm to pull her close.

"I'm sorry, Benny," she murmurs softly. "I wish you didn't have to go through that. It sucks." I press my nose into the top of her hair, inhaling the coconut scent of her shampoo. Of course, she knows how much that sucks; she's survived a similar relationship. Gabriela and I only dated for a couple of months before I couldn't take the uncertainty and broke things off, so I got off easy compared to the heartache Delaney experienced. Still, it was my first relationship following my divorce, and I really wanted it to work. I was convinced I had learned so much from my failed marriage that I knew enough to prevent any problems or fix anything that came up in any future relationship, but I couldn't. I took the breakup hard, even though at the time, I could see that it was for the best. Now, I'm even more convinced it was the right move, as I never would have met Delaney if things had worked out between Gabriela and me, or Justine and me, or any of the other half-dozen or so embarrassingly short-lived relationships I had prior to hearing the tinkling laugh of my future girlfriend.

Delaney and I end up staying up late, far later than planned. But between rounds of mind-blowing sex (because it's always mind blowing with her), we talk. We reconnect. We share a round of her newest concoction. We cuddle and fold our bodies into one another. We sigh into each other's mouths and lungs and skin. We can't get close enough and yet, I can't remember the last time I've felt so perfectly content. At some point, Kingston hops onto the bed and settles himself on my chest, next to Delaney's head, purring contentedly.

I start to feel Delaney drift off to sleep against me right as the sun starts peeking through my bedroom curtains. We've both been fighting sleep for the last hour, wanting to stay awake like teenagers at a sleepover, trying to wring a few more minutes of conscious togetherness out of these moments. Finally giving in to the weariness that's been threatening all night, I kiss her head and whisper goodnight.

"It's not nighttime anymore. It's the morning," she mumbles softly against my chest.

"Then good morning, Delaney."

# CHAPTER THIRTY-ONE

## *Delaney*

The Kai (A Delaney Kristoff Original): Silver Rum,
Pineapple Juice, Fruit Punch, Cracker Jack Garnish
*Can be made non-alcoholic

"You're really going to make me go alone?" The look Jamie gives me is the poster child for pathetic guilt trips. I'm not easily swayed by manipulation, but Benny's comments about his previous girlfriends have been playing on a loop through my mind ever since he told me about them last week. I find myself losing the fight against Jamie's fake puppy dog eyes and overly pouty lower lip.

"I'm considering letting you go alone, given that you look like an overgrown toddler." I cross my arms over my chest, staring down my bouncer. He grins, sensing my cracking resolve.

"Considering it, but you won't." When I stop fighting him, Jamie claps his meaty hands together, the sound reverberating in the nearly empty bar. I announced last call a minute ago, but only one patron took me up on it, the rest of the clientele slowly shuffling out the door. "I'll ask Sloane to get our shifts covered."

Jamie turns on his heel and walks into the back offices, leaving me alone with the three remaining barflies. I huff an annoyed sigh at him.

"You're going to leave me alone with this rowdy bunch so you can arrange your social calendar?" I call after him. Jamie's laugh fades as he walks further away from me. Two of the last three guests are Julian and Carl, the world's most harmless men, finishing their last round of darts. The third man is sitting at the bar. He's spent more time frantically typing on his phone than nursing the single beer he ordered forty-five minutes ago. I've never felt safer at work, but that doesn't mean I'll willingly let Jamie off easily, especially if he's planning on dragging me to a Foxes game tomorrow. Benny promised him tickets whenever he wanted, and apparently Jamie wants them for when the Foxes play Cincinnati, Jamie's childhood team.

I finish putting away the latest round of clean glassware Jeff brought up front. I've already inventoried our liquor stash. There's not much left for me to do, other than to wait out the last few customers. I feel my phone buzz in my back pocket.

Benny

What's this I hear about you coming to my game tomorrow?

> Jamie finally wore me down.

> I'm glad he did. You have tonight and tomorrow morning to brush up on your baseball knowledge, baby.

> Never gonna happen. I hope you aren't embarrassed by your girlfriend being the most ignorant fan in the stands.

> You could never embarrass me.

"Row three," I tell Jamie, glancing at my electronic ticket, as he descends the stairs in front of me. He not so gracefully slides into the middle of the row, apologizing along the way for jostling the fans who have stood up to let him pass. I mumble my "excuse mes" and "thank yous" as I sidle through as well.

Jamie is not a small man; there's a reason he's employed as a bouncer. He rarely needs to throw around his bulk at Sip, but on the rare occasion he does need to get involved in an altercation, we're all grateful for his size. I wonder briefly how comfortable these seats are for a man of his stature, but he's not complaining.

Instead, he's spreading his food across his lap and on the floor near his feet.

Jamie insisted on the full baseball experience, loading up on nachos, hot dogs, popcorn, and Cracker Jacks. He somehow managed to balance all of that while carrying a drink holder with four beers–the maximum we were allowed to purchase at once. He hands me my drink, suds sloshing sloppily down the sides and over our fingers. I put the drink in my cup holder, wiping my fingers on my shorts. I'm too nervous being here to take a drink. I know no one knows who I am, or how I'm attached to Benny, but I still feel like I somehow need to make a good impression. On whom, I'm not sure.

An usher glides into the mostly empty row in front of us and asks to see our tickets. When I show him my phone, confirming we are in the right spot, his personality warms.

"Welcome to Foxes Field. My name is Dale; let me know if there's anything I can help you with."

"Oh, thanks, Dale," I say, taken aback by his change in demeanor. Jamie nods along, his mouth filled with an enormous bite of hot dog. As Dale turns to leave, he greets the other fans in the row by name. I knew Benny would put us in the "family section," as he called it, and it seems to be aptly named. A woman on the end hugs Dale tightly, and I wonder if I should have introduced myself after Dale told me his name. He initially seemed suspicious of our presence, but once he confirmed we were in the right spot, he warmed instantly.

We stand for the national anthem, Jamie fumbling awkwardly with half of the concession stand on his lap. I crane my neck to peer into the dugout, but from this angle, I can't see inside. I guess the only way I'll be seeing Benny tonight is if he comes onto the field. Admittedly, I did not study up on baseball like he suggested, so I have no idea if Benny walking onto the field is even possible in this sport. I've seen coaches on the sidelines on television for basketball and football games. Are there sidelines in baseball? He did get thrown out that one game when he went onto the field.

"Maybe there will be a benches-clearing brawl today, and you'll be able to see your man," Jamie suggests.

"Does that happen often?" I ask, less alarmed about the prospect of a fight than I thought I would be. In fact, I'm not sure I'm turned off by the idea, envisioning Benny cocking a tattooed fist back, muscles rippling as he demonstrates his strength and pas-sion.

Jesus. *Down girl,* I tell my libido. *You're in public.*

"Nah, but it is fun to see when it does!" Jamie assured me he would help me understand this sport. I made him promise not to let me look like an idiot in front of anyone while we were at the game, but this isn't exactly the tutelage I thought I'd receive.

"I haven't seen you here before," the pretty blonde woman one seat down from me says, turning my way. "Who are you with?"

"Oh, this is Jamie," I say, gesturing toward my coworker, confused by the lack of introduction from this woman who wanted to know his name.

"Sorry, that was a dumb way to start this conversation," she says, shaking her head. Her long ponytail swishes with the movement. "Let me start that over. My name is Amy. My husband is Jackson–JJ–Jeffers, the shortstop. Are you friends with someone on the team?"

"Oh, um, I'm dating Samuel Benjamin. The manager. I'm Delaney." I stutter my way through the world's most awkward greeting. Amy, however, takes it in stride. She clasps her hands in front of her chest, her brown eyes shimmering with excitement.

"You're Delaney! I'm so excited to finally meet you! Benny couldn't stop talking about you at our last team dinner! I've been wondering when we would finally meet!" This girl's excitement is going to turn her into a walking exclamation point, but her happiness seems genuine.

"Yeah, I've been really busy with work." I cringe as I supply the lame excuse.

"Girl, I get it. Summer tends to be a busier time for me, too. Although the school year is busy with field trips, too, so I don't really have a slow time for work, so I don't get to come to many day games." After the tiniest of pauses, in which she sucks in a breath, she continues. "I'm a museum educator, so we have all these STEM summer camps right now. And my job is to coordinate field trip experiences across all the museum campuses downtown during the school year. No one really knows what a museum educator is or what they do, so don't feel bad if you've never heard of one. Alicia, at the end of the row, is a museum educator, too. She is engaged to Warner James, the right fielder."

I lean forward, taking in the brunette I saw both at the party last year at Sip and at the airport after the midseason break. She's deep in conversation with the woman seated between her and Amy. My mind is reeling with all the information Amy just rattled off. I don't know what to say to any of it, so I nod and smile.

"Um, well, like I said, this is Jamie. He's my coworker. We work at Sip. It's a bar a few blocks from here."

Amy is nodding along but her gaze is focused on the game, where it appears her husband is at bat. I don't know what the proper etiquette is here. Do I shut up while she watches her husband at work, so I don't distract her? Do we keep talking like this is totally normal? Most spouses don't watch their significant others at work, so I don't know what to do here. I'm saved from having to figure it out as number nineteen watches the pitch sail by below his knees before it reaches the catcher's glove. He quickly removes a strapped-on thing at his ankle and trots off to first base.

"Good eye, baby!" Amy shouts. It didn't look like the batter did anything other than stand there, but the crowd seems to agree with Amy. I clap along like an idiot, not wanting to seem unsupportive.

Amy leans forward, tapping the women next to her on their knees. "Guys, this is Delaney. She's with Benny!"

Both women mirror Amy's delighted smile and speak at the same time.

"Delaney! We've heard so much about you!"

"It's so nice to finally meet you!"

We all laugh at the awkward greetings. They introduce themselves as Alicia, Warner's fiancée, and Jenny, the second baseman's wife. Apparently, my reputation as Benny's girlfriend precedes me. I'm not sure what they've been told about me, but they clearly all knew I existed prior to this game.

As the innings drag on, we chatter along. Jenny invites me to join the WAGs' (wives and girlfriends) book club once she finds out I listen to audiobooks. Amy insists on exchanging numbers so we can get together when the guys go out of town. Alicia asks me my shirt size so she can make me a matching shirt; she wants me to feel included in some themed events later in the season. During occasional lulls in conversation or following particularly exciting plays, Jamie fills me in on random baseball trivia.

It feels weird and comforting all at the same time, being here, making friends. I'm not a total hermit, but my social circle tends to be small. I've never had a problem with that. It almost feels weird that it *doesn't* feel weird to find myself connecting easily with this group of women. They're all roughly my age and Amy and Alicia both work. Finding out they still have their own careers is somehow comforting to me; it somehow makes them more approachable, more down to earth. Even Jenny, who doesn't seem to have a job, isn't some rich, snobby, unwelcoming person.

By the time the game ends, I've agreed to attend next week's book club meeting. Jenny walks with me and Jamie, showing us how to enter the field after games. She flashes a smile at a security guard before stepping through the gate and onto the field as if she belongs there.

We trek across the field before walking through a wall hidden near the foul line. It takes us up a set of concrete stairs and through another door, before shooting us out near an exit on the concourse. We merge with the throngs of fans exiting the stadium. Jenny grabs my wrist and directs me across a pavilion and into the lobby of a nearby building, where she explains that everyone waits for players and staff to finish up. She swipes a badge across a key card reader, allowing us access to the building.

"Deb can make you one of these. We call them our WAG badges, and they basically let you into the building here, the gated parking lot," she points out the window to an enclosed lot. "And onto the field. I can shoot Deb a text and ask her to make one for you, if you want."

"Oh, um, sure, I guess. Thanks." I assume Benny would be fine with me having one of these.

It's another hour before any of the Foxes employees start trickling upstairs to the lobby. When JJ Jeffers comes up, Amy makes a point of introducing me to her husband. His eyes twinkle with mischief, but he otherwise greets me normally. Warner James and Caleb Andrews greet me similarly. I'm happy that Benny's players are happy about their coach's relationship status. I'm also happy Jamie offered to stick around and wait with me for Benny; everyone else seems to have dispersed.

When the man of the hour finally makes an appearance, Jamie thanks him for the tickets and gushes over the win. Benny tucks me under his arm, casually walking down the sidewalk as we discuss the game. Every block or so, he is stopped by a fan looking for an autograph or a photo. He obliges each time but makes a point to return his attention to me as soon as the fan interaction is over. As we walk to his townhouse, I'm yet again reminded how precious, how cherished, Benny makes me feel, and for once, I don't fight it.

# CHAPTER THIRTY-TWO

## *Delaney*



"Obviously, the library scene was my favorite," Jenny mumbles with her eyes closed. We're gathered at her and Caleb's house, discussing the newest book club selection; I've been officially adopted into their club, and, apparently, their friend group. Evidently, whoever is hosting the discussion gets to choose the book, and Jenny has a particular affinity for dark mafia romance. We all mumble our agreement with Jenny's assessment, trying not to move our mouths too much, lest our cucumber face masks slip.

"Salvatore is for sure the hottest MMC we've read this season," Amy murmurs, pressing her mask into her cheeks as her mouth moves. "He reminds me of Jackson's brother's friend, Killian. There's something dark and brooding about a man that I can get behind." Alicia snaps her fingers in agreement.

"I'm giving up on this mask. I need to eat." Hailey, Elijah McClintock's wife, pulls her mask from her face, swiping the extra moisturizing goo from under her eyes before dragging a potato

223

chip through an unholy amount of onion dip and shoving it in her mouth. I close my eyes and lean my head back against Jenny's couch, hoping gravity will assist me in keeping the goopy mask on my face.

"Warner got an advanced copy of Erica Kathleen's newest mafia release; he's going to be the male main character in the audiobook version, so he's been reading up. He may have read a scene and wanted to try it out on the balcony the other day before he left." Alicia's face is covered by her mask, but her neck flushes.

"Ooh, did he let you read any of it?" Amy asks, completely ignoring Alicia's spicy revelation.

"No," she pouts. "He signed an NDA. But from what I can tell you from the reenactment, this one might be her spiciest yet."

"Oh! Speaking of spicy!" Amy rips her mask from her face and zeros in on me. "I want to hear about Benny's latest gift to you! I hear you're the one we all have to thank for some *custom* souvenirs."

It takes me a moment to catch on to what she is referring to. Benny gifted me a juicer on the way home from the midseason break, but that's clearly not what Amy is referring to.

"Wait, Delaney was behind that?" Hailey squeals. "Girl, we all owe you a debt of gratitude. These road trips are not quite as lonely these days." She tosses a wink in my direction, and the pieces finally click together.

"You guys know about that?" I shriek.

"Girl, how do you think we know about it? We all got similar ones after JJ found the DIY kit in Benny's hotel room!"

This mask's cooling properties are not enough to combat the flaming of my cheeks. At the same time, a weird sense of pride surges in my chest.

"Elijah made mine neon green! I'm a big fan of the BYOD project." Hailey announces proudly. At our blank looks, she explains, "Build Your Own Dildo!" I choke on my wine, but Amy plows forward, unfazed.

"Mine is rose gold. Apparently, JJ had to call to specifically request that color, but they made it for him." After a brief discussion, we learn we all have different colors: Alicia, a deep red, and Jenny, Foxes blue with orange swirls. It's a ridiculous conversation, and one I never thought I would have in my entire life, but it's funny and absurd all the same. We dissolve into a fit of laughter, and Jenny refills our wine glasses.

By the time we resume our actual discussion of the book, we're all three sheets to the wind. My cheeks hurt and my belly aches from laughter, but my heart is so, so content.

# CHAPTER THIRTY-THREE

# *Benny*

The Genesis (A Delaney Kristoff Original):
cinnamon Whiskey, Apple cider, calvados (french
Apple Brandy). *can be served warm or chilled.

It hasn't been that long since I saw my kids during the mid-season break, but it's still been too long. When Genesis and Kai were little, they, along with Keeley, traveled with me during baseball season, relocating every six months or so to wherever I was playing at that point in my career. I loved it. I loved being able to come home and wrap my babies in my arms, or look into the stands and see them standing on their seats, waving at me. It was a lot of work—and a lot of pressure—on Keeley, but having them with me during the season allowed me to raise them, too, and I'll forever be indebted to Keeley for those incredible years.

Once they started school, though, Keeley and the kids restricted their in-season time with me to the summers. It was still great, having three continuous months with them. After the divorce, however, Keeley and the kids made Nashville their permanent, year-round home. As much as it broke my heart not to have them near, it made sense. Genesis and Kai were getting older, getting more involved in sports and extracurricular activities. It wasn't fair of me to ask them to uproot their lives for weeks or months on end, and I knew the stability of one permanent location was in their best interests, even if a piece of my heart chipped off and remained with them. Now, they try to come out to visit me in Chicago whenever they have more flexibility in their schedules, but even those times are becoming few and far between. It's the reality of my kids growing up, and I hate it on so many levels, as much as I accept it.

All that being said, their trip to see me this week is that much more exciting. As independent as Kai and Genesis are, Scarlett is not, which means Keeley and Ricardo will be bringing them. I feel a little bad that my ex and her soon-to-be-husband have to tag along to ensure Scarlett is cared for while I'm at work, but they insist it's fine. Every moment I'm not at work this week, I will be with my babies, which means Keeley and Ricardo have their nights free. I insisted on putting them up in the five-star boutique hotel near the ballpark. It's expensive as fuck, but the location is convenient and it's the least I can do.

Delaney offered to take my car to pick up my family from the airport, which made me want to stop time so I could spend the rest of the night showing and telling her how much I appreciate her. I know some people view dating a single parent as coming with a unique set of baggage, but I found myself a woman who not only accepts my family, no questions asked, but embraces them. I know

I'm falling for Delaney hard and her enthusiasm for my loved ones makes me fall that much harder.

The last few nights in bed together, when she's wrapped around me as much as I've wrapped my body around her, I've been so tempted to tell her how I feel, but each time, I've stopped myself. I don't want to ruin the good thing we have going and telling her the depth of my feelings might complicate things. For her, not for me. I'm all in, and I know she is devoted to me, but given her initial resistance to being called my girl, I can't help but feel like her knee-jerk reaction to exposing all of my heart to her might make her want to pull back.

While I didn't take Delaney up on her offer to pick up my family from the airport, I did invite her along. She declined, knowing that once Keeley and Ricardo saw the kids safely into my vehicle, they would head off to their hotel. She told me she wanted to give me some time alone with my children. I think she's not quite sure how they feel about her, but I know they're as happy in Delaney's presence as I am. Still, it's a thoughtful gesture to be so consider-ate of their feelings. That's why I'm alone in my car, circling the arrivals level of Terminal One at O'Hare, waiting for a glimpse of my family before security shuffles me along again.

A flash of wild, auburn hair indicates my favorite redhead has surfaced from baggage claim. Throwing the car in park, I exit the vehicle and barely make it onto the sidewalk before her tiny body barrels into me. Lifting her and crushing her to my chest, I want to drown in her giggles. When Kai and Genesis arrive, a little more subdued in their enthusiasm to see their old dad, I crush them to me with equal fervor. Scarlett shouts out that she's being squished, but my grip on my babies doesn't waver. When I finally release the embrace, they clamber into the car, Genesis helping Scarlett strap into the car seat I fitted into my vehicle earlier today.

Greeting both Keeley and Ricardo with (admittedly slightly less enthusiastic) hugs of their own, we load the car before the kids say goodbye to their mother. Tomorrow morning, we'll all walk to the ballpark together, where I'll drop the kids at the hotel. They have plans to visit the Humanities Museum; Amy Jeffers has hooked them up with a behind the scenes tour. They'll join up with Delaney for the game tomorrow night, but for now, my kids are mine.

I navigate us to Alfredo's, my favorite pizza place, followed by milkshakes at Moon Shadow. Scarlett is entranced by the shiny, red, retro barstools at Moon Shadow, having no memory of coming here last year. Kai and Genesis, on the other hand, are old pros at Moon Shadow, requesting specialty customizations to their shakes without even glancing at the menu. They settle on a caramel and apple combination for Genesis, strawberry/raspberry/pineapple for Kai, and vanilla with rainbow sprinkles for Scarlett. Of course, my trusty peanut butter milkshake makes an appearance as well. Our tastes are varied, but each shake tastes great, and we make a point of sampling each others' concoctions before declaring our own to be the best.

By the time we settle in at my place, our bellies and hearts are equally full. Genesis and Scarlett share a bedroom, while Kai takes the loft. My place isn't huge, but it works for all of us. When I finally drift off to sleep, my arms empty, I vow this will be the last night Delaney and I spend apart, no longer willing to be in separate beds when we're in the same city.

# CHAPTER THIRTY-FOUR

## *Delaney*

The Benny 2.0 (A Delaney Kristoff Original):
Champagne, Rose water, Peach Simple Syrup

Having Benny's kids in town is surprisingly fun. I knew I liked them when I first met them, but a small part of me forgot how much. Having them here, at Benny's house and at his games, is a pleasant reminder. When I tentatively asked Benny if he was okay if I proposed a day at the beach while he was at work, I swear he cracked my rib with how hard he hugged me. I felt like Keeley and Ricardo could use a break and use the time to relax or reconnect or do whatever touristy stuff they felt like doing. Apparently, my suggestion went over well because the words were barely out of my mouth before Keeley agreed, practically shoving the kids at me.

We're spending the morning at the zoo before we head to the beach after lunch. It's a long day, and I'm not sure if the kids will want to go to Benny's game tonight. A night game means that Benny can join us for part of the zoo trip. He made pancakes for breakfast this morning. I thought it might be awkward for the kids to wake up and find me in the house, having come over after my shift last night when they were already asleep. Scarlett is too young to understand the implications of her father's girlfriend spending the night, but the older two surely picked up on it. Kai tried to hide his smirk behind his glass of orange juice, but Genesis hugged me with an enthusiasm she clearly inherited from her father.

Now, we're strolling between monkey enclosures at the zoo. Scarlett is on Benny's shoulders, loudly imitating primate calls as he and Kai chat easily below her. Genesis and I stroll along. I don't say much, but Genesis keeps up a steady stream of gossip about teenagers I don't know and her plans for college when she starts in two weeks.

"So now that Brianna hooked up with Tyler, they're trying to figure out if they want to date right before leaving for college or keep it casual." I don't know what to say to that, so I make a non-committal noise in the back of my throat and continue walking next to her. Benny catches my eye and tries to hide his smirk that clearly says *better you than me*. "Ugh, I'm so glad I'm going to college unattached. I don't want to hold myself back from meeting new people or trying new things. Garrett would have *definitely* held me back. Now, I can hang out with whoever I want, whenever I want."

I glance at Benny, relieved he seems to have missed his daughter's not-so-subtle hints at wanting to hook up with others at school. I'm all for (safe) hookups. It's better that she figures out what she wants—and doesn't want—before she settles for some guy who will cheat on her and break her heart. Of course, I don't say that to her, because even I can see that I'm projecting here.

After another hour of wandering through the animal exhibits, Benny says his goodbyes. Genesis and Kai promise to make it to his game, but I can't say the same for Scarlett. I reassure him approximately seventy-three times that I'll be fine staying home with Scarlett if she's exhausted before we pile, sans Benny, into his car and head toward the beach. It's not far from the zoo, but between our towels, beach umbrella, snacks, and other amenities, driving makes more sense.

As soon as we lay our towels out on the sand, we hear the ding of the bell for the paletas man. Digging into the pocket of my shorts, I pull out a crumpled bill and hand it to Kai, asking him to get us all popsicles. Scarlett is enamored with the idea of a popsicle cart; apparently, they're not prevalent in Nashville, or at least not at the establishments this five-year-old attends. Kai comes back with more than enough popsicles for all of us; apparently, he's inherited Benny's inability to say no to Scarlett as well.

We're several hours into our beach day, Scarlett curled up under the umbrella taking the nap she insisted she didn't want or need, Kai kicking around a soccer ball in the sand, and Genesis sunning herself next to me, when she turns to me, suddenly serious.

"You know, you're the first of my dad's girlfriends we've met."

"Really?" I don't know what else to say. I want to ask how she feels about that, but don't want to come off as desperate. As much as I pretended to resist Benny's initial advances, I don't think I can play it cool around Genesis.

"Yeah. It's nice to meet you in person, without having to find out about you from some website." Now I don't know what to say to *that.* I know Benny probably didn't tell his kids about his previous relationships for a reason, but that still had to suck for his children. My parents split up during the age of the internet, but they were never famous enough for the internet to ever be interested in their dating lives, despite how prolific my father's was. My mother never bothered to "take a lover," as she called it. I'm sure she's had her needs met, but anything even remotely resembling a relationship would make her run screaming from the state, so I never had to experience what Genesis has gone through.

"I'm sorry that happened to you," I say after a pause. She looks down and shrugs before locking her brown eyes with mine. They're one shade darker than Keeley's hazelnut color, but equally stunning. She takes a deep breath, as if she wants me to understand the seriousness she's about to convey.

"I'm really glad my dad met you. It's been a long time since I've seen him happy with another person. When my parents first got divorced, I had this dream that they would magically get back together." *Oh.* I'm not sure if I should be hearing this. "It wasn't easy for me to understand. I had friends whose parents were divorced, and they had all these stories about their parents fighting and hating each other. My mom and dad were never like that, so for a really long time, I had convinced myself they would eventually find their way back to each other."

Kai slows his kicks of the soccer ball nearby. I hadn't noticed the rhythmic tempo until it suddenly slowed, then stopped. Out of the corner of my eye, I see him shuffle around with the ball, clearly listening to what his sister is saying. Genesis glances over and picks up on his slowed movements, too, but doesn't seem bothered.

"Anyway, when mom met Ricardo, I thought it was just a phase, until they got engaged. It was really, really hard on me. I was mad at my mom for so long." She swallows, her eyes suddenly overbright. "At its worst point, I came out to stay with dad for two weeks. I missed two weeks of school to stay with him last year. I did my assignments online, but I still can't believe my parents allowed it. During those two weeks, my dad didn't hold back on telling me how disappointed he was in the way I was treating my mom, but even more than that, he told me how much he loved me. Every night, he told me how proud he was of me. Here I was, being absolutely awful to him for not loving my mom enough, and being horrible to my mom, and every night, he told me he was proud of me."

A tear rolls down her cheek. Behind my sunglasses, my own tears threaten to spill over my lash line. Not that I expected him to impart the details of family drama to me, but I had no idea how stressful things were only a year prior. I reach across and squeeze Genesis's hand, if only to let her know that I am still listening.

"During that time, though, Dad was also really honest about why he and Mom didn't work out anymore. I didn't want to hear it, but eventually the message got through. Now, all I want is for him to be happy." She pulls in a deep, shuddering inhale, but no more tears fall. Movement in my periphery tells me Kai has stopped pretending not to eavesdrop and is sitting on the edge of the towel, fully invested.

"Don't cry, Gen," Kai whispers, and my heart cracks at the sound. Growing up an only child, I never realized what I was missing, but I sure could have used a brother like Kai when I was younger.

"No, it's okay." Genesis shakes her head. "My point is, he's really happy with you. I'm glad he has someone like you in his life."

Then, as if she didn't just totally shake my foundation, she flips over onto her belly and opens her book. I glance at Kai, who looks equally confused and somewhat embarrassed. He nods once, as if to say he agrees with his sister's statement but is unsure what else to say or do, before picking up his phone and scrolling away. Meanwhile, I sit in silence, staring at the waves rolling in off Lake Michigan, and try to wrap my head around Genesis's blessing.

"Yes!" I whisper cheer, throwing my fist into the air. My voice wasn't loud, but my eyes still dart toward Scarlett's mostly closed bedroom door. I could have watched the end of the Foxes game in Benny's bedroom, but I didn't want Scarlett to wake up and think she was alone. Kai and Genesis are at the game, which just ended in a walk-off homer from Caleb Andrews in the eleventh inning. Jenny already sent me an adorable photo of Genesis and Kai in the stands together. I send her another quick message, thanking her for the picture and congratulating Caleb on the win.

I'm glad Scarlett didn't fight me on not attending the game. After several hours in the sun, we came back to Benny's place to shower and change. Scarlett's eyes were droopy after her bath, so I suggested she and I hang back and watch a movie instead. Thirty minutes into *Moana 2* and Scarlett passed out faster than a drunk in the back corner of Sip. She didn't even wake when I carried her to bed.

When I returned to the living room, I flipped on the game, which was only in the third inning, and alternated between messing around on my phone, munching on the mostly uneaten bowl of popcorn, and watching the game. Occasionally, the television feed showed close ups of Benny looking as hot as ever, and my mind replayed Genesis's words from earlier in the night. She didn't tell me anything that surprising. I know I make Benny happy; he's told me as much himself. I know that he is a fantastic father; I've never suspected otherwise. But there was something about her delivery, the way Genesis seemed to want me to know more of her own personal history in relation to her parents and their relationship, that made me want to lock her words away in my heart. I never needed Benny's kids' permission to date their father, but now that I have their blessing, I seem to have unlocked a deeper meaning to my relationship with their dad.

I'm still thinking about Genesis's words as I watch the team stream onto the field, celebrating the walk-off win. I watch as they jump around Caleb at home plate before lining up to give each other high fives before departing the field. The camera pans across all the players before resting on Benny's handsome face.

"Things seem to be going well, as usual, for manager Samuel Benjamin," the announcer declares. "The Foxes are on a five-game winning streak and are currently in first place in their division. After making the postseason the last two years, the only question seems to be not if the Foxes will make it to the postseason, but how far they'll go."

I smile, nestling further into the couch cushions as the announcer continues to sing Benny's praises. I've always known Benny was good at his job, but it's nice to hear others agree with me. He deserves all the praise and recognition for a job well done. I know he's worried about his tenure with the Foxes, but given what I'm hearing now, it sounds like he doesn't have much to worry about.

I find myself growing tired, sleep threatening to pull me under. I pull up my phone and tap out a quick message to Genesis and

Kai, letting them know they can stick with Jenny, and she will bring them to the lobby to wait for Benny after the game. Genesis responds immediately with a thumb's up emoji, and I close my eyes.

"Wake up, gorgeous." Warm, calloused hands caress my cheeks as I'm slowly pulled from slumber. Benny's face swims in my vision as I blink him into focus. He's smiling softly down at me. "Goodnight, you two," he says over his shoulder as Genesis and Kai make their way to their respective bedrooms. I stretch, knowing I've got pillow lines marring my cheeks.

"Why didn't you go to bed, baby?" His voice is barely a whisper, cognizant of Scarlett sleeping a room away.

"I didn't want Scarlett to wake up and think she was alone. I wanted her to see me if she left the room in the middle of the night." Benny pulls me close, my lower body still on the couch, as he roughly presses a kiss to the top of my head.

"You're perfect, you know that?" he says gruffly. There's so much emotion laced in his voice that I can't bring myself to provide a snarky reply. Placing my hand in his, I let him pull me to my feet, guiding me to his bedroom. We climb in together, Benny dragging me across his chest and holding me tighter than he has before. We couldn't be closer together if we tried. He molds his body to fill in the spaces between my curves; it's as if even an inch of space between our bodies is too much for him tonight. I can't bring myself to fight him or tease him about it because it feels too right. I don't know if it's because his kids are leaving in the morning and he's feeling extra emotional, but the way Benny is holding me right now feels a lot like love.

# CHAPTER THIRTY-FIVE

## *Benny*



My kids left this morning, and I can't help but be a little mopey about it. I'm surprised Delaney hasn't kicked my ass out of her apartment, but she's been nothing but compassionate. We both have the day off, and while I wish my family could have taken a later flight back home, Genesis was itching to get back to Tennessee to make the most of her limited time left of summer to hang out with her friends and finish packing.

Delaney is poking around her kitchen, mixing and matching various liquors while I'm supposed to be working on tomorrow's lineup. Instead, I find myself watching her. Humming to herself, she flips through her scrapbook, verifying she hasn't repeated a flavor pairing. Seeing her hard at work is fascinating; the sight could be featured in its very own nature documentary.

*The elusive Delaney stirs the nectar, attempting to bring forward the finest tasting notes. This remarkable creature is hard at work. Her ample bosom and large posterior on display to her mate, she has no idea she's engaged in a dangerous mating ritual. Her mate watches her from across the room, preparing to woo her. She throws her dark mane behind her shoulder, unaware that the action stirs something inside her partner...*

She catches me grinning at her across the room.

"What?" she accuses self-consciously. When I don't respond, she falls back on her signature snarkiness, exactly like I knew she would. "Take a picture, it'll last longer."

I swallow a laugh. Stalking over to her, I sit down across the center island from her. She makes a weak attempt at ignoring me before she grows self-conscious again. She can't even help it, but everything she does is adorable.

I was falling for Delaney before this past week. But seeing her interact again with my kids? Something happened—I don't know what—the day they spent time together at the beach. They seem to have deepened their relationship, at least between Delaney, Kai, and Genesis; Scarlett gets along with everyone. But there seems to be a mutual respect, a deep care, the three of them hold for each other, that wasn't as apparent before.

Delaney is an hourly employee; she's not salaried. So, for her to take off multiple days, forfeiting pay and tips, to be able to hang out with me and my family, hasn't gone unnoticed by me. That, and the way she treats my kids and my ex, make me completely certain I'm not just falling for her. I'm so far gone I have no hope of climbing back up. I'm done for. I've fallen too far.

I almost told her I loved her last night, when I brought her to my room after finding her camped out in the living room on the off-chance Scarlett needed her. Instead, I tried to infuse my love into her pores, as if there was a way she could feel it through osmosis.

"Are you seriously just going to watch me do this, weirdo?" She's getting unnerved, and I kind of like it. I like that I have the power to throw her off her game, at least a little bit. Maybe then she'll realize the power she holds over me every second of every day.

"Delaney." She shifts her focus to me, stopping mid-pour of a dark liquid. It drips onto the counter in front of her, narrowly missing her scrapbook. I pull the book toward me and out of the splash zone.

"Benny, what's your deal today? You're making me nervous!" She sets the shot glass and bottle down, fixing me with a stare.

"Nothing's my deal," I tell her innocently. "I just wanted to tell you I love you."

# CHAPTER THIRTY-SIX

# *Delaney*

The Delaney (A Samuel Benjamin Original): Fresh
Squeezed Apple/Lemon/Ginger Juice, Bourbon,
Cinnamon Stick Garnish

*Nothing's my deal. I just wanted to tell you I love you.*

*I just wanted to tell you I love you.*

*I love you.*

It's official.

Benny has short-circuited my brain. I think I'm hearing things.

I swear he just told me he loved me.

But that can't be right, because he's looking at me with a soft expression and I'm pretty sure I'm just hearing what I want to hear.

# CHAPTER THIRTY-SEVEN
## *Benny*

Communication Breakdown (A Delaney Kristoff Original): Gin, Orange Marmalade, Lemon Juice, Orange Bitters

"D. Firecracker. Are you okay?" Shit. I think I broke my girlfriend. It's not a statement I ever thought would pass through my mind, but here we are. I would be a lot happier about this if my breaking Delaney had something to do with my dick and breaking the bed as well. She's still not saying anything. Is there maybe a power button I can press? Can I turn her off and back on again? How do I reboot my girlfriend?

"Sorry, I think I spaced out for a minute. What did you say?"

Fucking of course. The first time I tell a woman I love her since my divorce, and she doesn't even hear me. I run a hand down my face and take a deep breath, preparing to repeat myself.

"I love you, Delaney." I wait expectantly for a reaction—*any* reaction—and get nothing. It's like she's frozen and I'm watching her glitch in real time.

Then she starts laughing. It's a nervous sort of giggle, but a laugh nonetheless.

What the fuck?

When I said I was waiting for any reaction, I didn't mean laughter.

"I'm so sorry, I thought for a second you told me you loved me," Delaney says, gasping between giggles.

"I did," I tell her flatly. She takes a sharp inhale. "I guess I'm not getting the joke." Delaney pales and becomes frantic.

"You don't mean that. You're just saying that because I took care of your kids yesterday." Her words are coming out rushed, frenzied. It's hard not to be a little defensive.

"Yes, in a way. Seeing you take care of my kids solidified that I love you. I guess I didn't realize you'd be so averse to hearing it, though."

Delaney shakes her head, coming to stand in front of me. I move to stand, to walk away. I suspected she may not have an overly enthusiastic response to my words, to my feelings, but I didn't expect this.

"No, I'm sorry, Benny. I just...wasn't expecting you to say that."

"It's okay, we can forget I said anything." I need to get some fresh air. I don't regret telling her, but this conversation isn't fun for me. I have no desire to continue it.

"Benny," she pleads, placing her hands on my chest. She's my Kryptonite. I want to leave, even for a little bit, to get my head on straight, but I can't bring myself to leave her. Not when she's looking at me, her stunning green eyes wide and pleading. I sigh, looking down, wanting to avoid the inevitable heartache when she retreats into herself. "Sam."

I look up sharply. Delaney has never called me by any version of my first name. I'm not sure how I feel about it, but I brace myself for whatever she's going to say next. I suspect it's going to be something along the lines of "it's not you, it's me."

"Tell me again, Sam." When I hesitate, her tone is even more pleading. "Please, Benny. Tell me again. I promise I'm listening." The look on her face is so earnest, so beseeching, that once again, I can't deny her.

"I love you, Delaney," I tell her again, hiding my internal wince at the prospect of rejection. She closes her eyes, savoring my words. When she opens them again, there's a slight sheen to the intense green.

"I love you, Samuel Benjamin."

Five words.

Five words are all it takes for my heart to stop beating. The look on my face must be showcasing my shock, because Delaney giggles, but this time it's a relaxed, tinkling sound, not the nervous tittering sound she was making only moments earlier. She slides her palms up my chest, linking them behind my neck. I'm still staring at her in disbelief when she presses her lips softly against mine. When her tongue licks against the seam of my lips, I pull her close to me. She steps between my widened legs as we deepen the kiss.

Pulling back, Delaney is breathless. "I'm so sorry, Benny. I had no idea you were going to say that. I had no idea you felt that way about me. I didn't think it was possible you could feel the same way as I do."

"Get the fuck out of here," I murmur against her lips. "How could I not be completely in love with you?" Standing, I glide my hands down her curves. Palming her ass, I lift her and set her gently on the island in front of me, never breaking our connection. "Delaney, you are my perfect girl. I need to make one thing clear. Yes, I fell further in love with you, seeing you interact with my children. But I was already so far deep, there was no going back for me."

She closes her eyes at my words, as if she was waiting to hear me say them for so long. I pull her hips to the edge of the counter, pressing my hardness into her center. She moans at the contact.

"Sammy," she whimpers. No one, not even my mother, has ever called me that. The nickname, coming from Delaney's perfect mouth, goes straight to my cock. I groan.

"Call me that again," I demand. She pulls back, her eyes full of mischief, knowing damn well what she does to me. She licks her lips.

"I love you, Sammy."

# CHAPTER THIRTY-EIGHT

## *Delaney*

The Gardener (A Delaney Kristoff Original Exclusively for A Night Out in Nature): Mezcal, Whiskey, Beet Juice, watermelon Simple Syrup, Blueberry Garnish

"**T**his is seriously the best margarita I've ever had," Jenny slurs, the best margarita she's ever had, three times over, making its presence known. The guys are on another road trip, and I'm hosting book club. I was originally going to hold it at my tiny apartment, but when Benny found out, he insisted we do it at his place, since it is much bigger.

"Thanks," I say with an air of fake cockiness. "I do take my job very seriously."

"We need to plan a night out at Sip soon!" Amy announces, then promptly hiccups very loudly. These girls need to learn to hold their liquor. I'm not much better though; the two shots of tequila I took while "recipe testing," along with my own two margaritas, are catching up to me.

I groan. I wouldn't mind the girls coming to Sip, but I'd much rather hang out with them when I'm not working.

"I'm sure Delaney would love serving your asses," Hailey says with an eye roll. I knew I liked her the best.

"Well fine, but we should go out bar hopping or something soon, when you're *not* working," Amy stresses.

"I'm good with that. I like visiting new bars and seeing if they've got any new signature drinks."

"Oooh!" Alicia's voice is loud. Clearly her margaritas have gone down a little too smoothly as well. "Have you guys been to The Bookstore? It's a speakeasy Warner took me to!" Jenny and I nod, but Amy and Hailey have never heard of it.

"Benny took me there once." I debate telling them the next statement but then figure I should probably start opening myself up to these women if we really are going to be friends. That, and they may be too drunk to remember in the morning, so who cares? "I, uh, actually created one of the drinks on their menu."

"Tonight? I don't know if I should be mixing my liquors at this point." Jenny slurs. She's not wrong about the liquor, but she doesn't understand my meaning.

"No, I mean I invented a drink and sold the recipe to them. I didn't make it tonight."

There's a brief pause before Alicia screeches, "What?"

"I, uh, like to invent new cocktail recipes. Make my own signature drinks. It's dorky, but it's what I do for fun. Benny took me there to meet with the owner and head chef, and I made him a drink and he asked to buy it from me so he could put it on the menu."

"Holy shit, you're like, famous," Amy elongates the words. Out of all of us, she's the drunkest. She starts petting my hair gently. I snort a laugh. Amy is married to one of the most famous baseball players in the world, yet she's starstruck because I have one teeny mention of my name on a menu at a bar in Chicago.

"What other drinks did you make?" Hailey prods, eyes wide. Alicia is tapping on her phone and in record time, she has pulled up the cocktail menu from The Bookstore.

"Holy crap, there's your name!" Alicia passes her phone around, as if to prove I wasn't lying. "I didn't notice it when we were there. I wish I had ordered it!" She pouts, but I think she's genuinely disappointed and not being overly dramatic.

Amy rests her head on my shoulder when Jenny passes the phone to me. This girl is a lush.

"Forget book club nights, why aren't we having cocktail tasting nights?" Jenny asks.

"You guys would really want to do that?" Four pairs of eyes blink back at me in disbelief. Okay, three pairs in disbelief. Amy's eyes are glassy and unfocused.

"Of *course* we want to do that! We'd happily be your taste testers! What's the best thing you've made?" Jenny rearranges herself on Benny's couch so she can look directly at me. She looks like the star pupil in grade school, attentive and ready to absorb any wisdom I can impart.

"Uh, well..." I think. "I'm playing around with summer flavors right now. Benny and I went to a farmers' market the other week, and all the fresh produce really inspired me. He gave me his old juicer, so I've been playing around with fresh juices and seasonal local produce."

"Oh my God! Alicia! The nature museum event!" Amy is gripping Alicia's forearm, and her panicked tone makes me think they forgot something related to work. Alicia, however, seems to speak Drunk Amy and understands instantly what she's saying.

"Great idea!" Alicia gushes. At my blank look, she says, "This year, the nature museum–you know, the one by the zoo? They're holding this evening fundraiser. *A Night Out in Nature*, they're calling it. They're getting all these local vendors to set up booths and people can explore the outdoor museum after hours. They're getting these art installations for it, too. You should design some cocktails for it!"

My first reaction is to downplay my skills. To tell them I wouldn't really know how to go about marketing that to the museum. Suddenly, an image of Benny's face pops into my mind. I remembered how it glowed with pride after Ernie Young offered to buy my recipe, and his gentle scolding when I tried to minimize my skills and talents. I decide to own this.

"That would be really cool. I was playing around with a fruit and vegetable cocktail yesterday. It had watermelon and beet in it, so it was this really pretty color. I liked it for a rustic, earthier style cocktail."

"That sounds amazing. I love beet juice." When Hailey gives Jenny an incredulous look, she exclaims, "What? It was one of the few vegetables I could tolerate during chemo. Don't ask me why; I don't make the rules."

"Let me shoot Eva, one of our directors, a text and see if she can connect you with the event coordinators! It would be so cool to have you at our event!" She looks meaningfully at Hailey and Jenny. "You guys should come, too. We've gotta support our girl!"

Amy nods, resuming her stroking of my hair. It's weird, but it feels nice, so I don't stop her. It also feels nice to hear promises of support from my new friends. It's been a long time since I've had such a supportive circle of friends, even if they are a bunch of lightweights.

# CHAPTER THIRTY-NINE
# *Delaney*



It takes us about two days to fully shake our hangovers from the margaritas at book club, but once we do, we plan to hit up The Bookstore together while the guys are still out of town. Technically, they come home tonight, but they probably won't be landing until close to midnight. If book club the other day was any indication, they will make it to their cars at the airport in time to pick up our drunk asses from the bar.

We got what looks like the last reservation for a group of five. I was worried we wouldn't be able to get in on such short notice, but there must have been a cancellation at the last minute, allowing us to swoop in and scoop up the reservation. We decided to make a night of it by dressing in 1920s style clothing, to match the speakeasy theme. Luckily, I had a black sequin dress from my last trip to Las Vegas. Tilly lent me a flapper-style headband from an old Halloween costume she had, so all I needed to do was pick up a pair of retro panty hose, the kind with a line down the back of the legs. There's no shortage of unique clothing stores in Chicago, so finding them wasn't as difficult as I thought it might be.

When we arrive at The Bookstore, we're a little early for our reservation. We take several moments to ooh and ah over everyone's outfits. Hailey went all-out with an art-deco inspired dress; she even brought a long cigarette holder. She insists on speaking in a mid-Atlantic accent all night, and I can't say that I hate it. Jenny curled her short hair into tight waves reminiscent of a flapper style. Alicia's thin frame supports a gorgeous drop-waist, sleeveless dress the same ivory color as the scarf around her hair. Amy's dress is like mine, but she's paired it with black gloves and chunky earrings. Altogether, we look incredible, and we ask the couple in line in front of us to take our photos. I send the picture to Benny, knowing he won't see it for a few more hours since the game has already started.

When we reach the front of the line, we squeeze into the tiny front room of the bar. The receptionist confirms our information before pulling a hardcover novel from her hostess stand. She turns and presses a sequence of three books on the shelf behind her. The hidden door swings back, and Amy and Hailey, the newbies to the speakeasy, gasp in delight.

We're brought to our table, the hostess setting the book in the center of it. Opening the book, Alicia directs us to the menu pasted inside.

"Look, there it is!" She points and squeals loudly. The diners at nearby tables turn to look at her, but she is unfazed. She snaps photo after photo of the menu, focusing in on the words "The Audiobook, crafted by Delaney Kristoff exclusively for The Bookstore." I have to admit, even I am a little awestruck.

After Ernie bought my recipe, I didn't really think to come back to check if he made good on his promise to credit me in the menu. Not that I doubted him, but I guess I didn't quite believe my drink was good enough.

"Good evening ladies, my name is Melissa, and I'll be your server tonight." Melissa runs us through the specials, tells us a brief history of the speakeasy, and welcomes any questions. She explains that due to the heavy volume of customers tonight, our seating will be limited to ninety minutes. It's disappointing to put a time limit on our revelry, but a place like this is in high demand, and turning over tables is the only way to make everyone happy. I'm hoping we can find another nearby bar once we're done here, so we won't have to cut our night short.

"I think we're ready to order our first round then," Hailey announces, still in her accent. "We'll take a round of Audiobooks, seeing as this beautiful lady right here," she gestures up and down my body, "invented it!"

"Is that right?" Melissa asks, clearly amused by Hailey's theatrics.

"Guilty as charged," I admit, ducking my head. It's been a long time since I've been publicly embarrassed, but it's been even longer since I felt a genuine sense of pride in my skills.

"Five Audiobooks, coming up," Melissa says, punching the order into her electronic device. It's not very on brand with the speakeasy theme, but if it helps us to get our drinks faster so we can make the most of our ninety-minute time slot, who am I to complain?

We fall into easy chatter while we wait for our drinks. Occasionally, we get smiles and looks from other patrons, clearly amused by our dedication to tonight's theme.

"Delaney Kristoff!" Ernie's booming voice reaches my ears a second before his round belly filters into my periphery. His white chef's coat is pristine, save for a small tomato sauce splatter near his chest. I can't help the wide smile plastered on my face. Ernie Young is simply not a man you can be anything but joyful around; his ebullience is contagious.

I stand and accept Ernie's offered hug before introducing him to my friends. Not that they had any doubts about my cocktail invention story after seeing my name on the menu, but seeing Ernie really seals the deal.

"Oh my God, I've seen you on Food Network," Amy gushes unabashedly. "You are incredible!" Ernie's eyes twinkle at the praise.

"It's so nice to meet a fan," he tells her graciously. "And here I was, coming out to meet someone *I'm* a fan of." He nods toward me; my cheeks flame.

Melissa brings our drinks, setting them on the table. She smiles at Ernie, pleased to see he made his way out to greet us.

"I have to head back to the kitchen, but I'll send Melissa here out with some snacks, on the house. You ladies stay as long as you like." He winks at me before striding back into the kitchen.

"Oh my God, oh my God, we just met Ernie Young!" Amy whispers, mostly to herself, I think. "I have to tell Danny!" She pulls her phone out, her fingers flying rapidly over the electronic keyboard.

True to his word, Ernie sends Melissa back out with a charcuterie board overflowing with marinated olives, dried fruits, nuts, cheeses, and cured meats. I don't even think this is on the menu, but it's incredible. I make sure to snap a photo of the board, with my drink in the background, and send it to Benny.

The table we're seated at, and most of the tables in this section of The Bookstore, for that matter, are small and spindly. Known more for cocktails and snacks in this room, rather than complete meals, there's typically not a need for large tables here. Ernie elected to use smaller tables to allow for more customer seating, which is a smart idea except when you decide to send a giant charcuterie board to a table of five women who somehow need to fit both the food and five cocktails on one small table. We elect to hold our drinks in hand while grazing with our free hand until enough space on the board is freed up to use for cocktail real estate.

If I'm honest with myself, I initially felt a lot of pressure in meeting the other baseball wives and girlfriends. I'm not generally someone with low self-esteem, but I can't help being a little self-conscious in the face of these gorgeous, successful women. They're all stunningly beautiful with solid partnerships. Amy and Alicia have impressive jobs. I'm a bartender, a college dropout. My relationship with Benny is new. So it's nice to be able to offer something impressive to these women, even if they haven't so much as hinted at wanting or needing that from me. It's almost like I needed to prove to myself that I have something to offer.

Hailey's phone buzzes from its position on her lap. Glancing at the screen, she announces that the Foxes game has ended, right on schedule. The boys will be leaving for the airport in exactly an hour, meaning they will be home in less than three. We sip our drinks slowly, pacing ourselves, now that we don't have to leave in the normally required time span.

My phone vibrates against my lap. I can't help smiling when I see Benny's name flash across the screen.

Sammy

You gonna be drunk when I pick you up, superstar?

> Maaaaaybe.

You deserve it, seeing your name in print on that menu. Warner showed me the picture Alicia sent him. How's it feel to be famous?

> Not so bad. Fighting off the paparazzi was tough, but I managed.

That's my girl.

I look up to catch Jenny eyeing me, a sly grin across her lips. "You tell coach you love him yet?"

"As a matter of fact," I say, snagging an olive from the board, "I did. Last week. After he told me he loved me." The sounds of whoops and cheers from my girlfriends could be seen as embarrassing. It draws the attention of more than one table, its patrons turning to stare at our unseemly cheering. I can't find it in me to care.

# CHAPTER FORTY

# *Benny*

Firecracker (A Samuel Benjamin Original): Aperol,
Ginger Simple Syrup, Peach Vodka, Prosecco

Delaney and the rest of the girls are going to be the definition of hot mess by the time we arrive to take them home. When we are on the road, some of the guys elect to drive to the airport and leave their cars there, but there's always a bus that shuttles back and forth from the ballpark for those who don't. Wanting Delaney to have access to my vehicle while I was gone, I rode the bus. I typically take the bus anyway; I feel like it's good for my players to see me with them.

My normally solid plan leaves me in a bit of a jam tonight, though, since I want to get to my girl sooner rather than later. Stopping home to pick up my car would have only added time to the clock, and since we're all heading to the same location, I grab a ride with Elijah. Between the increasingly sloppy texts we've each gotten as the night has worn on, we've been able to piece together most of the girls' shenanigans and prepare ourselves for the states of our significant others when we arrive at The Bookstore. Noth-

261

ing, however, could have prepared us for the scene we were about to stumble upon.

JJ, Elijah, and Warner all toss their keys to the valet upon pulling up, Caleb having ridden with JJ. I had texted Ernie when we landed to see if he could let us in without a reservation but haven't heard back. I'm sure he's busy working. I shouldn't have bothered though, because as soon as the receptionist lays eyes on JJ's pretty-boy face, she promises to find a way to put some tables together for us.

"That won't be necessary," JJ assures her. "Our wives are already in there, we'll just join them, if that's alright with you?" The hostess gives JJ a beaming smile; I'm sure he could have requested the moon, and she would have done everything she could have to make it happen. It's a good thing my shortstop has a level head, or I'd be concerned about his ego inflating from the way people— not just women—trip over themselves to make things happen for him.

*Our wives are in there,* JJ had said.

Hmm. I like the sound of that.

It's been a long time since I thought of myself in relation to the word "wife." I rarely refer to Keeley as my ex-wife, preferring the shortened term "ex." It wasn't something I consciously did, but maybe that separation in my mind was more meaningful than I realized. More important, though, is my reaction to JJ referring to Delaney as my wife.

Sure, he mostly did it for ease of communication. He wasn't going to explain semantics to a stranger, that Delaney was only my girlfriend, and that Warner wasn't married to Alicia yet. Still, the privilege of calling Delaney my wife? That does something unexpected to me. Some men swear off marriage following their divorces. Some even go so far as to swear off all relationships. I've never been that guy, but my stance on remarriage has always been relatively neutral. If I find it, I find it, and I'll make it happen for the right person. Based on the horde of butterflies taking flight in my stomach right now, I'd say the chances of Delaney being that person are high.

My thoughts are interrupted by a loud shriek, which turns out to be Jenny launching herself at Caleb as we enter the main dining room. He widens his stance and plants his feet immediately before his wife flies through the air. He catches her with ease and spins her around, seeming not to care that the handful of patrons finishing their last calls are staring.

My eyes take in the rest of the scene. Delaney and Hailey seem to be engaged in some sort of debate with the group of twenty-somethings at a nearby table. Hailey is wildly gesticulating, as if to really drive her point home. I don't miss the way at least two men and one woman rake their eyes appreciatively over my girl's exposed cleavage, where she seems to have put...is that a fake cigarette holder? I smirk, half in response to Delaney's makeshift pocket and half in response to her adoring fans. They can look all they want. I'm not jealous; I know she is coming home with me tonight.

"Hey, firecracker," I say, bending low and whispering in her ear. She jumps, clearing the seat of her chair by at least an inch. Once she collects herself, pressing a hand against her racing heart (I see three sets of eyes at the next table track the movement), she bestows a radiant smile on me. Her eyes may be somewhat unfocused from the copious amounts of alcohol I have no doubt she consumed tonight, but her grin is genuine. She throws her arms around my neck.

"Sammy!" she squeals loudly, unaware her voice volume is about four notches too high, but I don't care. I'd kill for this kind of reception every time I come home from a road trip.

I don't miss the way Elijah mouths "Sammy" to Caleb, nor do I miss my second baseman's responding grin. I'm sure there will be plentiful use of my newest nickname in the clubhouse tomorrow.

The lights in The Bookstore slowly lift, indicating the patrons better hit the road. Ernie saunters over, several bottles of beer laced between his thick fingers. He passes them out to each of us.

"I was wondering when my favorite manager was going to visit me again!" Delaney and Jenny needn't have worried about their voice volume; they've got nothing on Ernie's naturally loud amplification. "And you've brought friends," he remarks jovially. I make a round of introductions, although I have no doubt Ernie–and half of Chicago–recognize my players on sight.

The table next to the girls', where Hailey and Delaney were holding debate club, looks reluctant to leave. This isn't the first Chicago bar to stay open late for the Foxes, and it won't be the last, but most average patrons don't get to see that side of things. I tip my beer bottle at Delaney's opponents before shifting my attention back to our group. A loud scraping noise tells me Ernie is dragging a particularly large, high-backed chair to the table. It's a sturdy looking piece of furniture, but I still have my doubts about whether it will hold all his weight. I pull my own seat easily over and sit down; Delaney perches herself gracefully on the arm of my chair. I tell myself my arm snaking around her hip is to help her maintain her balance after a night of drinking, but I'll take any excuse to touch her.

Amy is curled up in JJ's lap. I'm fairly certain she's already asleep, but her face is tucked into his neck, so I can't be sure. Alicia is sitting on Warner's lap. The look on her face as she gazes at him tells me she wants to climb him like a tree. I hide my grin behind my beer bottle, taking another swig. Elijah rests his hand possessively against the back of Hailey's neck, where she's seated beside him. Caleb and Jenny have both disappeared to god-knows-where, which more than likely means the bathrooms. Caleb is lucky the place is empty; I'm sure his publicist would have a heart attack if the media found out he was engaging in public sex in a bar. All in all, I'm glad Delaney has found a good group of women, because I'm glad to be surrounded by a good group of men.

Some managers might balk at hanging out with their players, and at times, I do have to be more mindful of my boundaries. When I started managing, though, I was coming in fresh off a playing season, so some of my former teammates became, technically, my subordinates. I've always maintained a closer than average relationship with my players, and tonight is no exception. It helps that everyone here is not only incredibly talented, but incredibly hardworking, so I don't have to worry too much about my closeness with them clouding my judgment when it comes to playing time or trade potential.

Not that any of these guys were considered for a trade this season, anyway. The Foxes are still (barely) clinging to first place in a notoriously competitive division. Cincinnati, the second-place team in our division, has several more wins than the next winningest team in our league, so things are looking good for the postseason, as long as my guys can stay healthy and keep doing what they're doing. Most of the activity before the trade deadline consisted of minor league transactions with an eye toward maintaining our winning projections in the next several years to come. The closest we came to trading a major leaguer was New York's interest in Asher Incaudo, the relief pitcher who has been straddling the line between our Triple-A affiliate and major league playing time since last season. In the end, New York let us keep Incaudo and we offered a few minor league pitchers for cash and players to be named later.

Delaney wobbles on the arm of my chair for the third time. Giving up the fight, she slides onto my lap with more grace than I was anticipating, given the slight slur to her voice. The guys are filling Ernie in on the game today, and he listens with rapt attention.

After several minutes, Caleb and Jenny reappear. Jenny grabs a glass of water from the table, drinking deeply for several moments. She presses a hand to her sweaty forehead, which only serves to call attention to her curls, which are significantly more disheveled than they were when we arrived at the bar. Caleb takes a seat next to me, the smug smirk on his face making his foray into the bathrooms with his wife that much more obvious. We all pointedly ignore him, knowing he's practically daring someone to make a comment so he can even more openly display his satisfaction.

Part of me is a little jealous, if I'm completely honest. It was too long of a road trip for me not to want to take Delaney into the bathrooms and bend her over the sink, but I'm pretty sure she can't even stand right now, so we'll have to save our reunion for tomorrow, or whenever Delaney's probable hangover subsides. As much as my cock is protesting right now, I'm happy to settle for holding her close, pulling her back into my chest and letting her warmth seep into me.

By the time we leave The Bookstore, the girls have sobered slightly, all except Amy, who is still asleep on JJ's lap. Hailey has given up on the weird accent she's been using most of the night, sleepiness taking over her normally excitable features. The valet workers brought our keys an hour ago, letting us know they moved our vehicles into the small but now mostly empty employee parking lot. The Bookstore staff have long since cleared out, Ernie having shooed them away hours ago, promising to lock up himself. Alicia presses several crisp bills into Ernie's hand, making him promise to tip out Melissa tomorrow.

I lag behind, saying goodbye to my good friend, before joining Elijah and the girls at his car. Ernie had pressed a meaty paw into my shoulder, congratulating me on winning the series on the road and expressing how I must be less worried about the possibility of being cut from the franchise now. As much as I'd like to tell him I'm less nervous, the fact is, the relief from winning the series is minimal and temporary. Obviously, I want to win; losing is terrible for morale, and when we're this close with Cincinnati in the division, we need all the clubhouse optimism we can get. Still, I know if we can't pull off a strong performance in the postseason, I'll be in the hot seat. And we still haven't clinched *going* to the postseason yet. It will likely happen in the next two weeks, but what that playoff berth looks like won't be clear until shortly before the season ends. I've been in this game long enough to know you don't count your chickens before they hatch.

Delaney and I wake late the following morning, which is to be expected when you hang out at a bar until four in the morning. I only had a few beers over the course of two hours, but the travel and late nights are wearing on me. I pride myself on acting and feeling younger than I am—age is just a number, after all—but I can't keep up with my younger players and my even younger girlfriend. Delaney isn't excessively younger than me, but on mornings like this, I'm reminded exactly how much more spry she is than I am, at least in terms of our sleep needs.

She's rebounded from her hangover like a champ, and I mentally pat myself on the back for all the glasses of water I nudged into her hands throughout the night. The minimal headache she experienced before we eat brunch is worth the frequent eye rolls she gave me each time I pressed the glass back toward her. I knew she wasn't feeling too bad to begin with when we woke up and she pulled the covers back with a mischievous look in her eye. She spent the next several minutes sucking my soul out through my dick and I've never been more grateful for such an enthusiastic welcome home.

Now, several orgasms later, we sit at what is rapidly becoming our booth at Moon Shadow, while Delaney soaks up the remaining alcohol residue in her stomach with cheesy potatoes courtesy of her favorite breakfast skillet. She's in the middle of enthusiastically telling me about book club and Alicia's idea to pitch some cocktails to the nature museum for their event next week when a shadow falls across our table.

"Delaney Kristoff," an unfamiliar voice calls.

If I could freeze time, I would have in this moment. I wish I had a button where I could pause the world around us, if only so I could shove this guy away from our table and out of Delaney's mind, because the look on her face is one I've never seen before and one I never hope to see again. It's a mixture of disgust, shock, and nausea.

"Wow, how long has it been?" The owner of the voice looks innocuous, but I'm already on guard, having caught Delaney's expression. The man stands slightly under six feet tall but looks like the kind of guy who wears lifts in his shoes. His brown curly hair does nothing to offset the acne scars marring his cheeks. He shifts, crossing his arms in front of his chest and using his fists to press his biceps up, giving the illusion of having more muscles than he does in his ridiculous cutoff shirt. This guy is trying so hard. I'd laugh if I weren't so concerned about my girlfriend's well-being. I don't miss the way her fist clenches tighter around her fork.

"You know exactly how long it's been, Bob," she grits out.

This fucker? *This guy* is the infamous Bob?

Why is it always the ridiculous-looking guys that think they can take advantage of beautiful, perfect women like my Delaney?

"What? No hug for me? Not even a smile?" This asshole really is pushing his luck. My muscles tense, but I don't say anything yet, ready to watch Delaney deliver the verbal tongue lashing that I know is coming.

Except it doesn't come.

Bob completely ignores me, his body angled toward Delaney. I'm not offended by this rude motherfucker, but I am pissed off on Delaney's behalf. I've seen her put drunk barflies in their place so fast their heads spin, but she's not saying or doing anything. It's almost as if I can see her warring with herself internally, debating whether she should give in to this asshole's request for a hug to get him out of here faster. Not on your life, sweetheart.

I'm not a jealous guy; I trust Delaney implicitly. That doesn't mean I'll hold my temper in check while this guy walks all over my girlfriend. *Again.*

I stand, unfolding myself to my full height. I'm not incredibly tall (I was a catcher, after all), sitting at six foot two, but I easily have three inches on this douchebag. What I lack in height, I make up for in strength. This guy clearly thinks he spends enough time in the gym making himself look muscular ("vanity muscles," my strength coaches call them). I've spent more than twenty years in professional sports, honing my body into a fast, strong, and efficient machine. I may have been sitting behind a peanut butter milkshake at the table, but that's only because I'll be running four miles when I get to the ballpark, not to mention the postgame lift I have planned.

Bob blatantly ignores me. Again, it would be laughable how hard he's trying to ignore my presence, a fully grown man standing literal inches away from him, but I can't erase Delaney's stricken expression from my mind. She's fighting for composure and I can't stand it. I angle my body, wedging myself between Bob and the table so that he's forced to look at me instead of her.

"Hey man, I'm Sam." Normally, I'd hold my hand out in introduction, but I'm not really looking to be polite here. "Delaney and I always appreciate a fan, but as you can see, we're sharing a meal. If you'd like an autograph when we're done, I'll swing by your table on our way out," I lie. There's no way in hell I'm doing anything for this guy, but I fall back on my old PR habits to avoid causing a scene and potentially embarrassing Delaney. I see Emilio, the day shift manager of Moon Shadow, hovering on the periphery of this conversation. I want to tell him I'm not going to let anything get out of hand, but I don't want to take my attention off the troglodyte in front of me.

Bob sputters. He's clearly trying to assert his dominance over someone who can't be dominated (except behind closed doors by Delaney). He straightens up, throwing his shoulders back and puffing out his chest.

"I was talking to Delaney."

"And now you're talking to me." There's a smile on my face, but it doesn't reach my eyes. Bob attempts to look around me at Delaney. I shift again, blocking his view.

"Delaney, I thought we could be friends. My wife, she's in the Navy and stationed overseas. It'd be nice to hang out and catch up with you."

I fight not to drop my jaw. Did this dipshit allude to wanting to cheat on his wife–with my girlfriend–*while she is serving in the military overseas?* In no scenario in my mind did I envision Bob to be worse than Delaney had already portrayed him to be, but he's gone ahead and surpassed my expectations.

"Alright, it's time for you to go. Here's what's going to happen. You will not be contacting Delaney again. You're going to walk out of here and erase this entire interaction from your memory. In fact, go ahead and erase every memory of her you've ever had."

Emilio steps beside me. "Sir, I've taken the liberty of boxing up your lunch. It would be best if you took it to go." I make a mental note to tip Emilio accordingly.

Bob gapes at Emilio, which is pretty fucking ballsy, given that he is openly talking to *my girlfriend* about cheating on his wife. Emilio presses the white plastic bag to Bob's chest, giving him no choice but to accept it. I give him a hard stare and, in my periphery, I can see Emilio doing the same. Bob mutters something under his breath about just wanting to be friends before stomping out the front door.

Emilio turns away, wiping down a nearby table and doing a decent job of pretending like an altercation didn't almost happen. I would have been glad to throw a punch at this guy, but I suspect Delaney would have wanted to get the first shot in, and she wasn't moving.

"Scoot over," I tell her gruffly, sliding into the booth next to her. I grab my milkshake from the other side of the table and take a sip. The few other diners in Moon Shadow return to their meals as if nothing happened. Delaney, however, is shaking ever so slightly. If her fork weren't still hovering in midair, it wouldn't have been noticeable.

Gently, I pry her fingers off her fork, setting it down in her skillet. I wrap my fingers around her hand, placing it on our laps, where our thighs are pressed together on the bench.

"I fucking froze," she whispers. "I've had years to fantasize about all the things I've wanted to say to that genetic U-turn, and I said nothing." I squeeze her hand in solidarity.

"I got you covered, baby."

"But I don't *want* you to have to cover me!" Delaney is whispering, but her words hold a vehemence.

"I know, baby. And I promise, I'll always give you first crack at the assholes. But if, for whatever reason, you're unable to defend yourself, I will always, always have your back."

Delaney gets lost in her thoughts for a while. I know better than to press her right now. I want to give her time to process not only the interaction with Bob, but what I have said about always having her back. She's been a strong, independent woman her whole life, and when she finally let her guard down, Bob stomped on her soul a little bit. I've finally broken through some of her defenses, but I need her to know that I mean what I say, and promising to defend her without question is no exception.

In the back of my mind, I know I'm in too deep. If, for some reason, I'm no longer in Chicago next year, I don't know what I'm going to do or how I'm going to hold on to Delaney. But you better believe I'm going to formulate a plan.

# CHAPTER FORTY-ONE
## *Delaney*

Sex on the Beach: Vodka, Peach Schnapps, Orange Juice, Cranberry Juice, Cherry Garnish

"**S**o anyway, all you would need is recipe cards and any non-standard bar materials or ingredients, and the booth is yours!" Alicia's enthusiasm bleeds through the phone, straight into my ear holes, and warms my heart. Today started out great, getting tangled up in the sheets with Benny, before turning terrible when I encountered, for the first time since the breakup more than seven years ago, the biggest waste of oxygen and a sorry excuse for an ex-boyfriend.

Dammit! That's what I should have told Bob!

*"Somewhere out there is a tree tirelessly producing oxygen for you. You owe it an apology."* Or, *"Your mom should have swallowed and saved me from dealing with your morally repugnant ass."*

I swear, since we left Moon Shadow earlier this afternoon, I've thought of a thousand things I want to scream at Bob. I would have won the verbal sparring match ten times over and shown Bob that I'm so much better off without him. He would have been simultaneously impressed by my wit and vitriol and chastised by his horrible existence. Instead, I sat there catatonically and let Benny take one for the team.

Not that I'm not grateful for it. Benny redirected the growing tension–and unwanted attention from other diners–away from us and, along with Emilio, sent Bob packing in a professional, graceful manner. But, god, I wanted to prove to him I won the breakup! It sounds petty, knowing we broke up so long ago, but Bob altered the course of my life in such a drastic, dramatic fashion. While I'm happy with where I'm at now, for years post-breakup, I was reeling while he suffered no negative consequences for the way he treated me. He's fucking married, for god's sake. Obviously, it's not a healthy marriage, but I wouldn't wish Bob as a husband on my worst enemy. His poor wife.

"You're in, right?" Alicia's voice pulls me back from my thoughts of revenge and Bob's poor, unsuspecting wife.

"Yes! Definitely! Thank you, Alicia," I tell her sincerely.

"Good, because I already told Eva you would do it." I huff a laugh at Alicia's overconfidence. "The only problem is that the budget has already been set and the caterers booked, so they don't have any wiggle room to hire more bartenders to staff your booth. But! Don't worry! I'll work the booth with you and I'm sure the girls will be happy to help too!"

My phone vibrates a moment later, followed by several more vibrations, indicating enthusiastic responses to Alicia's request via group chat. I pull the phone away from my ear to read them.

Of course! Tell me the details and I'm there!



Ooh, yes! Love this for us!



Practice run tomorrow night? The guys have another night game so D, you can teach us while they're at work.

I tap out a text response, confirming everyone can meet at Benny's place on my night off. I then immediately send another text to Sloane and Tilly, requesting a last-minute change in the schedule for my shift this weekend. Sloane agrees to make a rare appearance behind the bar to cover my shift while I work the event. Sure, this day has been a roller coaster of emotions, but at least I'm ending it on a high note.

When Benny makes it to my apartment after the game, I share the good news with him.

"I'm so proud of you, D! I'm not the least bit surprised they want you at the event. You're a mixology genius." Benny's eyes crinkle at the corners. His unyielding support for me is quickly becoming one of my favorite attributes. "I wish I could be at the event Saturday night."

He's already opening his laptop to look for tickets. Kingston parades himself across the keyboard, looking for ear scratches. I pull my attention whore of a cat away from the technology, giving in to what he wants. He purrs contentedly while still reaching out for Benny. What a little jerk.

"I'm buying a ticket now, but as you know, I'll probably be late. We have a day game on Saturday, so who knows when it will end. But I promise I'll make it."

I press a kiss to his shoulder in gratitude as he finishes the online transaction. His email dings with confirmation of his electronic ticket.

"Want to do breakfast and a walk on the beach tomorrow morning to celebrate?" It's well past midnight already, and I don't have any wiggle room in my work schedule to take another night off, so Benny and I have resorted to breakfast dates. We've become experts on all the local weekday brunch spots near our respective houses, but aside from Moon Shadow, our favorite is a tiny beachfront restaurant on the shore of Lake Michigan. It's only open during the summer, and with fall quickly approaching, Benny and I are taking any excuse we can get to visit before it closes for the season.

"Always," I tell him with a smile.

"Oh, hey, by the way, I've got a surprise in the works for you." I swear, Benny's eyes twinkle.

"A surprise? What is it?" I'm the kind of girl who loves surprises while also being unable to stand suspense. I tend to beg the secret keeper to tell me what the surprise is until they give in. Then I am secretly disappointed that they told me. I know it doesn't make sense, but it's what I do.

"Nuh uh," Benny tells me, gently tapping my nose. "If I tell you, it won't be a surprise, and then you'll be disappointed." Sometimes I hate how well he knows me. "I'll tell you at brunch."

# CHAPTER FORTY-TWO

## *Delaney*

*Dark and Stormy: Dark Rum, Ginger Beer*

Weekday brunches, especially when they fall on my days off from work, are my favorites. Prior to dating Benny, I didn't have much of a social life; my life consisted of work, relaxing at home, playing around with my cocktails, and more work. I had friends, but aside from Sloane and Tilly, who I honestly never really saw outside of work anyway, my small circle of friends was scattered across the country. We'd loosely keep tabs on each other's lives via social media and occasional texts, and it didn't really bother me. Now, my social life is robust, between dating Benny and hanging out with the Foxes WAGs, of which I guess I now consider myself one. Prior to Benny, I worked all the time, living for vacations and setting short-term goals to get me to my next travel destination.

It was a rare day, prior to Benny's entrance in my life, that I was awake early enough for anything resembling breakfast *or* brunch. Now it's a regular staple and something I find myself missing when he's on the road.

Today, we opted for smoothies to-go and a longer walk, rather than sitting down for a lengthy meal. Benny woke to a text asking him to attend a last-minute conference call before his regularly scheduled meetings, meaning he needs to be at work even earlier than usual. We're walking along the beachfront, in the sidewalk lane designated for walkers, but it's such a gorgeous day out that we still have to dodge foot traffic as runners and bikers swerve around us. The paths are congested with everyone wanting to enjoy the last dregs of summer before the cooler fall weather prevails.

"So, what's this surprise?" I nudge Benny's shoulder. He had to have known it was only a matter of time before I began pestering him again. He laughs and guides me over to a set of concrete bleachers near Belmont Harbor. I'm sure there's an architectural or environmental reason for them to be there, since they're generally not all that aesthetically pleasing, but all I've ever seen them used for is people lounging on them or resting after a run.

"Okay, so," Benny sits next to me, angling toward me. I'm facing him, and out of the corner of my eye I can see the splendor that is the lake, and further in my periphery, the edges of the city skyline. Still, I have the best view from straight on. "I've been thinking a lot about us. These road trips have been getting harder on me, being away from you. As much as I'm excited to be with my kids in Nashville for the offseason, I'm also dreading being away from you. Which only makes me further dread what might happen to us if I'm not with the Foxes next season."

I nod, waiting. If I'm totally honest with myself, I agree with him. At least about road trips getting harder; I don't honestly believe he'll be let go from his job, but what do I know about these things? Until a few weeks ago, I didn't know the difference between an error and an out. Still, it's hard not to have the knee-jerk reaction to pull away at Benny's hint of getting more serious. The thing is, I wouldn't mind getting more serious with Benny, if we did it the right way. I don't want to be forced into anything prematurely just because of his job (or potential lack thereof).

"I did some research and talked to some people in admissions. I found out there's a great opportunity for you to go back and finish your degree, since you were so close to finishing." My heart drops out of my chest, tumbling down these concrete steps. I can practically hear it splash into the water, but Benny keeps going. "If you get your degree, you can do a lot more online marketing of your skills or even work entirely remotely. Then you can relocate to Nashville or join me wherever I might be next year. I want you to be with me, wherever I land."

The blood whooshes in my ears. It's almost loud enough to drown out the disappointment coursing through my body, traveling up and down my entire nervous system. I don't want to burst Benny's bubble; his eyes are so hopeful. Even through the haze of crushing dismay, I know he made this plan out of love. I know he thinks he's doing what's best for me, even if I hate this plan. I gently extricate my hand from his grip.

"I know you think college is too expensive, but I'd happily foot the bill. And if that bothers you, I can pay upfront and you can pay me back over time, whenever you're comfortable with it. I think with a degree, you're afforded a lot more freedom to go wherever you want, do whatever you want."

I'm a bartender, not the mayor of Chicago. If there's any job that affords me freedom, it's the one I've already got. I can pick up and transplant myself wherever I want; I would know, I've done it before. There will never be a shortage of bars and pubs in this country–in this world–so there's something to say about job security in this field. Sure, my marketable skills are somewhat limited, but I don't need a degree to do my job. And I'm already doing whatever I want. Slinging cocktails and being on my feet at all hours of the night may not have been my childhood dream, but being a bartender affords me the freedom to make decent(ish) money so I can travel and hang out with my suddenly larger group of friends.

I feel myself physically and emotionally withdrawing from Benny. Even though I can see his heart is sort of in the right place, I know I've specifically told him college wasn't for me. It's not only because of Bob that I dropped out; I didn't enjoy myself there. The classes were hard, I hated living on campus, and I couldn't see the value in getting a degree when I didn't even have a career I wanted to pursue.

Benny pauses, looking expectantly at me. I swallow, my mango peach smoothie suddenly feeling like lead in my belly.

"Benny, I don't want to go back to school." My voice is quiet but firm. We're seated in the middle of these stupid concrete bleachers, and I suddenly wish we were seated near the periphery. Each level of seating is unnaturally high, which I suppose adds more privacy for people to spread out and enjoy a picnic on them, but it makes for a slow and awkward getaway. I'd have to scramble ungracefully up or down, jumping or scooting on my butt to move down toward the sidewalk, or stretching fully to clamber over the rows to move upwards, if I didn't want to zigzag my ass uselessly back and forth before reaching the edges.

"Oh, okay." He pauses, then doubles down. "But if you go back to school, you'll be a lot more marketable in the future. You can be more than just a bartender."

I suck in a sharp breath. *Just* a bartender? Never has he given me an indication that he's bothered by my job and his statement has me suddenly questioning all our interactions.

Who is this man and what has he done with the unwaveringly supportive Samuel Benjamin I used to know? I guess he's technically still supportive, but *I don't want this.* I didn't ask for this, and now that I've explicitly told him it's not what I want, he's still pushing it.

Suddenly the fresh air and wide-open spaces are claustrophobic. Tears of frustration prick the backs of my eyes. Why am I crying?

It only serves to frustrate me more. I want to go home and curl up with Kingston, so I don't have to think about this anymore.

"No thank you," I tell Benny politely, as if he's some door-to-door salesman hawking useless wares. He looks startled at my response. Clearly, I'm not giving him the reaction he was expecting.

"Delaney, what's wrong?" When I press my lips together, he urges, "Come on, don't be that way."

I bite my tongue hard enough to taste pennies. I need to get out of here before I say something I can't take back. My disappointment is quickly morphing into anger, and I've never been one to hold back on expressing myself (the run-in with Bob at Moon Shadow notwithstanding).

"I'm gonna go home. I have a lot to do before the girls come over tonight." I stand to leave, deciding that going down is my best bet. I don't know if my legs are long enough to climb up this structure, and I'll probably die of embarrassment if I try and fail. I can catch a cab if I climb down and follow the path to the frontage road of Lake Shore Drive.

Benny stands and offers me his hand, helping me to clamber down. I'm being petty, but I don't take it. At this point, it's less about showing Benny how mad I am and more about preserving myself. I'm afraid if I take his hand and allow him to apologize, I'll let him convince me to enroll in school, something I *know* I don't want to do. I'll be letting another man control my life. But the second I don't take his hand, I regret it. Benny's face flashes briefly–is that pain?--before he quickly shutters his emotions.

I finish my awkward half-hops, half-steps down to the bottom of the bleachers before turning quickly and walking north. Benny follows, calling out after me, but I don't slow down. When I reach a trash can, I toss my still-mostly-full smoothie in; there's no point in drinking it now when I'm on the verge of throwing up. I don't look behind me, but somehow, I know, the moment I throw the smoothie Benny bought me in the garbage, he stops following me.

# CHAPTER FORTY-THREE

## *Delaney*



Making fun, summery, nature-inspired cocktails when you feel like absolute garbage isn't a pleasant task. It's made approximately one thousand times more difficult when you have to pretend you wouldn't rather be curled up in bed, stewing over the non-fight you had with your boyfriend.

The girls took the last-minute change of venue in stride, completely buying my excuse that lugging my juicer and cocktail tools all the way to Benny's was going to be too much work. We're all squeezed together in my tiny kitchen, huddled around my even smaller island, while I demonstrate my recipes and wait expectantly for feedback.

"I knew this coming into the night, but the beet one is my favorite," Jenny insists. Hailey wrinkles her nose, despite informing me a few minutes ago that my beet-inspired cocktail was "surprisingly delicious."

"I like the pink one," Amy says, holding up a champagne coupe with a lavender-prickly pear concoction. I had a feeling she would like that one the best. Amy is a girly girl, through and through, even if she pretends to hide it.

"I do, too," Alicia agrees. "The floral notes are well-balanced without it tasting soapy." I appreciate the thoughtful feedback, but Amy snorts into her drink.

"Okay, you've been spending too much time with Anita James if you're bringing out tasting notes."

Alicia sticks her tongue out at her best friend and pokes her playfully in the arm. "Says the girl who fangirled over Warner's mom the first time you met her," she mumbles under her breath.

"I did not!" Amy's voice is indignant, but she answered way too quickly for any of us to believe her.

"You answered her with 'Yes, Chef!' every time she spoke to you," Alicia reveals and we all dissolve into giggles. I personally find Amy's fangirling adorable, if a little awkward. It feels good to laugh with friends. A little bit of the tightness in my stomach loosens.

Later, when we're all squeezed into my living room (Alicia and Amy insisting they don't mind sitting on the floor), Alicia eyes me suspiciously. We've switched to espresso martinis, which was probably a bad idea, given how smoothly they're going down. The boys are going to get annoyed if they have to keep picking our drunk asses up each time we hang out together, I think. Then I remind myself that my boy isn't, because I won't be seeing him today.

"Spill it," Alicia instructs. "You've had this look on your face all night, like something is bothering you." Perceptive little wench.

"Nothing's bothering me," I say, but even I hear how my voice comes out slightly more high-pitched than usual. I sigh. "Benny and I had our first fight today. I don't even know if it was a fight. It was more of a non-fight, if that's a thing?"

Hailey nods sagely. Yep, it's confirmed: despite her beet judgment, she's my favorite. "Do you want to share what happened?" she asks gently.

"I don't know," I begin hesitantly. On the one hand, sharing it might help me process my thoughts about it. On the other hand...

"I get it. You don't want to shit-talk your man." How have I never realized how wise Hailey is? Alicia is usually the one in touch with her emotions and who can pick up how everyone is feeling, but Hailey might give her a run for her money. "I hate telling others when Eli and I fight, which doesn't happen that often, but I worry that if my girlfriends hear about the bad, they'll forget about the good when they see him next. I mean, he's still my husband. Just because we fight doesn't mean we'll get a divorce."

My mouth suddenly is drier than the Sahara, despite having taken a sip of my drink. Is this the beginning of the end with Benny? Surely not. I'd like to think it would take more than one non-fight to break us. But for him to push something I clearly don't want, something he *knows* I don't want? For what? To get what he wants, to get me to follow him around like a lost puppy? And what was up with that "just a bartender" statement?

Alicia squeezes my knee. "You don't have to share. Just know we support you. I love Benny, but I'll be on your side if you need me to take sides." Amy nods fervently, while Jenny and Hailey verbalize similar attitudes.

"Thanks, guys," I say. Instead of saying more, I gulp another swig of espresso martini. I, of all people, know that this is a drink meant to be sipped and savored, but tonight, I need to get drunk and forget.

# CHAPTER FORTY-FOUR

# Benny

The Herbalist (A Delaney Kristoff Original Exclusively for A Night Out in Nature): Gin, Green Chartreuse, Muddled Mint, Muddled Basil, Muddled Lemon Verbena, Lemon Juice, Pomelo Simple Syrup

Sometimes I wonder if seeing grown men slap each other publicly on the ass is ever weird to people outside of sports. It's been such a normal part of my life for the better part of twenty or thirty years, but if anyone other than Delaney touches my ass off the field, we're going to have a problem. As a coach, my ass gets tapped in a completely sportsmanlike, professional way far less often than when I was a player, but still, it's a weird concept.

I know I'm avoiding thinking about Delaney when I allow my mind to wander to the concept of ass slapping in sports. I've kept my head in the game the whole time tonight, but now that the game is over, ending in a blowout win for us, I can't avoid thinking about my girlfriend forever.

What the hell happened earlier? Obviously, Delaney did not take the surprise the way I intended. But, seeing as she won't talk to me, I don't know what, exactly, was so horrible about what happened. I pride myself on my communication skills; it's something you have to do with your partner if you want to have any sort of healthy relationship when you're apart for as much as those in baseball life are. I have to be good at communicating with my guys and with the front office to get to where I've been in my career. So, when Delaney is giving me very little to go off, I don't know what to say to make it better.

All she told me was that she didn't want to go back to school. Is it because she's scared of failing again, after everything went down with Bob? I don't know if it's the money thing. She's been getting better about allowing me to pay for things, but maybe this is too expensive? I don't really care all that much if Delaney goes back to school or not, but I thought she might like some flexibility, instead of having to work hourly and be on her feet, dealing with drunken idiots and entitled patrons all the time. I get it; customer service is a tough gig.

"Yo, you going to Delaney's?" Caleb pokes his head in my office. "Looks like another shitshow for the girls." He holds his phone up to me as if to warn me of the drunken texts I've likely received. I pick up my phone. There are a bunch of work emails and a text from Kai, commenting on a play Edwards, our catcher, made earlier tonight. Nothing from Delaney. I school my features; the last thing I need is for my players to start crooning about trouble in paradise.

JJ's head appears over Andrews' shoulder. "Did you see the girls are at Delaney's, not your place?" My head snaps up so quickly I'm surprised it doesn't strain my neck. Sensing my confusion, JJ elaborates. "Yeah, something about Delaney not wanting to lug her supplies all the way to your place. Guess you'll be heading there instead of home. Maybe we'll see you there." He winks at me.

JJ and Caleb are already showered and dressed. I'm still in my uniform and now that I know Delaney isn't waiting for me at my house, I'm in no rush to leave. I don't know the best play here. Do I leave her alone and give her some space? Or do I show up at her doorstep and fight for her? Delaney has never been the kind of girl to play those types of games, but she's also been stuck with shitty boyfriends who have probably never fought for her or done anything remotely romantic.

With visions of *Say Anything* in my head, I hustle through my computer work and shower. I want to give the girls enough time to clear out, in case Delaney really doesn't want me there, but I don't want to waste so much time that Delaney goes to bed before I get there. She's a night owl, but who knows how much she's been drinking.

I make a quick sweep of the locker room and, as I suspected, it's empty of players. They tend to clear out quickly once they're done with their postgame workouts following a night game. No one wants to stick around longer than they need to after night games.

By the time I make it to Delaney's, Warner and Alicia are leaving. He tugs her close to him on the sidewalk, nodding in greeting as they pass me. Alicia gives me a knowing look; I don't know what she knows, but I suspect she's aware I'm somehow in the doghouse. If she could enlighten me on the specifics of *why*, that'd be great. Instead, they both keep walking, Warner's deep voice murmuring something against Alicia's temple. Looking up, I see Delaney watching me from the window. I race up to the third floor in time to hear the deadbolt click on her door. I cross my fingers that she's flipped it to unlocked, wanting me to walk in, rather than locking me out.

I try the door and thank my lucky stars when it opens with little resistance. That's precisely where my luck runs out, though, if Delaney's expression is anything to go off of. She's angrily gathering empty cocktail glasses from their scattered locations around her apartment and depositing them into the sink. Grabbing a nearby martini glass with some sort of frothy foam and coffee beans in the bottom, I bring it to the sink next to her.

"Why are you here, Benny?" she huffs on a sigh.

"I want to talk about earlier today." My response is simple, measured.

"I don't want to talk." She moves to walk past me, but I reach out to stop her. She could keep moving, shove my arm aside. Hell, she could push me away by the chest and I'd let her. She sighs deeply.

"Just give me something to go off of, baby." She stiffens at the nickname. *Okay*, guess I won't be sweet-talking her tonight. "I don't know what I did to upset you. All I know is that I did. I just want to make it right."

Delaney closes her eyes and, for a brief moment, I think we're getting somewhere. But when she opens them again, her resolve is hardened. "Benny, it's not a good idea to talk right now. I'm too angry and I haven't figured out how I feel. I'm going to say something I regret and you're going to end up getting hurt."

I plant my feet in front of her, not backing down. I'll take Delaney yelling at me, telling me everything I've done wrong, but what I can't take is uncertainty. I can't fix it until I know what's wrong.

"Maybe I came here to get hurt. Come on, baby. Do your worst to me."

She crosses her arms in front of her chest, and it strikes me that this movement is a small way for her to protect herself, to shield herself.

From me.

My insides want to crumble at the thought.

Instead, I stand open, my arms at my side, defenseless. Because the truth is, Delaney's worst is still better than not having her at all.

# CHAPTER FORTY-FIVE

## *Delaney*

Love Letters and Promises (A Delaney Kristoff Original): Vodka, Pink Lemonade, Passionfruit Juice, Champagne, Aperol

I don't know how I feel about Benny being here. Part of me is annoyed, angry even, because I need my space and he's not respecting that. But another, very real part of me is flattered that he's here, fighting for me. I hate myself a little bit for liking that he's here, wanting me. I've never had someone fight for me before.

But I meant what I said about not wanting to hurt him. I know I rarely back down from a confrontation, and I know I love Benny enough to not want him to be on the receiving end of my ire. So instead of lashing out, I do the opposite. I shut down. It's not an approach I use often, but it's better than hurting the best man I've ever known, especially when I haven't parsed through all my emotions yet.

"Benny, not tonight. Please." His face is so wounded at my final plea, but I need to stand strong on this. Bob never let me sort through my emotions when we fought; I always needed to move on and get over it right away. While I know that's not what Benny is asking me to do, I'm still not ready to talk at all. "Please go," I plead.

"No." His words are whispered, but they hit me in my chest. "Baby, I'll leave you alone. I won't force you to talk to me. But I'm not leaving you. I'll give you your space, but if you need me tonight, I'll be right here." He gestures to my lumpy old couch.

He can't be serious. Sleeping on that thing will destroy his back. It's not big enough for me, and Benny's got several inches both in height and width on me. I want to fight him, tell him he's being ridiculous. For the briefest of moments, I want to joke with him and tell him that at his age, that couch is a dangerous choice. But I can't.

Tonight, I need to shore up my defenses when I'm around him. Every fight with Bob (of which there were so, so many) ended with me crumbling first. Me forgiving him too easily, too quickly, until I came to realize that the problem was as much my fault for allowing him to treat me that way as it was his for doing it in the first place. I can't go down that road again.

Thinking about Bob spikes my anger again, and I harden my resolve further. If Benny wants to cut off his nose to spite his face and sleep on my couch, be my guest. I stalk across the living room and into my bedroom, shutting the door behind me as I go. It's immature, but I need to do something that allows me to feel at least a little bit in control of my emotions.

I don't leave my room all night. The only bathroom in my cramped apartment is attached to my bedroom, and I vaguely wonder what Benny will do if he needs to pee. I purposely don't lock my bedroom door for that reason, but he never crosses my threshold. When I wake in the morning, I can't decide if I'm disappointed or satisfied by that.

I fell asleep quickly last night, thanks in part to emotional exhaustion helped along by the booze. Taking a deep breath, I steel myself for Benny's presence when I open my bedroom door. Since I fell asleep faster than I thought I would, I didn't process what went on yesterday. But my stiffened posture is useless, because Benny isn't there. Instead, I find a note written on the back of textured scrapbook paper.

FIRECRACKER,

I'M SORRY. I DON'T UNDERSTAND WHAT HAPPENED BETWEEN US, SO I CAN'T FIX IT, BUT I WANT TO. KNOW THAT I NEVER MEANT TO HURT YOU, AND I'M HURTING KNOWING YOU'RE HURTING. I'LL GIVE YOU AS MUCH SPACE AS YOU NEED. WHEN YOU'RE READY TO TALK, I'M HERE.

PROMISE.

I LOVE YOU

## Sammy

My heart cracks at the signature. My Sammy.

I may not know how I feel about everything, but one thing is clear. I need to figure it out soon, because the idea of it being too late to fix things between us is awful. All I know is that I want to be back in my Sammy's arms. But I can't be if he doesn't respect me as I currently am, rather than who he hopes I'll be.

# CHAPTER FORTY-SIX

# *Benny*



I came to get hurt, but I didn't realize that the most effective way for Delaney to hurt me isn't her sharp words hurled at me in anger.

It's her shutting me out.

After three days of radio silence, my chest physically hurts. I press my hands against my sternum, as if to check that my heart, my chest, is still in one piece.

Worse than my chest, though, is my head. I'm in a constant war with myself. When is enough time? Do I wait for her to reach out to me or has enough time passed where I can say fuck it and go after her myself?

The last thing I want is for Delaney to forget about all the good we've had because she's mad about me fucking up. With each day that passes without communication, the risk of her forgetting the good and remembering only the bad goes up.

Tonight is Delaney's big event. There's no question in my mind that I'm going. The question remains what her reaction will be.

"This conversation never happened."

"Obviously," I say into the phone before hanging up. I'm not sure how to feel about this. I feel like one of those cartoon characters that was hit over the head with a hammer, tiny birds circling my dome.

Ultimately, I know this is a good thing, but with things up in the air with Delaney, it's hard to recognize it as such. When Robert Davis, my old manager and friend, called me, I knew something was up. Despite his somewhat advanced age, Davis always texts me, never calls. Given the nature of the conversation we had, I understand why.

Baseball has extremely strict tampering rules. While the intention behind them is good, the application of those rules to staff members is a little extreme, in my opinion. Teams cannot talk to a player or staff member in any capacity—official or unofficial—while said employee is under contract. It doesn't matter if they're talking to them about a future contract that won't even start until the current contract expires—it's all forbidden.

Most staff contracts expire on the last day of October in any given season, which means there's always a mad dash to either renew with your current team prior to that or scramble to apply and get an interview once you know you aren't coming back. And if your current team gives you no indication if they'll renew or fire you, you're basically shit out of luck, sitting on your hands until you get official (or, in this case, clandestine) information. I'm not even allowed to send my resume anywhere in baseball–it's enough to get me blacklisted from all thirty teams. If a team has the balls to reach out to me, they could get fined, lose draft picks, or even receive suspensions. I don't delude myself to think I'm important enough to warrant some of the more severe penalties, but if anyone finds out about my conversation with Davis, he and Los Angeles could be facing some hefty fines.

That being said, tampering and information sharing absolutely happens; it simply occurs in sneakier ways. Case in point: Davis's phone call alerting me to his retirement plans.

It wasn't a total surprise to hear he's riding off into the sunset. He's been in baseball for more than four decades. His wife has been bugging him to retire since I played for him. What *was* a surprise was to hear Davis tell me he's recommending me as his replacement.

It doesn't exactly work that easily, but I'm grateful and flattered, nonetheless. Seeing as the Foxes haven't given me an indication of whether they want me back next season, it's nice to have something to fall back on–assuming the position isn't snatched up by someone more available. And seeing as Los Angeles can't interview or talk to me until at least Halloween (or until the Foxes officially terminate my contract), the entire situation is out of my hands.

Still, Davis called me to give me an under-the-table head's-up. When he asked if I was interested, I didn't know what to say. Fuck yes, I'm interested on principle, but it's not that simple. Chicago has been my home for the last several years. I've been on both sides of the dugout, as a player and a manager. I love this city. But the thing holding me back from a more enthusiastic yes has nothing to do with that and everything to do with the black-haired beauty who currently won't talk to me.

If I had known Delaney would come with me, I'd have said yes in a heartbeat. Being on the other side of the country from the rest of my family would be tough, but the blow would be easier if I had my girl by my side. At this point, I don't even know if she *is* my girl anymore.

And if she's not? Maybe tucking my tail between my legs and retreating to the West Coast would give me the space to lick my wounds and mourn the loss of her.

But if she's mine and she wants to stay in the Windy City? I'll move heaven and earth to make that happen.

Glancing at my watch, I start when I realize talking to Davis has pushed me further back in my schedule than I'd planned. I'm late for Delaney's event, which I'm sure isn't going to do me any favors.

I sigh. Maybe one of these days I'll climb out of the hole I keep digging for myself.

"Why can't you get it yourself?" Elijah asks me accusingly.

"Man, just do it," JJ prods. Elijah stalks away toward the bar, mumbling under his breath about seniority breeding laziness. Normally, I'd quip back at him, but even if I could think of something witty to say, I don't have the energy. All the fight in me is gone.

JJ, Warner, and Caleb are left eyeing me suspiciously, but none of them ask me what they all want to know, which is why I won't go order a drink from my own girlfriend at her event. Even though I've put on a good show, they all know something is off. I'm glad they don't ask, because I don't know what to tell them. Still, I'm grateful the words "trouble in paradise" haven't crossed their lips. I'd hate to have to punch my own players.

From a distance, I watch Delaney mix drinks. The weather is nice, now that the sun has set, but I imagine the slight sheen of sweat on her forehead. I've been here for fifteen minutes and the line for her bar hasn't dwindled. As soon as one person steps away with a drink, another joins the queue. It's been at least ten people deep the whole time I've been here, and from what Caleb told me, it's been like that since he arrived about forty minutes before me.

I want nothing more than to brush my hand across Delaney's low back and force her to take a break, to drink some water, to let me pull her thick black strands back into a ponytail to give her a little relief from the late summer heat.

She looks beautiful tonight. She always looks beautiful, but the proud expression underlying her features makes her glow. She's dressed professionally in black pants and fitted black tee, her vibrant green eyes the star of the show. Her septum ring glints in the last rays of the sun.

If she would let me, I'd crawl to her right here and worship at her feet.

Elijah returns shortly after, shoving a drink in my hands. I know he dawdled at the bar, flirting with his wife as she made the drinks. Jenny, Alicia, and Amy are back there too, spread out across the long bar. Alicia and Amy are collecting drink tickets, leaving the bartending to Jenny, Hailey, and Delaney, but it's clear Delaney is running the show.

"Here. It's called The Gardener. It's got beet juice and watermelon and some other shit I can't remember." I look down at the red drink in my hands, swirling it with the blueberries on a toothpick Hailey garnished it with. "Hails said it was Delaney's most adventurous drink. It also has the most alcohol, in case you were looking for liquid courage, she said to tell you."

I grunt a response. It's the best I can do tonight. I sip my drink, allowing the flavors to burst on my tongue. When Elijah told me it had beet juice in it, I was surprised, but I never doubted Delaney's ability to pull it off. It's smokey and slightly sweet, the contrasting flavors somehow marrying together in a way that works unexpectedly. The result is a really fucking good drink. It's a shame this one is the most alcohol-laden, because I could drink about ten of them. I stupidly drove tonight, because I am secretly hoping Delaney finally responds to my texts and wants to come home with me.

As the night wears on, I realize that was wishful thinking. When my phone vibrates with a text near the end of the night, I nearly spill what's left of my drink (mostly half-melted ice at this point) on Warner in my haste to pull my phone from my pocket. I should have known better. It's a text from our travel secretary, reminding us of the itinerary for the road trip after tomorrow's game.

I pull up my text thread with Delaney, in case something came through that I missed.

> I had to leave for an early meeting. I left you a note in the living room in case you didn't see it.

> It's been two days, and I hate sleeping without you. Good morning, firecracker.

> Good luck tonight, baby. I have complete faith in you; I know you'll kill it. This will

launch you onto bigger and better things. I love you.

She hasn't responded. I try not to let my dismay show. A small hand clasps my forearm tightly. I whip around, hoping it's Delaney. Instead, I find Alicia's face looking back at me in concern. My shoulders sag in disappointment. Alicia looks pretty tonight, her brown hair twisted into some sort of elaborate braid, but her beauty is nothing compared to Delaney's.

"Give her time. She'll come around. She needs to realize you're not Bob." Alicia gives me a tight smile and another squeeze before releasing me to walk with Warner toward the exit. I look up to see JJ studying me carefully. Caleb and Elijah are oblivious, off arguing whether the annotated display is showing monarch or tortoiseshell butterflies, despite the sign in front of it proudly announcing they are painted ladies. Idiots.

"You good?" JJ asks with an expression that says he knows I'm anything but. I sigh.

"I don't know what I did. I offered to pay for Delaney to go back to school to get her business degree. She's been getting really into mixology and inventing new cocktails, and I wanted her to have as many options as possible to be successful." JJ nods thoughtfully. "She never finished school, and she's kind of defensive about it, so I thought she'd want to go back if I paid for it. I guess that wasn't what was holding her back, but like an idiot, I assumed it was."

"And you don't know why she's upset about your offer?" He asks it without judgment, but I bristle all the same.

"I love her. I just want to make things easier for her. I want her to be happy and successful and to never have to worry about the world not seeing her as perfectly as I do." I sigh heavily, well aware that I'm uncharacteristically dragging the mood down. JJ doesn't seem to mind. He waits patiently for me to continue as we walk amongst the various outdoor exhibits. By now, the crowd has mostly dispersed, but the event is still technically ongoing, so Amy and Delaney are still behind the bar. There's still a line for their drinks, despite other bars having no wait.

"I was trying to help her," I say lamely, not knowing what else to say.

"Did she ask for your help?" Again, JJ's question is presented without judgment, but he's somehow hit the nail on the head.

"Fuck. No, she didn't." I drag my hand down my face. I stare at the butterflies flitting from one flower to another, but I don't really see them. After a long pause, I say, "I wanted to fix the problem before it even came up. Now I look like a dick who's insulted her, trying to force her to go to college when she told me it wasn't for her."

Could Delaney's reason for not wanting to go back to school really be that simple? She told me it wasn't for her, and like an idiot, I assumed there was more to it. Sure, it might have been wrapped up in Bob and his mess, but it's been years since they broke up. If she really was committed to going back and earning her degree, she probably could have figured out a way to do it in the years since.

I'm such an asshole. I pushed my single-minded agenda because I thought it would help, but all it did was push her further from me.

Throughout my life, I've been good at identifying problems and fixing them. It's what made me a top tier catcher when I played, figuring out which pitches to call. It's the reason I was behind the dish for three of my pitchers' no-hitters. Solving problems is what makes me a good manager, too. But my own marriage was a problem I couldn't solve. It was one I wasn't meant to solve, because after eighteen years, the pieces no longer fit together. It was a jagged pill to swallow, but I did anyway, because it was best for Keeley, the kids, and ultimately, me. But it didn't stop me from vowing that I'd search harder, find the problems earlier, and solve them before they became an insurmountable issue. Instead, I've been so consumed with solving problems that I created them where none existed.

JJ shakes his head slowly. "We've all been there, man. It takes a lot to get over a bad breakup, and from the little Ames has told me, Delaney had a rough one. Maybe she's trying to figure out what she wants."

What was meant, I'm sure, to be a reassuring statement has the opposite effect on me. The last thing I want is for Delaney to figure out what she wants and it be someone other than me. But it would be worse if she doesn't figure out that she doesn't want me now, only to break my heart later when she does work it all out. I can only hope I am what she wants, and that she figures it out before my heart completely splits in half.

# CHAPTER FORTY-SEVEN

# *Delaney*

can't Deny Me Love (A Delaney Kristoff
Original): St. Germain, cava, Grapefruit Juice,
Rosemary

K ingston walks toward me, meowing loudly, as I enter my apartment and toe off my shoes. I'm exhausted. Between running around, getting everything set up for the event, to nearly forgetting the laminated recipe cards I made, I felt frazzled before Amy even arrived to pick me up. Then, once we got to the museum, I ran around getting our station set up. Twice, we ran out of garnishes and had to have Amy switch from ticket collecting to garnish making. She did a great job, and I'm exceedingly thankful I had the foresight to double the number of mixers I originally planned to bring.

My brain is still processing the success of the night. Hailey told me repeatedly she couldn't believe how successful my "beet drink" was. I'd be offended if she wasn't gushing equally hard about how much she loved my other two drinks. I guess I can't blame her; the girl is simply not a fan of root vegetables.

My bar was consistently more crowded than the other stands throughout the night. At any given point, the line averaged about ten to twelve customers deep, which is saying a lot, seeing as they could have easily left and used their drink tickets at another, emptier bar. But no other bar had my drinks, so I know they were there for what I had to offer.

The feeling was overwhelming if I dwelled on it too long, so I didn't allow myself to think about it too much. I savored the moment, but since every moment was spent with someone else clamoring for another drink, I wasn't able to step aside and take it all in. Immediately before the event started, Kristen, the event coordinator, introduced me to Pascal, who owns a molecular gastronomy restaurant in the Loop. After trying each of my drinks, he handed me his business card and told me to get in touch with him.

I stood there in shock after that, before Hailey pulled me from my reverie by reminding me guests were starting to arrive. I didn't have time to think about what Pascal could have meant when he invited me to get in touch with him, but all I wanted to do was call Benny and share the news before I remembered I haven't talked to him in several days.

What my brain is not processing anymore are my feelings about Benny. I want to be stubborn. I want to still be angry at him for being a presumptuous, entitled asshole. But mostly, I just miss him. I also know he needs to give me an explanation about the "just a bartender" thing. He's never openly judged me for my job before, so I'm hoping there's an explanation. Because if there isn't? If my job suddenly isn't good enough for him anymore? It's going to break my heart.

I miss the way he cares for me. The way he does so much for me, without expecting anything in return. He brought me to Ernie, pushed me to charge him more for my one drink recipe, and encouraged me to develop more, even if it was only to hone my craft and didn't have a financial outcome. Benny always makes a point to make sure I am well fed. He ensures I drink enough water and pulls my hair back every time I forget a hair tie.

Even in my most stubborn moments since our fight, I knew, deep down, that Benny was only trying to help me.

Still, my mother's voice hisses in my ear. *Men are only there to take.* And didn't I know it, after everything with Bob?

A niggling doubt burrows its way into my brain. What if Benny is the exception? Maybe that's wishful thinking, but I realize I want it to be true so, so badly.

Maybe it's because I can't get my mother's voice out of my head, or because I need to talk to someone about everything, instead of trying to sort my thoughts on my own, but I find myself scrolling to my mother's name in my phone.

"Âllo, Delaney," my mother's voice purrs. "Ça va?"

"Alors, non," I tell her honestly. I launch into everything, suddenly no longer able to hold back once I start talking. A dam breaks behind my mouth, my teeth no longer able to contain my thoughts and emotions. I spew them all out, and my mother listens. I flip rapidly between English and French, code switching at random, but my mother keeps up, responding mostly in French, but rattling off occasional English phrases as well.

"So, then he just offered to pay for the rest of my schooling, like it was no big deal. As if money was the reason I dropped out to begin with. I *told* him college wasn't for me, but there he goes, imposing himself and his ideas on me. Isn't that ridiculous?"

"Actually, no, Delaney. It's not. It's not a bad thing for the person you love to want what's best for you." I scoff. I haven't told my mother that I love Benny. "It's also not a bad thing for the person who loves you to want to be there for you in all capacities."

I scoff again. My mother sighs, deeply and wearily.

"Delaney, I'm sorry that my poor experiences with love have colored your own experiences. I didn't want to turn you into a cynic; I only wanted to protect you from the heartache I felt. Your father and I started out so strong. When things fell apart, I was destroyed, and he was hardly affected at all. I had uprooted my entire life for him, and while I wouldn't change it, because it brought me you, it also brought me incredible pain and a strong distrust of love. But when I was in love, it was the greatest feeling in the world. I was invincible. I could take on anything. Suddenly, moving to a new country and settling down there weren't the terrifying prospects they should have been. To know that my attitudes and my misplaced defense mechanisms have prevented you from experiencing the incredible power of love is the biggest disservice I could have done for you."

And then, my normally stoic, jaded, and cynical mother sniffs.

# CHAPTER FORTY-EIGHT

## *Delaney*

walking cliche (A Delaney Kristoff Original):
French champagne, Grand Marnier, cassis,
cigarette on the side

I'm stunned. I sit in silence for a long time, soaking up my mother's words. I had no idea she harbored guilt in the aftermath of her divorce from my father. She was always so straightforward, to the point of being flippant, about their separation. To be honest, he was kind of a dick at the end, too, so that probably made it easier. It's been a long time since I've heard my mother speak positively about love in general, and especially the love she specifically held for my father, that I'm momentarily silenced. Her words swim through my brain as I try to make sense of it all.

My mother, though, is apparently not done imparting her wisdom.

"Delaney, men fuck up. That's what they do." After a pause, she adds, "Women fuck up too; they just look better when they do it. And he's going to fuck up again. You're going to fuck up again, too. It's part of life."

I hear her suck in a deep inhale and can imagine the cigarette smoke curling from her lips. My mother is a walking French cliché.

"The part of life worth living, though, is how you decide to move past it. You can call it quits and move on alone. Sometimes that really is the best course of action. Trust me. I know. But sometimes, you pick yourself up and decide to move on together. Only you can decide what the right way is for you. But I would hope that you make your decision based on what you want, not on what you *think* you should want."

Walking cliché or not, she's right. Ninety-nine percent of my life, my mother's advice has been terrible or just generally not the greatest. But today, she finally hit that one percent.

# CHAPTER FORTY-NINE

## *Delaney*

It's a Marathon, Not a Sprint (A Delaney
Kristoff Original): Strawberry Soju, Coconut water,
watermelon Puree, Strawberry Garnish

I went to bed last night, my brain swimming with my mother's words and my own emotions swirling in my chest. I slept terribly, waking every few hours, only to be reminded that Benny still isn't here to hold me.

The truth of the matter is that I want him here to hold me. I let go of my anger a few days ago, but my stubborn streak is still clinging strong, not quite willing to call him yet. There's a very real fear that if I give in to the forgiveness I so badly want to dole out, he will do this again. Especially if he really does judge me for being a bartender. I know that's Bob's MO, and not Benny's, but old habits–old fears–die hard.

I can't lie to myself anymore. I've been avoiding Benny because I'm a coward. If I see him, I know we'll have to talk about us. I'll be forced to confront the fact that I am *this close* to letting a man change the course of my own destiny. And if I don't let him? That option sounds almost worse. Nope. I'll just live in denial, maintaining this awkward, potentially heartbreaking limbo, because *this* unknown is better than getting my heart broken–again–for real.

I'm in the middle of the Sunday day shift, working only a few hours, when realization hits me. I was less angered about Benny's actions and more scared that they might change the course of my life. Which is a ridiculous thought, in a way, because Benny already *has* changed the course of my life. He has irrevocably shaped me into a more self-assured, adventurous woman. He's also connected me with Ernie, which has given my confidence in my own skills and abilities a much-needed boost.

If the universe hadn't set me on a collision course with Samuel Benjamin, where would I be now? Sure, I'd more than likely still be working at Sip, wiping down the same spot of the bar while waiting for my next customer to flag me down for another round. And yes, the Foxes game would still be playing in the background of the bar, but I wouldn't be keeping one ear out for the score, silently hoping for a Foxes win. And I wouldn't be mulling over my future with quite the same level of added pressure.

Because that's what it comes down to right now. My mother, in her occasional wisdom, was somehow right. What is done is done. It's how we move forward that matters. Now I need to figure out how I want to move forward regarding Benny.

It's that thought that tumbles around in my head for the next few hours, as I finish my shift at Sip, as I walk inside my silent apartment, as I fill the space with the sounds of the ninth inning of the Foxes game.

I can't help it. I've turned on every game since our fight. Maybe I'm a masochist, but I needed to see Benny's face, even televised from miles away, to know that he's still out there, breathing the same air as me.

I sit on my lumpy couch, absentmindedly stroking Kingston's fur, staring at the television but mostly spacing out. My gaze catches on the note Benny wrote to me, his messy scrawl carving into the paper. I read the words again; this time letting them carve their way into my soul.

WHEN YOU'RE READY TO TALK, I'M HERE.

PROMISE.

I LOVE YOU

SAMMY

My gaze slides to the television, where Foxes players are walking onto the field in a single file line, high-fiving the defensive players walking off. They pulled off another win. The on-field announcer interviews Warner, but I tune out most of the words. Before she signs off, however, she notes that Benny will be first up on the postgame press conference. My hand freezes on the remote, stopping myself from turning off the television.

I settle back further into the couch, needing to see Benny the way an addict needs their next hit. I really am a masochist.

As my eyes catch on the note again, I realize he's made me so many promises throughout the time I've known him. In nearly eleven months of knowing Benny, I'm confident in saying that he made me more promises than Bob made me in our two-year long relationship. All Bob did was break them, but Benny has kept them all.

Every. Single. One.

A sob catches in my throat when the commercials end and Benny's face appears on my screen. He looks as good as ever, if visibly tired. Purple crescents ring the skin under his eyes, but he's still breathtaking. The microphone in front of him is on, capturing the scratchy sound as he rubs a hand across his stubble. It's my favorite sound in the whole world.

I couldn't tell you a single question they asked him during the interview. I watched the whole thing with bated breath, but I mostly stared at the way his beautiful mouth formed what I'm sure were perfect words. The way his pale blue eyes shined when he smiled. The way he arched an eyebrow in response to a question. And, of course, the way the world's sexiest rose tattoo stood out among the veins and sinew on the back of his hands.

I may have been staring mindlessly at Benny, but my brain was churning away, processing thoughts and plugging puzzle pieces together.

I finally realize my own self-preservation, my self-imposed defensiveness, stopped serving me the moment I met Samuel Benjamin. At that moment, it turned from a helpful, protective factor into an ouroboros, that coiled snake that unknowingly gorges itself by eating its own tail.

In trying to avoid harm, I closed off parts of me that I'm no longer willing to keep behind closed doors. Specifically, the pieces of me that embrace love.

I spend so much time listening to romance audiobooks because I secretly love love. Don't get me wrong, the spice is often top-notch entertainment. But I keep coming back to the romance genre because love always wins in the end. Because the heroes and heroines transform themselves into something better when they enter the selfless throes of love.

Here I have my very own sexy, perfectly imperfect MMC, and I'm pushing him away due to my own stubbornness.

Suddenly, I have to get to him.

Glancing at the screen, Benny is walking away from the postgame interview. He's probably going back to his office to finish working for the night. I'd go to him now, but I'm disgusting. There's no way I'm making a love declaration with greasy hair and unshaved legs.

My shower is quick but thorough. I don't waste time drying my hair, instead throwing it up into a messy, wet bun. I briefly consider at least swiping some mascara on, but whether Benny accepts this love declaration or not (the idea of him rejecting me makes me want to throw up), I know I'll end up crying, so what's the point?

After throwing on shorts and a tank top, I shove my feet into my Converse and take off.

Delaney Kristoff was not made for running.

Especially not in jean shorts and a tank top.

But I have little time to pick apart my impractical wardrobe selection as I take off toward the ballpark. My boobs are bouncing dangerously with each perilous stride. I try to hold them down with my arms, turning what might have otherwise been a normal, albeit frantic, jog into a laughably embarrassing T-Rex-looking joke.

I don't even care. My thoughts are consumed with reaching Benny.

I make it to the L right before the doors slide closed, and I take the time to catch my breath, heaving and wheezing and being a general embarrassment. The Chicagoans in the subway car with me have seen far worse, I'm sure, so no one pays me any attention. Foxes Field is three L stops away from my apartment, and I'm grateful for the extra time on a mostly empty train. I can catch my breath and organize my thoughts.

I don't even know what I'm going to say to him. I mean, obviously I'll start with 'I'm sorry,' but whether I blurt it out or go into it with some sort of preamble, I have no idea. Unfortunately, I don't have time to decide before the doors to the L are opening again, spitting me out at the station across from the stadium.

The platform is crammed with Foxes fans in various stages of inebriation and revelry from the win. I'm a salmon swimming upstream trying to get out of here while everyone else jostles forward, attempting the same thing, but in the opposite direction. If I wasn't so frantic to get to Benny, I might appreciate the few extra minutes without the screaming burn in my quads and hamstrings.

Descending the stairs, I finally break free of the crowd and break back into my humiliating dinosaur gait. My boobs were not made for this kind of cardio. After today, nothing more strenuous than hot girl walks, I promise my bruised breasts. If my boobs had eyes, they'd be shooting daggers at me. As it is, they're stretching and bouncing and about ready to smack me in the chin. My lungs are tight and my legs are on fire.

So much for that shower; I'm a fucking mess.

I round the corner to the back of the stadium where I know Benny and his players will exit. I don't have a plan. Do I go inside? Wait for him out here? It's long after the game, and the crowd has mostly dispersed, so I no longer have to dodge my way through an obstacle course of pedestrians.

As if on cue, the door from the clubhouse lobby opens and a familiar laugh reaches my ears. Benny steps out, Mac following close behind.

Either I've watched too many rom coms and listened to way too many audiobooks, or the angels in heaven decided to throw old Delaney a bone, because I swear everything happens in slow motion.

I swear I hear a choir of angels herald his appearance.

He's never looked so handsome. Even though I saw him on my television screen not even an hour ago, he still looks breathtakingly beautiful. His stubble is sexy, reminding me of its feel between my legs and against my neck. His blue eyes are icy and clear, crinkled at the sides as he laughs at something Mac says. His muscled arms and dark tattoos are on full display as his short-sleeved polo stretches across his broad chest. I want to kiss him and hold him and trace every inch of his tattoos with my fingers. But the choir stops singing and this slow-motion reverie suddenly speeds up.

Benny turns and starts walking in the other direction, toward the two large buses idling further down the block. To be fair, he wouldn't be looking toward this side of the street, expecting to see his girlfriend on death's door thanks to the surely impending heart attack going on over here.

Gulping in a shallow breath–it's all my lungs will accommodate right now–I scream his name. He turns instantly, his eyes somehow automatically locking on mine. A smile breaks free and the effect is dazzling.

He starts moving toward me, waving a half goodbye to Mac and breaking into a jog toward me. I pick up my pace, which absolutely must be against the laws of physics or anatomy or something, as tears stream down my face.

Delaney Kristoff runs for no man.

But she'd sprint a fucking marathon for Samuel Benjamin.

# CHAPTER FIFTY

# *Benny*

Romantic Gesture (A Delaney Kristoff Original):
Rye Whiskey, Amaretto, Ginger Ale

She's here. She's running to me. She's here, and she's running to *me*. In my very own version of *Say Anything*, Delaney is romantic gesturing me.

At first, I think it's a mirage, some weird dehydration-induced hallucination, but when Mac murmurs, "Go get her," I know she is real.

"Tell them not to wait for me. I'll drive up tomorrow," I instruct Mac with a half-hearted wave behind me. I'm already moving. I stole a decent amount of bases in my career, but I swear, my feet have never moved as fast as they do now.

Delaney slams into my chest, wrapping her legs around my waist, her forward momentum causing me to stumble, but I stay true to my word from so many months ago. *I'm not going to drop you.*

Tears are falling down Delaney's beautiful cheeks faster than I can catch them with one hand, the other supporting her against me.

"Don't cry sweetheart. I'm so sorry. I should have–"

She cuts me off, shaking her head briefly before slamming her lips against mine. I've never tasted anything so sweet. My hand threads into her hair, which I'm only now realizing is wet, and thrown up into a bun. Delaney never wears her hair up unless I put it up for her. Pulling back, I assess her new look.

"Your hair is up," I say simply.

"I didn't want to wait for it to dry. I'm glad I didn't. It looks like I barely caught you." She frowns, her eyes filling with tears again. "Where are you going now?"

"Right now? I'm taking you home to my bed, where I'm going to show you just how sorry I am and how much I missed you."

She tugs against me, and I loosen my hold, allowing her to slide down my body until she comes to standing on the sidewalk. I immediately miss her heat and vow to press her body into mine as soon as she lets me again.

"But...the bus is leaving?" Sure enough, the first bus is pulling away from the curb, following its police escort. The second bus follows immediately after. I don't miss Asher's goofy face, along with a couple other rookies we recently brought up from the minor leagues, looking out the back window to gawk at me.

"We have a three-game series in Milwaukee. I'll drive up tomorrow at the last possible minute." I cradle her face in my hands. "I want to spend every second with you that I can." I duck down, pressing my lips to hers. This kiss is less intense, less sloppy than the one we just shared, but it's not any less passionate. I'm going to need to wrap this up soon if we want to make it back to my place. I don't have any qualms about fucking Delaney on the street corner just like this, that's how badly my body is calling out to hers. However, I have a feeling Delaney and the Chicago Police Department would have some thoughts about that.

An idea strikes me. "Come up with me. Come to Milwaukee. Spend the series with me. Stay in the hotel room with me. Come to the games or don't, but I need you in my bed every night."

Delaney pretends to think for a minute. "We do love road trips, don't we?"

# CHAPTER FIFTY-ONE

## *Delaney*

Twenty Minutes in Heaven (A Delaney Kristoff Original): Gin, Apricot Brandy, Lime, Simple Syrup, Soda Water

Benny practically drags me to his townhouse. It's not a far walk from the ballpark, but my thighs have already chafed from my earlier foray into ill-advised athleticism. As much as I despise the cardio-induced chub rub, I'd do it again in a heartbeat. Benny side-eyes my bow-legged walk, raising his eyebrows in question of my new gait.

"It hurts. I wore the wrong shorts to go running after you in eighty-degree weather. My fat legs chafed."

Benny stops walking and pulls me roughly to him by my belt loops. "You better not be insulting those thick thighs. They're one of my favorite parts about you." He pauses, looking thoughtful. "Them, and your perfect tits, your amazing ass...don't get me started on that talented mouth, and your gorgeous, sexy, brain."

I shove him away from me playfully, but I'm secretly thrilled. Heat courses through my veins. Thank goodness we're only a block away from his house.

"Let me see, baby," Benny urges, and I lift a leg for him to inspect my inner thigh. He reaches his fingers toward the pinkened skin.

"Don't touch!" I exclaim. He pulls his hand back instantly and shoots me a grin.

"Don't worry, I'll kiss it later. My tongue will soothe it all better."

"Don't you dare," I threaten without bite.

"What? You love when I wear your thighs as earmuffs," he taunts, and I practically tackle him to throw my hand over his mouth. We're on a public street; as much as I enjoy Benny's bedroom talents, they're for me alone. Luckily, there's no one within earshot. He chuckles, licking my palm. I pull it back and smack him lightly on his chest.

Standing in front of me, he slings his backpack toward his chest and crouches low. His muscular thighs strain against the fabric of his jeans and I'm momentarily distracted as I stare at them. Benny catches me and smirks.

"Hey, pervert, hop on."

Benny carries me piggyback style the rest of the way home and into his bedroom. When he walks me to his bed, I release my hold on his neck, falling with a soft "oomph" onto the mattress.

Benny is hovering over me in an instant, my legs automatically wrapping around his waist and pulling him closer. I want him to sprawl out over me, drop his whole weight onto me and never get up. I can't get him close enough to me.

His kisses against my neck grow frantic, frenzied. My fingers clutch his shirt, desperate to ground myself in some part, any part, of this glorious man. His palms find my breasts, his thumbs and index fingers plucking both of my nipples at the same time. I arch desperately into his hands.

"Delaney. My perfect girl. I never meant to make you feel–"

I cut him off. "Talk later. Please, Sammy."

Everything about right now is wild, feverish, crazed. Now is not the time for words. It's a time for action and heat and pleasure. Benny groans at my use of his nickname, rutting roughly against me. I cry out, both in pleasure–because it feels so good–and pain, because his jeans rub against my freshly abraded skin. He curses, pulling himself off me and I whimper at the loss of him.

Jesus, I'm not even *trying* to play it cool right now.

Benny doesn't seem to mind. He undresses himself quickly, tossing his clothes aside. Slowly, painstakingly, he unbuttons my shorts and pulls them down my legs, careful not to touch the raw skin on my inner thighs. The care and devotion in which he strips me down is so intense, tears prick my eyes again. I can't help it; I pull in a shuddering sigh.

"Shh, baby," he soothes. "I'll take care of you." He slides my panties down with equal care before spreading my legs and pulling back to gaze lovingly down at me. With any other man, I'd be self-conscious, being exposed like this. But with Benny, my Sammy, I feel worshipped.

He dips his head and begins to feast. In the days without him, I've forgotten how incredible his mouth is, in all senses of the word. As if reading my thoughts, he grins up at me.

"I've missed the way you taste, Delaney baby. I'm going to spend the next twenty minutes down here in this perfect cunt, and you're going to come on my tongue as many times as you can, do you understand me?"

I push myself up onto my elbows to stare at him in disbelief, to tell him twenty minutes is a ridiculous amount of time, to reassure him that I don't–I stop myself, because the *view* from up here, staring down at the hunger in his eyes as he stares back at me while he works me over with his tongue? It's the hottest thing I've ever seen. And then Benny, the cocky son of a bitch, winks at me.

I can't help it. I laugh. He chuckles along with me, and my laugh is quickly transformed into moans of pleasure, the vibrations of his laughter heightening each sensation. He doesn't slow; he doesn't break eye contact. For twenty fucking minutes, he keeps his mouth latched onto my pussy. Occasionally, he adds his fingers into the mix, curving them inside me and pressing his spit-lubed thumb against my back entrance. Over and over, I tumble headfirst into orgasm after orgasm. Each time, when the aftershocks subside, he gives my clit a brief reprieve, focusing on tonguing my entrance or pressing soft, open-mouthed kisses against my inner thighs before resuming his rhythm against my clit once more.

I'm a sweaty, babbling mess by the time he hauls himself up over my body. I'm glad I elected to forgo the mascara, as tears stream down the sides of my face and into my hairline. He gently swipes them away and pulls me into his body. I kiss his chest while I try to gain some semblance of control over my breathing. My poor heart really has been through the wringer today. She's earned herself a bottle or two of red wine later tonight.

"Are you okay?" Benny whispers into my hair.

"I missed you so much." My voice cracks on the last syllable as I start to sob. "I'm so sorry, Sammy. I know you were only looking out for me. I shouldn't have gotten so upset."

"Shh, shh, shh," he coos, running his large hands through my hair. "I missed you too, my love. Let's talk later. There's so much I want to say to you, but I need to hold you first."

I nod against him, pulling in gasping breaths. I don't cry often, but when I do, it's not pretty. I'm an ugly crier; I know this about myself. I'm glad to have my face smashed against Benny's chest, so he can't see the unflattering shapes my face is making. He wraps his leg around me, in addition to both his strong arms, holding me tightly and making quiet, soothing sounds. I don't know if I cry for minutes or hours, but I know we stay like this for a long time, wrapped up in each other. All the while, Benny's hands never stop their comforting movements, playing with my hair, drawing small circles on my back. If there ever was a heaven created exactly for me, this would be it. Cocooned in Benny's strong arms as he whispers sweet nothings to me and plays with my hair.

# CHAPTER FIFTY-TWO

## *Benny*

Rose Tattoo (A Delaney Kristoff Original): Cava, Orange Curaçao, Rose Water

Several times this evening I've had to check to make sure Delaney really was here, that this wasn't a dream. Each time I've wanted to pinch myself, she's proven that she's real. By kissing me, by nudging my arms tighter, by pulling herself closer to me. At this rate, I'd let this woman burrow into my skin.

Her sobs have long since subsided, and we can't avoid this conversation forever. I loosen my hold on her, pulling us both back toward the headboard and prop up against the pillows.

"Delaney, let's talk." A momentary glimmer of fear slices across her face, and I realize she thinks I'm going to break up with her. *Silly girl, I'm in it for the long haul.* "Come here," I say, opening my arms to her, and she happily wedges herself under my arm and across my chest. I press my lips against her hair, filling my lungs with the coconutty scent of her shampoo. She takes a deep breath as if preparing to talk, but I cut her off.

"D, you told me a while ago that college wasn't for you. I'm sorry I didn't listen to you. After everything you told me about Bob, I guess I blamed him for you dropping out, and I wanted to give you a second chance, thinking that you wanted one, too. I wanted to surprise you, which is why I didn't talk to you about it beforehand, but I should have listened to you earlier."

"Sammy, no. I mean, yeah, you're right. I don't want to go back to school. It was hard for me, but more importantly, I didn't *like* it. I don't think I'll ever change my mind on that." She pulls in a deep breath at the same time she pushes back from me a little bit, establishing eye contact. "But before we talk further, I need to know what you meant when you said I didn't have to be *just* a bartender?"

I rear my head back. Confusion colors my features. "When did I say that?"

"The same time you said everything else."

"Shit, baby. I don't even remember saying that. I'm so fucking sorry that I did. I absolutely didn't mean it like that. I have no problem with your job–you can do whatever you want. I think I meant that you could do whatever; that you didn't need to limit yourself if you didn't want to." She looks down, not fully convinced. "I'm sorry it came across like I didn't respect you or your job. I have nothing but respect for you, in every facet." I tug her chin up so she looks at me again, hoping she sees the sincerity in my eyes. I really don't give a shit what Delaney does for work, or whether she even works at all–I only want her to be happy.

She takes another stuttering breath and tucks herself back into me before speaking again.

"Part of the reason why I didn't like college was because I didn't see the value for me personally. I never had huge career aspirations. For me, a job is a means to an end, not a passion project. And that's okay. My job is great. I get to meet interesting people, and get to be creative with drinks, and earn a decent paycheck. And at the end of the day, if I don't like it, I can quit whenever I want. I don't have big projects hanging over my head, tying me to a dead-end job that I hate."

I take her in, never having considered these factors before. She lies back down.

"I get why you wanted me to go back, though. It's hard for people not to judge someone when they hear they're a college dropout. But I promise you, I'm happier in this job than in any college-created career I could have found." I nod against her, knowing she can't see me, but can still feel my movement.

"I'm sorry I pushed it on you. I saw a nonexistent problem in the future and wanted to fix it before it became an issue. I want good things for you, Delaney. I want you to be happy and not have to worry about anything."

"But there isn't a problem to fix," she insists.

"I know that now, but I can't help myself. If there's something I can do to make your life easier or better or happier, I want to do it. Making you happy brings me joy, baby."

She sighs against me, and I know she's choosing her words carefully.

"Benny, you're a giver. You've clearly always been that way. It's part of what makes you so incredible. It's part of your irresistible charm. And while most of the time, those are amazing attributes, I need you to recognize that you can't solve every problem, as much as you may want to. Sometimes, I only need you to listen to my problems. But if there's something I want you to fix, I'll let you know, okay?"

"Okay."

She scoots onto her knees, locking eyes with me. Her face is serious, and I find myself sitting up a little straighter, too.

"I love you, Sammy. I am sorry for losing it on you a bit when you were trying to help. Thank you for your patience when I wasn't ready to talk about it yet."

I close my eyes. I'm glad the time apart helped her to sort through her thoughts, but honestly? It killed me. I don't know if I can withstand another period of no contact if she gets upset with me again.

"Baby, look at me. Please." I open my eyes, knowing I can never deny her anything. "I need you to know it wasn't the college thing. I mean, yeah, that was the tipping point, the spark that lit the fuse. But the truth is, I stayed away, sorting through everything, because I was scared. I saw our relationship as something that would alter the course of my life, and I got freaked out. I already allowed that to happen to me once, and it blew up in my face. It took me so long to recover from the damage Bob did, and my feelings for him are nothing compared to the depth of my feelings for you."

I wait for her to say more, unsure if I should smile, knowing she loves me so much, or be concerned about her obvious unease.

"Your devotion to me is soul crushing." I can't tell if she means that as a compliment or not, but she's right. "And I want it all," she whispers. "You've already altered the course of my life. I already will never be the same, whether we stay together fifty years or break up tomorrow."

"One hundred."

"Huh?"

"We're staying together for one hundred years. At least." My voice is confident, unwavering.

"Okay, some of us don't have that much left in the tank," she says, poking my ribs.

"Watch it," I warn, flipping her onto her back and pinning her arms above her head. I kiss her deeply for a minute before pulling back. She arches her neck, seeking me again, and I know we've said everything we need to say. I watch as her eyes dilate as I press her into the mattress, holding her down as my cock slides fully into her on the first thrust. Her breath catches in her throat, and I give her a moment to adjust to my size. It's been a while since I fucked her properly. Far too long.

"You ready, sweetheart?" She nods, all traces of her fire muted to a soft burning crackle as she submits to me. I shift both of her hands into one of mine so I can toss a pillow behind her head. "I don't want you to hurt your head when I fuck you into the headboard," I explain.

"Oh, Sammy," she moans breathily, and I lose the thin tether of restraint I was holding on to. I shift both hands to her hips, and like the perfect girl she is, Delaney keeps her hands where I left them. I lift her hips, pulling them over me as I shift to kneeling, never pulling out of her. From this angle I can fuck her harder while watching that spot where I enter her repeatedly. It's like dinner and a show, my twenty-minute feast from earlier still in the forefront of my mind.

"Delaney, fuck, you're so perfect for me. I'm never letting you go."

"Never," she shouts, the syllables stuttering as I slam into her repeatedly.

Remember when I said it's been far too long since I fucked Delaney? I'm barely hanging on here, but I didn't reunite with her just to come inside her after two minutes. I grit my teeth and bite my lower lip. I clench my ass cheeks. I'm doing everything I can to stave off this orgasm, but I know I won't last much longer. Bringing my right thumb to her clit, I rub rough circles against it, the way I know she likes it.

"Sammy, Sammy, Sammy," she chants. I feel her walls tighten, and I know she's close. Thank fucking god. Her eyes are glued to my hand as it flexes against her belly, my thumb hard at work against her tight bundle of nerves.

"Come for me, Delaney. Let go," I instruct, and she does. I wonder vaguely if my neighbors can hear her, their dinners interrupted by her passionate screams, before spilling inside her with a roar of my own.

I collapse on top of her, catching myself on my elbows, but Delaney pulls all of me on top of her. The sweat on our chests mingles as we lie together.

"Fucking rose tattoo will be the death of me," she mutters.

"What's that, baby?" Lifting my head, I catch the flush on her cheeks.

"Your hand!" She attempts to gesture toward my hands, but her arms are pinned underneath my body, so the movement is stunted. "Your stupid rose tattoo is the sexiest thing I've ever seen in my life. I've always thought so." She ducks her head.

"Oh no you don't," I chastise, pulling her chin up. "You've always thought so but never told me?" She attempts a shrug, but again, I'm mostly still crushing her. I attempt to shift away, but she wraps her legs around my waist and holds me in place. "Hmm, it was probably a mistake telling me that, you know. Now I know your weakness."

"With great power comes great responsibility," she reminds me before kissing me softly.

# CHAPTER FIFTY-THREE

## *Delaney*

Hell or High Water (A Delaney Kristoff Original):
Rye Whiskey, Homemade Sour Mix, Seltzer,
Tobacco Bitters

We spend the rest of the night alternating between sex and deep conversations. Benny tells me he originally offered the college option because he was scared I wouldn't want to follow him wherever he'll be next year if I didn't have a viable career choice wherever he landed. I reminded him that I love him and that I don't need a reason other than that to follow him, which, admittedly, is a newer revelation I've stumbled across myself.

Because it's true; I'd follow Benny anywhere he asks me to. These last few days were hard enough without him, and that was when I was mad at him. I don't want to know what being apart from him normally would be like, although I suppose it wouldn't be too different from how we handle his current road trips: lots of texting and video sex. But I need those reunions after his road trips; if Benny isn't with the Foxes next year, I'm not willing to wait weeks or months between seeing him.

When I told him that I would follow him anywhere, it made me wish for a time machine, only so that I could go back and revisit the moment over and over again. The way his face lit up was so precious, so pure, that I want to do everything I can to put that excitement back on his face every chance I get. He told me about his conversation with his old manager, and the possibility of a Los Angeles gig. I told him I've always loved the beach.

It's nearly dawn before we finally give up on deep conversations and bodily coupling. Suddenly, I'm reminded of a nagging doubt. I want to shove it down, to ignore it, but I know it will only fester.

"Hey Benny?"

"Yeah, baby."

"How come you didn't come to the museum event?"

"What do you mean?"

"You sent me a text wishing me luck, so I know you didn't forget...but you didn't come. I wish you could have seen it." I'm trying to rein in my disappointment. There's no point in making him feel bad about something he can't change.

Two fingers under my chin tug it up so he can look me in my eyes. "Baby, I was there. I wouldn't have missed it for the world. You may have wanted your space from me, but I wasn't going to let that stop me from seeing you shine. I went, but I kept my distance. I wanted to respect your wishes."

"You were there?" I try not to let disbelief bleed into my tone, but apparently, I fail. Benny's eyes soften in compassion.

"Yeah, D. I was there. I saw you wearing your plain silver septum ring because you think it looks more professional than the elaborate gold one you normally wear. You had tiny jade earrings in, which brought out the color of your eyes. And you served your drinks with such pride that I've never seen you look more beautiful. I was there, D. And I saw everything."

There's a hitch in my breathing that causes Benny to tug me closer. I'm already mostly koalaed around him anyway, but it's apparently not close enough.

"Come hell or high water, I'll always support you, Delaney." The sincerity in his tone is enough to send me over the edge again, and a tear slips loose from my eye. Instead of swiping it away, Benny presses a soft kiss against it, and we both begin our surrender to sleep.

"Good morning, Sammy."

"Good morning, baby."

# CHAPTER FIFTY-FOUR

# *Benny*



We're both running on fumes, having only gotten about four hours of sleep last night–this morning, to be exact. I'm strangely energized though. Perhaps it's because without Delaney falling asleep in my arms, I've been averaging four hours of fragmented sleep lately anyway. I suspect my heightened energy has more to do with getting my girl back where she belongs, which, at the moment, is next to me in the passenger seat.

We have a game in Milwaukee late this afternoon, but several late-night texts with Mac assured me he's handling most of today's responsibilities. That still means I need to be at the ballpark several hours before game time, but it buys me more time with Delaney. I love my job; I wouldn't change it for hardly anything. It allowed me to remain faithful to my first love (baseball), while fulfilling all my childhood dreams. I've won a World Series, earned myself an MVP designation, and made countless friends and memories over decades in this sport. But at this moment, I'm hard pressed to find anything as satisfying as coasting up the highway, music playing, a beautiful woman to my right, her hand safely tucked in mine.

Still, my sporadic hours and long days (and nights) are really impacting the time I spend with Delaney. She's never complained, but it can't be easy on her. Maybe I'm overthinking things because we just made up, or maybe this is how I truly feel. Time will tell. What I am certain about, however, is my need to have her around more frequently. Year-round.

I pull her hand, still clasped in mine, toward my lips, pressing a gentle kiss to the back of her palm. Her smile is dazzling as she looks at me like I'm the most important thing in her world.

I'm enamored with her. I knew I loved her, but this last week without her solidified how much she's wrapped her essence around me, entwining it with my soul. I have been drawn to Delaney since the first time I saw her, the first time I heard her laugh, but I never expected to fall so hard for someone who was supposed to be a one night stand.

When I asked Delaney to come with me to Milwaukee, she didn't even hesitate. She immediately pulled out her phone to ask Hailey to keep an eye on Kingston, and the answer was an enthusiastic yes. Kingston is a pretty chill cat, and with the automatic feeder and watering dish Delaney has, I'm sure he would have been okay for a few days on his own, but she and I both want to make sure he doesn't get lonely without us.

Listen to me, talking about Kingston as if he's partially mine. As far as I'm concerned, he is. I'm planning on being in that cat's life till the day he dies, a grumpy, crotchety old twenty-something. As long as Delaney is willing to keep me around, I'll be there.

"Firecracker." She gives me a soft smile. "What are you doing from October through February?" She blinks back at me in confusion. "Tell me you'll come with me to Nashville. And then Phoenix in February and March for spring training."

I don't phrase them as questions because a very real part of me doesn't even want to give her the choice. I will, of course, but there's only one answer I'm willing to accept.

"I...Can I think about it?" I kiss her hand again.

"Of course. But while you're thinking it over, tell me what you're worried about and maybe I can put your mind at ease."

"It's just...I don't want to be dependent on you. Following you wherever you go. Giving up my job."

"You don't have to give up your job. You yourself said it was easy for you to pick up and go. I'm happy to support you financially, but I understand if you want your own income, your own independence. So, if you want to work, work. If you don't, don't." I shrug. I know I'm oversimplifying things, but sometimes simplicity is the solution. "And I'm asking you not because you'll be dependent on me. I'm already dependent on you. You make things better when you're around. You make me happier, more carefree."

Doubt flashes across her face. "But I'm so...messy."

I flick my gaze away from the windshield to her beautiful face. "Are you serious? You have never once given me anything I can't handle. You might think it's messy, but I think it's perfection. Neat and tidy is boring. I love that you keep me on my toes. So, give me messy, Delaney. Give me everything, because I want it all."

# CHAPTER FIFTY-FIVE

# *Delaney*



It's been two weeks since our Milwaukee trip. I don't know what was holding me back from joining Benny on more road trips before then, but now that I've experienced the types of hotels he stays at, you can bet I'll be joining him on a lot more. Feeling curious after he went in to work the first day, I looked up the hotel rates online and nearly choked. Knowing it's not something I could ever hope to afford on my own, I was happy to let the Foxes pick up the tab on that one. The games were great to experience as well, if not a little empty in the family section. When Alicia found out I was on the trip, she drove up to stay with Warner and attended the last two games of the series with me. We had fun bumming around the city when we weren't at the games.

Now that we're back in Chicago, Benny and I spend even more time together than before, which is really saying something. I still can't get over the way he took ownership of his "just a bartender comment" and the whole fight, even if he didn't remember parts of it. No gaslighting, no qualms about apologizing. Just acceptance and apology and moving on.

He's taken to setting up his laptop at Sip after games and finishing his reports there while I finish out my shifts. Sometimes Mac and a few other coaches join him. He's been so busy preparing for the postseason that even when he's in close physical proximity to me, I don't always have his attention. That's okay with me, because I've been equally busy when I'm not tending bar at Sip.

Pascal didn't immediately respond to my email when I reached out to him. Right as I was starting to convince myself he was no longer interested, he replied and invited me to L'Âme, his molecular gastronomy restaurant. As much as L'Âme in French looks like "lame" in English (despite being pronounced like 'lamb'), which makes for an interesting restaurant name choice, as soon as I researched their website, I understood why they chose the French word for 'soul.' It's clear to me a little bit of Pascal's soul is put into every aspect of his restaurant.

We have a meeting today at two o'clock at the restaurant, and I've been freaking out a little bit ever since the request for my visit came through yesterday. Tilly squeezed me extra hard into a hug when I shared the email and requested to come into my shift late. I have no idea how long this meeting will take or what to expect, but I figured it would be best to be prepared for it to run a few hours long, just in case. Tilly shook her head and told me to take the whole day. Apparently, Jeff has been itching to try his hand at tending bar, and she wants to give him a shot. I suspect Jeff's motives have more to do with socializing with a certain clientele, but he's been loyal to Sip and deserves a chance to earn more tips.

Benny is on the last road trip of the season, but it's been a lengthier one, heading up the West Coast and Texas before finally coming home to me next week. Last week, to no one's surprise, the Foxes clinched a playoff berth. The only downside is that Benny and the team were in Phoenix at the time, so I couldn't be with him and the guys to celebrate. From the increasingly incomprehensible texts he sent me that night, "celebrate" was an understatement for their postgame activities once they received the news.

I've already called him twice today, my nerves about my meeting with Pascal getting the better of me. My fingers itch to call him again, to have him talk me down from an anxiety spiral. It's probably nothing. Maybe Pascal only wants to chat, to network, and nothing will come of it. But I've still changed my outfit three times, trying to figure out what will convey "professional bartender" without coming across as desperate and forced. I've finally settled on the black slacks I wore to the nature museum event and a purple satin top. A small part of me cried when I tucked my Converse back in my closet, selecting a pair of plain black ballet flats instead. I've always bartended in my combat boots or Converse, and I have low tops in several colors, just in case. L'Âme is a five-star restaurant, though, and I'm afraid if I show up in my normal footwear, it will send the wrong message.

Fuck it. I need to call Benny one last time, just to make sure I'm making the right decision. My purple low tops would look great with this top, right?

"Good morning again, baby," Benny's laugh laces his voice and it immediately sets me at ease. It's morning for him in California, but early afternoon here. When I first called him, I was so worried about my own shit that I forgot about the time change and woke him up. He was good-natured about it, assuring me he was happy to hear my voice, but now that I've dialed him three times, I find it hard to believe he still finds the situation amusing.

"I'm sorry for calling again. I'm about to leave but now I'm second guessing my outfit." I've already called him for general advice and input on whether I should wear my hair up or down ("Down," Benny practically growled. The man has some sort of weird obsession about being the only one to put my hair up.).

"Don't apologize for calling. I love being the one you come to when you're stressed. Let me see your outfit. Switch to a video call." Suddenly, my phone is vibrating with a video call. I answer it, angling the phone toward the full-length mirror on the back of my closet door. "You look great. Don't change a thing."

Benny's firm, concise response leaves little room for second-guessing and is exactly what I need.

"Okay." I blow out a breath. "Thank you."

"You're welcome. What else do you need?" His incredibly handsome face smiles back at me from the screen.

"I don't know," I tell him honestly, then start to second-guess everything else. I set the phone down on my bed and pick up my backpack, rummaging through it. "Is it dumb to bring my scrapbook? I don't want to come off as presumptuous." Benny's voice is slightly muted against the comforter.

"Baby, look at me." I pick up the phone and sit on the edge of the mattress. "It's not presumptuous, it's called being prepared. You'll know once you talk with him when the right time to pull it out is. But it's better to have it and not need it than to need it and not have it, yeah?" I nod. "You are exceptionally well-prepared for whatever this meeting will entail. You are amazing. You're smart and capable and good at your job. You deserve whatever good things will come from this meeting. Do you hear me?"

Bossy Benny is what I need right now. Someone to get me out of my head. I nod again, but he's not having it.

"I need to hear you say it." I roll my eyes at him, and I swear his sparkle back at me.

"I'm smart and capable and good at my job," I grumble, not because I don't believe it, but because even when he's helping me, I still like giving him at least a little bit of a hard time.

"God, you're sexy when you agree with me." I can't help it; I bark out a laugh. Benny chortles along with me, knowing he's succeeded in getting me out of my head. "I know you were going to take public transportation, but can I please order you a rideshare instead?"

I turned down his earlier offer to have me use his car. Parking near my apartment is atrocious, so I would have had to pick up the car from his place, cutting down on the time I had to get ready. I also don't know if this meeting is going to involve alcohol, so I want to play it safe and not have to worry about driving. Chicago has a good system of public transport, between the L and city buses, but you never know if an accident or some sort of malfunction will interrupt its schedule. I didn't consider a rideshare, mostly because I rarely use them, preferring to take public transport and save myself money. Benny sees my hesitation.

"You haven't said no, which means the only reason you haven't said yes is because you don't want me to spend the money. Well listen up, Ms. Kristoff, it's my money and I get to spend it however I want. A rideshare is going to be much more reliable. So, unless you tell me no right now, I'm ordering it."

I don't fight him, mostly because I'm distracted by his use of my last name. "Ms. Kristoff, huh? What am I, your boss now?"

"Baby, you can boss me around as much as you want as soon as I get home." I can practically see the lust simmering under his skin. "Now go outside. Your Uber will be there in three minutes. You're going to do great. I'm not going to wish you luck because you don't need it. I love you."

I thank him before hanging up, triple checking my backpack has everything I need, and walking out the door.

"I've wanted to meet with you for quite some time, Ms. Kristoff," Pascal tells me.

"Please, call me Delaney," I insist. Ms. Kristoff is going to be reserved for Benny.

"Delaney," he corrects. The way he pronounces my name, with the stress on the last syllable, is the same way my mother (and every other French person) does. There's something comforting about it, and I'm marginally more at ease than I was when I first walked in the empty restaurant.

L'Âme is three hours away from opening, so the restaurant is devoid of the front of house staff. I can hear the soft clanging of pots and pans from the kitchen, but it's only Pascal and me in the dining room. We sit at one of the four-seater tables where the chairs have been taken down. Every other table has its chairs flipped upside down on top of the surface, allowing for easy cleaning of the floors. Aside from the faint noises from the kitchen, the restaurant is quiet and still. There's a particular beauty in seeing such a normally bustling atmosphere at rest.

"I was speaking with Ernie Young a few weeks ago, and I had a delightful fig and red wine cocktail at his restaurant. I believe you know the cocktail about which I am speaking?" Pascal raises his bushy gray eyebrows.

"I do," I squeak out before clearing my throat and trying again. "I do know the one."

"I am French, obviously, Ms. Kristoff. Delaney. So I happen to be very particular about any drink involving wine."

"I am too. My mother is from Lyon."

"Vraiment? Vous êtes française?" Pascal immediately switches to his mother tongue, and we continue the conversation in French. My mother would be thrilled.

"Oui. My father is American, but French is my first language. I didn't begin speaking English regularly until I started going to school." Pascal leans forward, suddenly much more invested in this conversation. His English is impeccable, but he's clearly more comfortable speaking his native language.

"Ernie informed me that you developed and sold the recipe to him. I have a very capable staff here at L'Âme, but I must admit, the idea intrigued me. I like the idea of sourcing local talent for guest spotlights, but molecular gastronomy does not generally lend itself to amateur chefs." I nod. I've never had the privilege of eating at L'Âme, or any other molecular gastronomy restaurant, but I know enough to recognize a strong understanding of science is blended with a love of all components of an ingredient. "I am wondering if you have ever thought about developing other exclusive cocktails? Would you consider developing a drink for us here, or perhaps more than one?"

Now it's my turn to be surprised. "Really? I would be honored!" It's the best case scenario for a meeting like this, but I never allowed myself to truly consider this possibility, lest I get my hopes up for nothing.

"What are your standard rates for consultation?"

"Oh, um..." I pause. Last time I was asked this, Benny told me I undersold my skills. But if I tell him too high a price, he'll withdraw his offer. "I'm currently reworking my consultation contracts to reflect the time devoted to each drink. Or each menu," I hastily tack on, in case Pascal thinks I'm limiting myself.

"Very smart," he says, dipping his chin. "I would love for you to send over a contract when you have finished revising it. Perhaps we can start with one drink and move forward after that?"

I nod eagerly, then wonder if I'm too enthusiastic. Maybe I should make Pascal work for it a little more? No one likes a desperate job applicant, which is how I'm starting to envision this meeting.

"Can you tell me about some other cocktails you have made? Perhaps those on the more adventurous side, to match the atmosphere of L'Âme? If you would like, we have the bar available for your use."

My hands are shaky as I unzip my backpack and drag out my scrapbook. I feel a little silly bringing out an arts and crafts project in the middle of this high-end restaurant, but Pascal doesn't bat an eye.

"This is how I keep my recipes for personal use," I hastily explain. "I would obviously develop something unique for you. For L'Âme, I mean." I shift awkwardly in my seat as Pascal thumbs through my scrapbook.

"Très intéressant," he murmurs, stopping on the page where I've featured The Nail and Bail. I cringe, hoping that bit of slang doesn't translate. I've decorated the page with relatively innocent decor, featuring pineapples and a particularly drippy honey jar. I'm hoping Pascal thinks the black and white rose in the bottom corner and the various red lip outlines on the page are there to denote how much I love the recipe and for no other reason. After another awkward minute, he moves on, lingering longer on some pages than others. He pays special attention to the final three recipes in the scrapbook, which are the ones I developed for the nature museum event. I've created more since then, but haven't had a chance to create the corresponding scrapbook pages.

I want to ask him what he thinks, but don't want to come off as impatient. His fingers ghost across a three-dimensional butterfly I glued to the last page. He finally looks up at me with a small smile.

"I think you will do well." I want to ask him what he means without coming off as completely dense. I take a gulp of my water. "Please send me the contract via email and we can get started right away."

# CHAPTER FIFTY-SIX

# *Delaney*



"Talk to me." Benny's rich, smooth voice comes through clearly on the phone, despite the buzz of background noise.

After Pascal handed back my scrapbook, he invited me to tour the restaurant. While I'm sure his intention was to focus on the bar, he also showed me the kitchen. By that point, cooking for the night was well underway, and the smells coming from the kitchen were nothing short of mouth-watering. The sights were even more impressive; I had to check multiple times that my jaw wasn't hanging open as I watched chefs-slash-scientists hard at work. The food preparation was more science experiment than cooking, I realized, as one of the employees casually tossed what looked like a mixture of herbs and lemon juice into a pot of dry ice, before covering it and shaking vigorously.

Pascal explained some of the aspects of the cuisine, sending me home with a paper copy of the menu so I could coordinate an appropriate drink. He asked me to develop something for their upcoming spring menu, which apparently was already in development, despite it only being late September. I suppose if new equipment or materials needed to be sourced, menus needed to be planned far in advance.

I'm glad Tilly insisted I take the day off, because by the time I finish at L'Âme, it is nearly two hours later, which explains the chaos and background noise coming from Benny's end of the phone. I know his game is starting soon and I am surprised he even picked up.

"Benny! It went so well! He wants me to design a new drink for L'Âme! Me! He even went through my scrapbook and told me there were lots of interesting ideas in there, and I don't think he was just being polite."

"Of course he wasn't, baby. You have amazing ideas in there." I appreciate the compliment but barely register it, still buzzing from my interactions with Pascal.

"Benny, he said if my first drink is successful, there's a possibility to design a whole drink menu!" I want to squeal, I'm so giddy.

"I'm so proud of you, Delaney baby." Benny's voice is genuine, and I can picture his eyes twinkling as he says it. I've never had someone champion me the way he does, and I'm surprised to find the realization has tears pricking against my eyelids. I swear if I didn't get my period last week, I would be concerned that I'm pregnant, given how emotional I've been in the last month.

The thought occurs to me that I could get pregnant in the future, and I find that it doesn't terrify me as much as it probably should. It's probably because I know Benny's kids already and know what an incredible father he is. We stopped using condoms a long time ago, but I've been religious about taking the pill. I shake my head, wondering where these thoughts are coming from. I haven't considered parenthood, or marriage, or moving across the country with a man, in so long. After my past experiences, I shut myself off completely to the possibility. Since meeting Benny, my life has evolved in so many new and exciting ways.

"D? Are you still there?" His voice breaks through my day-dreams.

"Yeah, sorry. I'm processing a lot."

"I get it. Did you eat anything yet today?" As if on cue, my stomach emits a loud rumble. I wouldn't be surprised if he can hear it through the phone, but it must have been contained enough because he doesn't comment.

"I was too nervous," I tell him honestly. The adrenaline from the meeting is wearing off, and I know it's only a matter of time before I turn annoyingly hangry.

"Get yourself some lunch before heading home. Really treat yourself, baby. I'm buying." I glance around me. I'm in the Loop on a weekday, so there's no shortage of great options, even if it is that weird time between lunch and dinner.

I spy a Japanese restaurant across the street. It looks like an elevated type of cuisine, if the white tablecloths are any indication. I'm glad I didn't switch to my Converse; I'm not sure they'd let me in with such casual footwear, but my interview outfit will fit right in.

After hanging up with Benny, I shoot off a quick text to Alicia, knowing she lives nearby. She responds almost immediately and agrees to meet me for sushi and sake. I take a deep breath as I pull open the door to the restaurant.

My life is on an entirely different trajectory than I imagined before meeting Sammy, but I couldn't be happier about it.

# CHAPTER FIFTY-SEVEN

## *Delaney*

Friends Like These (A Delaney Kristoff Original):
Champagne, Mango Nectar, Passionfruit Juice,
Edible Gold Glitter

I've never really had the type of friend I can call up on a whim and invite to lunch, but I have to admit, it's nice. I didn't expect Alicia to be available on such short notice, but she was. And I didn't expect her to be so genuinely excited for me when I told her my news about L'Âme, but she was. I need to stop underestimating the people in my life.

After we ate our weight in California rolls and gyoza, Alicia asks if she can drive me home. I was planning on getting another Uber, but she insists that she has a few of Warner's cars at her disposal and has been itching to drive a particularly sporty green little number, so I agree. She also insists on paying for lunch as a way of celebrating my accomplishments and only agreed to let me pay when I told her Benny already made me promise to send him the bill.

When we pull up outside my apartment, Alicia parks in front and turns off the car.

"I want to see Kingston really quickly, then I'll be on my way." I agree, but am a little nervous about her leaving Warner's nice sports car on my shitty street. She assures me she's not worried about it.

When we get up to my apartment, I try to unlock the deadbolt and find it already unlocked. I frown. Normally, I triple check that I've locked my place up, but I must have forgotten with my nerves jangling around in my head all day. Nothing looks out of place in the hallway. My welcome mat isn't even askew, but I can't help feeling a little on edge.

"Surprise!"

I blink, taking in Hailey, Jenny, and Amy standing in the middle of my living room. Alicia hugs me from behind while Jenny pops open a bottle of champagne, causing Kingston to scurry under the couch at the unexpected noise.

"What is this?" I ask stupidly.

"We are so proud of you! Benny texted us the news about four seconds before Alicia did, and we want to celebrate you!"

I can't help it, the pinpricks that threatened my eyes earlier return as I burst into tears. The girls rush to hug me as I dissolve into my feelings. I cling to my friends as my emotions overwhelm me. It's not only the success from L'Âme, but also having someone—multiple someones—to celebrate it with.

# CHAPTER FIFTY-EIGHT

# *Benny*

Tastes Like Victory (A Delaney Kristoff Original):
Champagne, Chambord, Vanilla Simple Syrup

The end of the season wrapped up about as nicely as I could have wanted. While our wins after clinching technically didn't matter, as we were mathematically secure in our playoff berth, we went eight and two in the last ten games of the season. The wins, and their resulting morale boost, launched us into the first and second rounds of the playoffs, where we swept Arizona in three games and are hoping to beat Miami in four.

I've never made it this deep into the postseason as a manager. I've felt pressure all season to get here; some of it was self-induced, but it was stressful all the same. Now, we need to do more than maintain our successes. We need to prove it.

We're down to the last out of the game, and if we can hold on, we'll move to the next and final round of the postseason: the World Series. I nervously gnaw on sunflower seeds. I don't particularly like the taste, and if I think about it too long, the concept of eating while playing a sport is gross, but it gives me somewhere to channel my nervous energy. On the outside, I'm calm and collected, but inside, my stomach is roiling. I have confidence we can pull off the win, but my nerves are omnipresent nonetheless.

The win yesterday fuels us today. Our forward momentum has been evident from the first crack of JJ's bat in the first inning to the last out smacking neatly into Carter Perez's glove in the ninth.

Mac jumps on me, screaming about four more wins. He's saying something else, which can't be heard over the roar of the crowd. Their volume is only matched by the screaming of my players and staff, huddled around Asher Incaudo on the mound. The poor kid's face when he gave up that fly to left field was almost comical. We were already up by six runs, so even if Perez didn't catch it, it wouldn't have cost us the game, but he looked so panicked I thought he was going to puke right there on the mound.

It takes us a long time to make our way to the locker rooms, the team preferring to celebrate on the field where the fans can see. I know the locker room is already covered in plastic sheeting in preparation for the champagne and beer showers that will inevitably occur, but I'm happy to let the fans feel like they're a part of the celebration. On the field, Delaney joins us, donning a pair of ski goggles to protect her eyes from the alcohol quite literally flying everywhere. The wives and families aren't allowed in the locker room, even for celebrations such as these, so I'm glad we're sticking on the field for now. And while Delaney isn't my wife yet, I'm hoping to bring that change about sooner rather than later.

# CHAPTER FIFTY-NINE

## *Delaney*

*Foxes Frenzy (A Delaney Kristoff Original Exclusively for Foxes Field): White Rum, Blue Curacao, Lemonade, Orange Curacao Float*

I've never seen Benny so quietly stressed. The Foxes have been killing it in the postseason, and tonight could potentially be the final game, where the Foxes finally win the World Series, if they can hang on and eke out a win tonight. So, I get why he's stressed. Plus, they're going into tonight's game fresh off a loss, so it's not an ideal situation. The Foxes are up, three wins to two, and the game returns to Foxes Field.

Benny has been home the last two nights, the Foxes having flown back from New York late after the loss two nights ago. It was a somber plane ride. The WAGs got to accompany their significant others on the flight, which was a first for me. Benny sits up front with the other members of the coaching staff in the first-class seats and even though the mood was depressed, it was a little exciting for me.

"The good news is that you can win at home now," I tried to reassure him quietly on the flight back. What do I know, I'm

371

repeating what I've been told, although my baseball knowledge has admittedly grown exponentially in the last few weeks.

While not exactly grumpy, Benny's grown increasingly quiet over the last few days, so I know the stress is getting to him. He's been tossing and turning in his sleep, when he does manage to catch a few hours. My heart aches for him. My confidence in his ability to pull off the win has never wavered, but it's hard to see his own confidence on shaky ground. Part of me will be glad when this is over, regardless of the outcome.

The game tonight isn't until seven, but Benny is dressed and ready to go by nine this morning. I've offered everything I can to reduce his stress, from alcohol to massages to morning blow jobs, but he's turned down each one with a small smile that doesn't reach his eyes. I never grew up believing in a god, but if there's one out there, she better make sure the Foxes win, or I'll have several bones to pick with her in the afterlife.

He kisses me gently on the cheek before tossing his backpack over his shoulder and heading out the door. He normally walks to work, but the hysteria surrounding Foxes Field has reached a fever pitch, so he's been driving in during the postseason. He'd never make it into the office on time otherwise. As it is, he gets stopped every few feet by fans looking for photos and autographs on the walk from the parking lot into the clubhouse lobby.

In addition to the extended season, which means more games and more workouts, there have been increased promotional media obligations and an endless stream of meetings among the coaching staff and front office. It's been fun to see Benny's handsome face on more billboards and bus stop ads than ever before. There wasn't a game yesterday, but he still went into the ballpark and came home late, completely exhausted. The man barely made it into his bed before collapsing.

Kingston and I have been spending all our time at Benny's townhouse. I put in my two weeks' notice with Tilly and Sloane and the rest of the Sip crew. My official last day is next week, but I've taken most of last week and this week off to travel with Benny to the games. I could have worked yesterday, but I had hoped Benny and I could spend some time together as a couple. With him getting called in to work, that didn't happen, but that's okay. It gave me time to finalize the finishing touches on the cocktail I created for L'Âme.

I've been working off and on over the last couple weeks to develop the drink. Not being a science nerd myself, it's taken me a little bit to figure out some of the techniques (at least, the easier ones that I can do from Benny's kitchen). I'm happy with the finished product, and I'm hoping my drink, which I've named Lost Soul, will make customers happy. I learned how to make these incredible little popping bubbles using aquafaba and dry ice, so I'm hoping the presentation will also live up to the very high standards of L'Âme.

I hit send on the email to Pascal after uploading my attachment. The file is hefty, containing lots of photos, not only of the finished product, but of the various steps in the creation. Benny had put me in touch with his lawyer, who connected me with another attorney in his firm. Cian helped me to write a contract for consulting that I used for L'Âme and can use for any other restaurant moving forward.

It took some convincing, but Benny encouraged me to request a more generous fee for my services than I was originally planning. We conducted some market research to help us narrow down an appropriate rate, but most mixologists consult with restaurants to overhaul their whole menu, rather than single drinks at a time, so we went in a little blind. Pascal, however, didn't even blink at the price I set, agreeing to it immediately. Fortunately, that part of business was done via email, so he couldn't see my eyes bug out of my head when he elected not to negotiate and simply paid my asking price.

Benny, when not totally exhausted from work, has been encouraging me to devote more time to my newest idea: my own mixology recipe book for sale to the public. After my success with The Audiobook and the drinks at A Night Out in Nature, and hopefully soon to be bolstered by Lost Soul, I'm hoping there will be enough interest to market the book, at least to the local scene in Chicago. Ernie and I have lunch scheduled in a week and a half, after the postseason hullabaloo dies down but before Benny and

I move (together!) to Nashville, to discuss my options. Ernie is no stranger to cookbook publishing, having written several of his own.

My phone dings with a group text.

Hailey

I can't handle this anxiety. Who wants to get drunk right now?

Jenny

I'll drink with you, but I'm not getting drunk. I need a clear head for this game.

Amy

Alicia, Danny, Tim and I already started. I've been nervous since we flew back from New York.

Alicia

Babe, you came out of the womb nervous.

Hailey

Ooh, she went there. <embarrassed emoji>

Jenny

<wide eyed emoji>

Alicia

> What? You all know it's true.

> Just come over to Benny's. I can whip up espresso martinis so we can take the edge off and stay awake.

Amy

> Danny's way ahead of you.

> <photo of oversized mason jar with dark liq-uid inside>

> Great, get your asses over here. We'll walk to the ballpark in two and a half hours.

It will still get us there early, but it will take us some time to get through security and to fight the crowds to get to our seats. I pop a couple of frozen pizzas in the oven in preparation for snacking while we drink. I'm not sure pizzas really go with espresso martinis, but we're aiming for function over taste at this point.

Yes, the Foxes have held a narrow lead all game. Yes, they look composed and professional and not at all like they're experiencing the nerves we are in the stands. But it doesn't matter, because I still want to throw up. The guys have worked so hard, and they deserve this win (despite knowing that New York has worked probably equally as hard, but I don't know them personally, so screw them).

I'm not the only one who wants to puke. Hailey has a permanent ridge dug into her bottom lip from her teeth. Alicia looks like she's having trouble breathing as she squeezes Warner's sister's hand–Eden looks like she hasn't even registered the risk of amputation to her fingers due to a lack of blood flow. Jenny has ripped her napkin to shreds, and Amy? I'm genuinely concerned about Amy's well-being. She's sitting in the row in front of me while JJ's brother rubs soothing circles on her shoulder blade. JJ's other brother, who apparently is an agent for a bunch of guys on both teams, is glaring at the game unfolding in front of him as if he can will it to swing in his brother's favor. He might be on to something, because JJ's latest at-bat looked great, resulting in a stand-up double and allowing Caleb to score.

The extra run should calm my nerves, but it doesn't. I have a sneaky suspicion I'll feel like puking until the Foxes finally win. I focus on breathing in and out through my nose, which is only marginally helpful.

The sixth inning ends, and shortly after, the top of the seventh wraps up. The Foxes will be back to bat after the seventh inning stretch. Throughout tonight's game, local Chicago celebrities (and not-so-local-anymore celebrities with Chicago roots) have been featured on the jumbotron in center field. Most I recognize, but some I do not. When they announce Take Me Out to the Ballgame will be sung by Adalina Esau, lead singer of the pop-punk band Lake Shore Losers, I gasp. Mostly inactive for the last decade, Lake Shore Losers recently began touring again. They were the voice of my generation, at least when I was in high school. I can't help but fangirl a little bit as Adalina belts out the least punk-rock song in the world but still makes it sound good.

From where I'm sitting, I can only barely see Benny from his post near the top of the dugout stairs. Even with his back to me, I can tell he's focused. He moves through a complicated set of pantomimed motions, some of which are returned by his first base coach. I'll have to remember to ask him to teach me some of his secret code; maybe he'll let me join his boys-only treehouse if I know the secret handshake.

Whatever Benny communicates, Warner seems to understand it well, because as soon as the first pitch of the inning sails out of the pitcher's fingers, Warner sends it deep into the corner of left field. It doesn't have the height to fool us into thinking it's a home run, but it has a deep enough placement to rile up the crowd. When Elijah comes up to bat after Cota draws a walk, he sends the ball bouncing into a double play, but Warner scores easily. The last batter, Tyler Edwards, strikes out swinging.

Two more innings left to play. One and a half if we can maintain the lead.

A lanky relief pitcher comes in for the Foxes in the eighth inning. Even he looks on in disbelief after the third out is called and he gets out of the inning unscathed (despite allowing two runners on base). The threat of New York scoring takes a year or two off my lifespan, but the Foxes make it out of the inning alive. The bottom of the eighth is unremarkable, as three batters come up to bat, and three batters immediately strike out.

Which brings us to the top of the ninth inning and three outs away from the biggest accomplishment of all our men's careers. The Foxes have Jameson Bates on the mound, who is normally unflappable under pressure. Amy is now watching the game from between her fingers. I'm fairly certain JJ's brother has cracked a tooth from grinding his jaw. The rest of us are just as much of a mess. I tug my hat lower on my ears, even though I have so much adrenaline coursing through my body, I wouldn't be able to feel the cold weather if I tried.

The New York center fielder strikes out.

Two more outs left, but the top of their order is due up, which means their best players are about to hit. I've taken to gnawing on my fingernails simply to have something to do with my nervous energy.

A huge, brawny batter steps up to the plate. The public address announcer declares his name to be Devin Demoranville, and his stats are as intimidating as his physical stature. I find myself shrinking back into my seat; I want to curl into a tight little ball of anxiety and resurface only when the coast is clear (AKA, when the Foxes have won).

*Crack.*

I crane my neck as the ball goes careening into right field. Warner races toward it in a full-on sprint, but he doesn't make it in time. He plays it off a bounce and throws the ball into the infield quickly, limiting Demoranville to a single. The good news is, this guy looks too big to be a fast baserunner, but again, what do I know about this sport? I'm learning quickly, but my "baseball IQ" isn't nearly strong enough to make solid predictions during a game of this magnitude.

I gulp down some air, swallowing thickly, which somehow makes me want to throw up even more. How can *breathing* make me want to vomit?

The next batter pops the ball up into the infield. JJ swings his arms wildly while running underneath it. The crowd is cheering even before he catches it, knowing we're only one out away from a World Series win.

One.

Out.

Away.

I stretch, trying to decipher Benny's body language but can't make anything out other than his broad shoulders. He leans forward, his front leg on the step above his other leg. If Mac moves to the side, I'm sure I could check out my boyfriend's ass, which is wholly inappropriate in these stressful moments, but what can I say? I'm only human.

Bates delivers the next pitch and the batter swings, connecting with the ball and sending it into a screaming line drive...straight into Caleb's glove. He didn't even need to move an inch in one direction or another. I don't know how he knew to stand in the exact perfect placement, but he did.

I barely register the slump of the batter's shoulders as the crowd erupts around me. Caleb is swarmed by his teammates, swallowed up in the sea of blue and white pinstripes. I don't even realize I'm sobbing until Jenny grabs my cheeks, jumping up and down with me.

They've done it.

They've won.

The crowd is going wild, tears streaming down everyone's faces, hugs being shared between complete strangers. I've never experienced anything like this, the solidarity and pride and pure joy shared by forty thousand fans–and those are just the ones inside the stadium. I have no doubt the streets of Chicago are filled with the same displays of joyous exuberance.

Jenny and I cling to each other, only separating briefly to share hugs with the other WAGs and family members. Dale, the usher for the family section, moves closer to us to ensure our safety, his eyes shining with unshed tears. We pull him into a group hug with us and sob together. I lean forward, craning my neck upwards to see into the skyboxes above us. Benny's kids are in there somewhere, but I was never able to figure out which one.

Baseball season is long, one of the longest in professional sports, made only longer by the Foxes' postseason run, and now it's over. And the boys have gone out on top. My Sammy, after a year of self-created pressure, has finally done it. He's the one who has been calling the plays and calling the shots, and he deserves this win more than anyone in the world. And he's finally done it.

I stand on my seat, trying to find Benny in the crowd of uniforms jumping and dancing and hugging on the infield. Someone brings out bottles of champagne, and players are spraying them indiscriminately at their teammates. Camera crews are weaving their way in and around the celebration, which is being broadcast on the screen in center field. Gloves and hats lay scattered across the infield, getting trampled by revelers. It will be a long time before we can join our men on the field, so I try to take everything in. I'm doing my best to memorize the moment when Eric approaches us.

Alicia grips him in a particularly fierce hug before finally releasing him. He rubs his neck self-consciously, or maybe from the way she nearly strangled him. We form a chain with our arms, and he escorts us down to the field level. Fans are dancing in the aisles, which makes our journey take three times as long, but it's hard to complain.

The game has been over for more than twenty minutes, and the stands aren't emptying. I can't say I blame the fans. I'd stay until security kicked me out. As it is, I'm preparing for a long night of celebrating with my Foxes family.

Eric ushers us through the gate leading onto the field. Several large security guards crowd the entrance, forcing us to squeeze past, but the tight quarters are probably to ensure a random fan doesn't slip in with us. My tears have mostly dried, but I'm sure my mascara has run like crazy. Hailey and I do a quick makeup check of each other, smudging the skin under each other's eyes for any traces of black before giving each other the thumbs up. Hailey's eyes widen half a second before muscular arms circle me from behind. I'm lifted into the air on a squeal before Benny sets me down.

As soon as my feet touch the grass, I spin around, throwing my arms around my man.

"I'm so proud of you, baby! I knew you could do it!"

"Fuck yeah!" Benny's eyes are overbright, and his voice is already hoarse. He's never looked sexier. "I'm so glad I found you!" He plunks his hat over my beanie as Perez walks by, spraying champagne. The hat, already soaked with both booze and sweat, I'm sure, does little to protect my eyes from random droplets, but the gesture is still thoughtful.

Someone presses an open bottle of champagne into Benny's hands, and he drinks deeply, bubbles streaming down his chin and neck. It's sloppy and messy and all I want to do is lick it off him, but I'm all too aware of the plethora of cameras and media attention surrounding us. Plus, Benny's kids are still somewhere in the stadium. He grasps my chin, tilting my head backwards and pouring champagne into my open mouth. He pours too much, the liquid overflowing and spilling down my cheeks, soaking my coat. I can't find it in me to care. My giggles turn into sobs once more as I fling myself at my boyfriend, hoping he feels how proud I am.

In the distance, fireworks erupt, but they're nothing compared to the fireworks I feel when I look at Benny, surrounded by his team, as he hoists the trophy over his shoulders and lets out a wild roar.

# *Epilogue: Delaney*



The familiar buzz of tattoo guns emit a comforting white noise as we step inside I.N.K. in downtown Nashville.

It's been four weeks since Benny and the Foxes won the World Series, and things are just starting to die down. Two days after the win, the entire city turned out for the celebration parade. We got to ride on a double decker bus through my favorite parts of Chicago. Benny and the guys stayed on the top level for the whole ride, but eventually, the girls and I made our way to the first floor where we could experience the parade from the heated interior of the bus. Benny and I were probably drunk for three days straight following the win; from what the girls have said on our group chat, we were in very good company. The Foxes medical team arranged for intravenous hangover treatments to be administered to us at our houses on the third day, so the hangover was fairly manageable.

Benny and I have been fucking like rabbits ever since. We've always had a lot of sex, but he was so stressed the last week of the postseason that he seems to feel the need to make up for lost time. He's definitely not too stressed anymore; shortly after the World Series win, he signed a major contract extension, keeping him in Chicago for at least another three years. My poor vagina is probably bruised, but I can still never say no to that man, not when his ice-blue eyes smolder and he slides his right hand down the waistband of my pants. He's switched to doing everything sexual with that hand because he knows how I respond to seeing that fucking rose tattoo.

Aside from sex and hangover recovery, Benny's been busy with the media circuit following the win. I had no idea there would be so much demand from the public to see him on everything from local morning talk shows to national golf broadcasts to charity events, but he hasn't said no to a single one if he's been available.

His busy schedule has allowed me to finish the outline for my recipe book. The rest of the book will come together in due time, but I've got a general idea of how I want to structure it. I've even picked out a title: *The Cocktail Collector's Scrapbook*. Ernie convinced me to keep an artsy format to allow it to stand out from other recipe books, and his oversight and expertise has been invaluable. He introduced me to his publisher and a lot of his contacts in the book world. We've become fast friends and have started joking that he and I are closer than Ernie and Benny are.

We've been back in Nashville for a week and have been busier than ever. Leaving my shitty apartment was easy, but leaving my team at Sip? Not so much. Now that Benny's contract extension is secured, I know I'll be back in Chicago in the spring. Sloane and

Tilly have already asked if I'm open to picking up shifts once we're back.

Nashville has been just as busy as the last few weeks in Chicago. Benny's been working to get his backyard re-landscaped. I didn't understand why that was his priority until he woke me up yesterday morning with the softest, most gentle kiss and asked me to marry him. Through a fresh round of tears, I said yes. He told me he wanted to get married as soon as possible and offered the backyard as a venue option.

When he slid inside me after the proposal yesterday, he made love to me with such reverence, such worshipful devotion, that I never wanted it to end. But eventually it did. Until I asked him if he'd be interested in having children with me. I've never seen a refractory period disappear so quickly, and he was back inside me within a minute, promising to fill my belly with as many children as I could possibly want.

Later that afternoon, his kids came over and watched us commit ourselves to each other in the immaculately re-landscaped backyard.

"Are you sure you want to do this?" I ask for the hundredth time. Now it's Benny's turn to roll his eyes at me.

There's no shortage of beautiful ink in shades of black and gray on his body, but his fingers are surprisingly bare. His tattoos, collected sporadically over the years, are not all that dissimilar to my own floral sleeve. When he originally proposed the idea of tattoos instead of rings to showcase our devotion to each other, I balked.

If anything, I wonder why he didn't get Keeley's initials on his finger so many years ago? When I ask him, he shrugs and says, "I guess I never wanted to."

"But you want to get mine?"

He gives me a sweet kiss before answering. "Delaney, the only thing I've wanted more than inking a piece of you on me forever is making you mine forever."

## THE END.

# Want more?

Can't get enough of Benny, Delaney, and the Chicago Foxes?

Sign up for Meghan French's author newsletter to get access to an exclusive bonus chapter! Scan the code below:

*QR Code for Newsletter Sign Up and Access to Exclusive Content*

# Acknowledgements

This is my third book I've published as an indie author, and I'm still waiting for things to die down, when I don't have to teach myself new skills each week or problem-solve a little bit of "gentle chaos." However, I wouldn't trade it for the world, and I'm lucky to have a great team behind me.

Let me start by thank you, my readers, once again. Whether it's reading, rating, or writing reviews, I'm so thankful for you. Reviews are one of the best ways to support an indie author, and I'm so grateful for each and every one of them. Thank you to the Bookstagram and Booktok communities for supporting me and just making a girl feel so special. It's not easy being a faceless author; I really do appreciate all your support!

Thank you to Katie Grear at Inked and Bound, not only for immediately embracing me as a local author (truly, thank you!), but for designing the most kickass scene break images a girl could ask for. When I messaged you asking you to design a fine line tattoo that I could use as a scene break image—with literally no other guidance—you jumped right in with two feet and gave me something far better than I could have imagined. I should have expected nothing less from the genius behind a combined fine line tattoo shop and romance bookstore in one (seriously, I'm still waiting on my invitation to move in).

Kristen Cherry at Desert Bloom Books, for being a one-woman hype team. You're supportive and proactive, and most of all, kind. Thank you for everything you've done for me.

A million thank yous would never be enough for David Sebastian, my SCORE mentor and all-around business guru. You are an Excel wizard who introduced me to the newest love in my life: Gantt charts. I'm afraid to think about where I'd be without your support!

My alpha readers, Jill, Alexa, and Aleshia...you see the raw, ugly story and help me shape it into something passable. Thanks for the constant feedback, talking me off the ledge, and giving me endless song suggestions. Thanks for supporting me from day one. I feel lucky to know each of you and count you among my friends. (An extra shout out needs to go to Aleshia, for finding all the places I should hyphenate words. There's just something about having an attorney line edit for you!)

Jimmy, one of these days, you'll get tired of me asking you small business/entrepreneurial questions. That day, surprisingly, has not come yet. Brace yourself: my next series is set in New York, so you know I'll only get more intense.

To my friends and family who have supported me on this journey, from showing up at author events, to your word-of-mouth recommendations of my books, to simply embracing all things Meghan French, thank you!

Neil, once again, the cover design is fabulous. What else can I say, that hasn't already been said, other than my deepest thanks for your beautiful work.

Of course, I can't put hundreds of hours of work into being an indie author without thanking my right-hand man, Mr. French. From being the first one to test out my new website, to being the guinea pig on my newsletter mailer, to being my PA at author events...none of this would have been possible without you. Thanks for feeding me and hydrating me and rubbing my back when I spend all day staring at a computer screen. Most of all, thanks for loving me and embracing my dream. Love you.

# About the Author

Meghan French loves writing authentic romances about strong female characters and the swoonworthy, dirty-talking men who love them. Her stories typically feature accurate mental health rep, heat, and heart. A self-professed foodie and dog lover, she lives in Arizona with her husband. When she's not in a writing cave, she spends her time as a school psychologist, practicing yoga, and reading all the romance novels she can get her hands on.

Join Meghan's Facebook group, Meghan's Francophiles, for updates on all things Meghan French.

*QR Code for Meghan French's Facebook Group*

You can also stay up-to-date by following her on Instagram, Tiktok, and Facebook under @MeghanFrenchAuthor.

# *Also by Meghan French*

Casual Now

JJ and Amy's Story

Book 1 of the Chicago Foxes Series

I'll Look After You

Warner and Alicia's Story

Book 2 of the Chicago Foxes Series

The Way You Say Good Morning

Benny and Delaney's Story

Book 3 of the Chicago Foxes Series

Book 4 of the Chicago Foxes Series
(Coming Soon!)

Billionaire Spinoff Series
(Coming Soon!)

Mafia Series
(Coming Soon!)